Under Carico's Moons

Book 3

Tricky Ground

by

Nan C Ballard

Published in the United States by
Not a Pipe Publishing
www.NotAPipePublishing.com

Paperback Edition

ISBN-13: 978-1-956892-23-9

Cover art by Don Aguillo
Photo of Nan C Ballard by Jonathan Billing,
PNWPortraitEFX.com

Praise for
Under Carico's Moons
Book 1: Distant Trails

"This thrilling sci-fi Western rides the open range of another world with complex characters caught in a web of conspiracy."
-Karen Eisenbrey
author of the *Rage Brigade* duology and the *Wizard Girl* trilogy

"*Distant Trails* is a roller coaster ride of pain and despair, love and redemption. Ballard's characters embody both frailty and resilience as they redefine their lives from tragedy to hope."
-Mikko Azul
author of the *Demons of Muralia* series

and for
Book 2: Deep Canyons

"Exquisite portrayal of the landscape, vegetation, and fauna of a distant planet with two moons—and complicated people in love and in peril."
-Barb Lachenbruch
author and Professor Emeritus of Forest Ecology

To critique groups everywhere.

Who says writing has to be a solitary endeavor?

Nadine, Marilyn, Dave, Leon, Genny, Valetta

I had to manage this one without you,

but your voices were always with me.

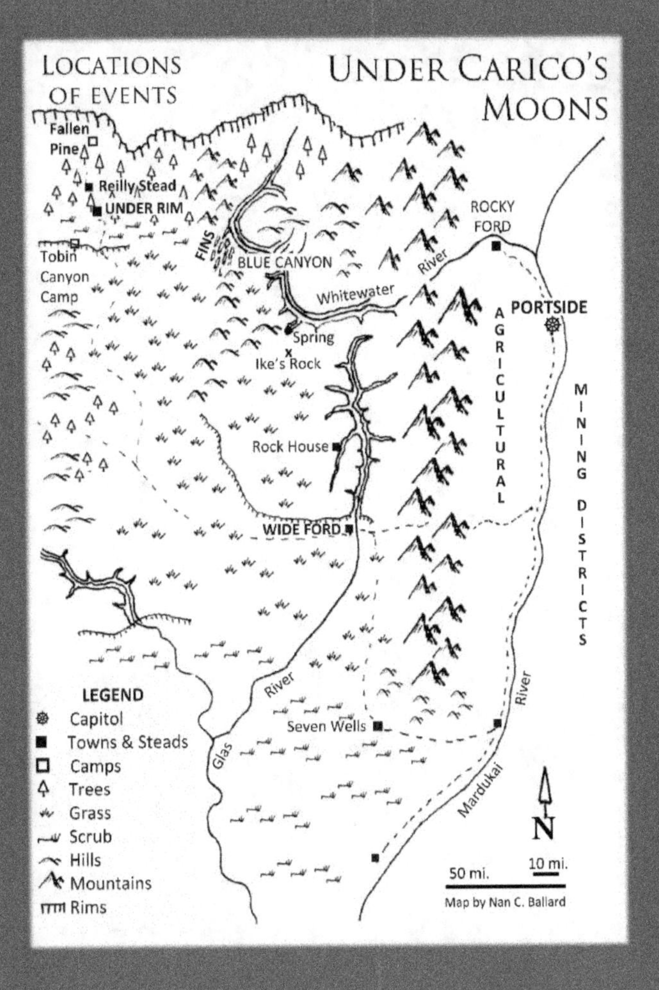

LOCATIONS OF EVENTS
UNDER CARICO'S MOONS
Fallen Pine
Reilly Stead
UNDER RIM
Tobin Canyon Camp
FINS
BLUE CANYON
Whitewater
Spring
Ike's Rock
Rock House
WIDE FORD
ROCKY FORD
River
PORTSIDE
AGRICULTURAL
MINING DISTRICTS
Glas River
Seven Wells
River
Mardukai River
LEGEND
Capitol
Towns & Steads
Camps
Trees
Grass
Scrub
Hills
Mountains
Rims
N
50 mi.
10 mi.
Map by Nan C. Ballard

Chapter 1

Eta'ak

Eta'ak watched from a high point as the two First-Comers, the humans, rode their horses out of the canyon onto the top of the plateau. They who called Eta'ak "Weaver" now rode to their home, bearing an invitation from Eta'ak's people to their own.

"It is done," Trrk said, twining his tail around hers and clicking his fiercely hooked beak.

"It is begun," she replied. "They must still reach their planetary administrative officer with the invitation and persuade her to accept it." The humans had given their word that they would keep secret the details of the hidden villages, revealing only that the Keloks were castaways upon this planet and wished to co-exist peaceably. But how would they feel once they were back among their own kind?

"I should have accompanied them as far as the hills." Trrk's sapphire eyes followed the distant riders.

"They called you Guard, but they do not need that service from you now."

"It might reassure the doubters among us to have a witness to their going."

"And some will never be convinced that this is necessary." She turned away from the view and reached down to preen his scarlet crest with her own blunt beak. "We have done all that we can."

Trrk was slender, agile, with a whip of a tail. He came to just under her chin when they stood upright and massed about half what she did, swift hunter to her steady gatherer here in this wild place. And his tactician's mind complemented her strategic planning perfectly. How lucky she was to have such as spouse.

He and his two brother spouses had carried out her plan to bring a human to her who could be convinced to act as a messenger. Without their efforts in support of her own, she — all of her people — would be waiting in fear of the day soon to come when the humans would discover them. She had chosen instead to initiate a meeting on equal terms so that they might have some control over the pattern of the weaving.

For they were not of this world. Her own purple-brown skin and Trrk's adobe plumage showed them to be out of place, contrasting sharply with the verdigris rock and green-yellow vegetation around them. They had come from elsewhere, lost in the tangled threads of space-time that allowed them to travel across the vastness of the universe. Nearly a third of their original complement nourished the gardens with their flesh before they learned to survive here, hidden in these cliffs and canyons, near but not too near the humans, where they had built new homes, a new life.

The humans had first claim to this world they named Carico by virtue of nearly sixty years and the authority of the Interstellar Coalition that adjudicated resources in this region of space. The Keloks had been there only ten years and were unknown to the Coalition. Now the humans were about to begin a satellite survey of the planet that would without a doubt reveal the Keloks' presence.

"May they go swiftly," Trrk said.

"Yes," Eta'ak replied. "Beyond our reach before the council rethinks their decision."

Chapter 2

Seth

Seth Reilly looked back over his shoulder. To check on the two pack horses, he told himself. But he half-expected to see hawk-beaked, feather-crested, snake-tailed hunters coming after them, coming to stop them. He didn't quite believe that Prime, the leader of the Kelok Gra'a Tral, would stand by the decision to send them back to their own people as messengers. She had only agreed when the head Kelok male had pushed her into it.

He turned his face ahead. They were free. No point in worrying over what ifs. The swinging walk of his roan horse carried him nearer and nearer the rising sweep of the hills, chartreuse with nutgrass flush from Carico's summer rains. Lee Vawn-Cory rode beside him on her harlequin-faced gelding. She smiled, and he grinned back. They were going home.

All they had to do was deliver what amounted to a diplomatic pouch from the hidden colony of previously unknown aliens to the Planetary Administrative Officer of Carico before the planned satellite survey discovered them. And get to the PAO without giving away the secret villages first. And make sure the meeting proposed by the contents of the pouch actually happened. Then they could go back to their own lives. With luck.

"If we don't hurry, we're going to get wet." Lee brought him back to the moment. A rumble of thunder reinforced her.

"Looks like a good spot up ahead," he said. They were nearly across the flats to the hills where they wouldn't be the highest thing in sight. He urged his gelding into a trot. The pack horses picked up their pace to stay with him.

They made it into a swale before the black clouds closed in. They stacked the packs and saddles under a clump of whipbrush, hobbled the horses to graze on the grassy bottom, and strung up a tarp for shelter. The summer storms had come early, and neither of them liked the idea of being out on the flats with lightning.

"We go south here," he said. "Along the foot of the hills until they swing east. Then up and over and we should come out right in the middle of the search for us."

"If anyone is still looking." She handed him a bar of dried meat mixed with berries. "It's been what, ten days since the boss should have gotten your message to come looking? And Guard's hunters didn't leave behind any clues when they took us."

"Not Guard. Trrk," Seth corrected. "Time to start using their proper names." Lee had come up with nicknames for the two Keloks who had held her captive. But now, if they were supposed to speak for the aliens, they should at least use their names.

"Right, and Weaver is Eta'ak," Lee said. "Point is, how long will Dougherty and your father keep looking when they find nothing?"

Searchers must think they had vanished into thin air. The Keloks had packed off every single thing either of them had carried when they had taken the humans captive. Lee's boss Kieron Dougherty, manager of the massive Seven Wells Stead, , and Seth's father Marshal Joe Reilly, would be going crazy.

"It'll be pretty obvious to them that we didn't just have some kind of accident," Seth said. "With no tracks to follow, they may have gone home to wait to hear from us. Dougherty probably left a couple riders at my place in case we show up there."

"So we shouldn't expect to run into anyone closer than that. Three more days if we push it." She leaned back against him. "On any other planet we'd have communications. You know, satellites overhead to relay messages, not antennas sitting on a few hilltops."

"We do," he countered. "At least the Keloks do. Hidden on Damele." The smaller of Carico's two moons, at that moment a crescent hanging in the western sky behind the storm clouds. Trrk's people had installed a communications relay there before permanently grounding on Carico when their starship had failed, leaving them stranded ten years earlier.

"Doesn't do us any good." Being raised on one of the central planets of the Interstellar Coalition, she had different expectations than Seth did. Carico was the frontier, struggling to meet the terms of its settlement agreement and prove up the humans' claim to the planet. Importing technology they couldn't manufacture for themselves weakened that effort. They mostly did without.

"We'll have lots of satellites soon," he said.

"Survey satellites, not communications."

Satellites documenting changes the human settlers had made, part of the measurement of their progress toward development goals. Satellites that would reveal the presence of the unauthorized Kelok settlements. That was what placed a time limit on delivering the message. Get the message to the planetary administrative officer before the survey began. But Seth didn't want to think about that at the moment.

"Hey, we're headed home," he said.

"Straight south from Blue Canyon would have been faster."

"They'll expect us to go that way," he said. "Besides, I hate being out on a flat in these storms." The first drops of rain hit the tarp overhead, and he slid farther under its shelter. He didn't mention that the swale also hid them from any followers. "Better rest while we can.

I'd like to get an early start in the morning." Before the heat; before the storms.

"I'm with you on that."

The rain drowned out conversation but that was fine with him. He didn't need words for what he wanted to tell her now that they were finally alone together.

Sometime in the dark of the night Seth woke out of a sound sleep and listened for what had disturbed him. Lee lay curled with her back against him and more than her fair share of the blankets, as usual. There it was again, the scuffling hooves of restless horses. Without trees to string up a highline, they had left the animals to graze with his roan and Lee's Clown staked out on picket ropes to keep them from straying.

He slipped out of the bedding, pulled on his pants and boots, and stepped away from their tarp shelter. The clouds had cleared. Damele had set behind the hills already. The bigger moon, Lander, was high overhead, waxing gibbous, giving him plenty of light. The four horses stood close together, their attention on the tall clumps of whipbrush on the far side of the little swale.

A warbling whistle pierced the night. The horses shifted uneasily. Seth whistled back, short and sharp, and knelt next to Lee. She jerked awake at his hand on her shoulder.

"What?" she whispered.

"I think it's Guard — Trrk," he said.

"Where?"

"The other side of the brush, out of sight of the horses." The animals had never had a chance to get used to the very unhuman Kelok before they had left the village. "I'll go see what's up."

"Can't be good." She reached for her clothes as he walked back out into the moonlight.

Chapter 3

Eta'ak

Eta'ak checked the settings on the bread maker, a strange implement left with her by the human female along with a crock of the essential yeast culture. She had mixed up her first batch of the bread earlier and left it to bake. If she was successful, tonight she would share it with the rest her clan here in the Village of Canes. This bread substance was new to them. The human had gifted a loaf to Prime during the discussion about the invitation, but most had not gotten to share in it.

She left the galley and looked out across the plaza of the cavern. Her three clan sisters and the four girl-children were returning from gathering fresh foods. They had been subdued for the few days that the humans had been present, uneasy with the aliens. It was good to see them relaxed.

The eldest child ran to her with a handful of fragrant stems. "See what I brought."

"Excellent," Eta'ak replied, her face feathers flashing purple and blue with pleasure. "I know just what to do with these. Please put them in the cool box for me."

The child trotted away. Children were of the clan, loved and cared for, females with females and males with males. She was not supposed to favor any of the girls, but she could not help some small pride in this one, all of seven years old and the first of Eta'ak's own hatching. Children, especially girls, were essential to their long-term survival on this world. They were the reason Eta'ak had been willing to pursue a strategy Prime opposed — so the children could one day travel among the stars if they chose.

Clan sister Yrrlt approached. She was the youngest of the adult females, a supporter of Prime, and had lived nearly a third of her life in this place. "I am glad your pets have left our village," she said and handed Eta'ak a basket full of mixed roots. "That we have our home back."

Eta'ak resisted a sharp reply and modulated her voice carefully. "It was a necessary disruption. The First-Comers are the thread to our future."

"Not everyone sees as you do."

"True." Eta'ak put the basket down. "But the council has decided. No more discussion is needed." She had to be wary. This one wished for leadership. "A fine gather," she said, using her tail to push the basket back toward

Yrrlt. "You may sort and clean these. I will use some of it for tonight's meal."

Yrrlt drew herself up tall and still for a breath before giving a very slight nod and picking up the basket. "I serve the clan," she said and sauntered away.

Trrk crossed the plaza to Eta'ak without hurry. But his crest wavered unevenly.

"What is it?" she asked.

"A broadcast you must see."

"Let us go then." She took her cue from him as they crossed the plaza, walking calmly, apparently unconcerned. He led her past the male quarters and the vine tree arbor at the front corner of the cavern to an opening in the woven-mat wall leading to a room against the rock. She was struck, as always, by the contrast between the array of communications equipment on the counter and its primitive surroundings.

Trrk nodded to one of his co-spouses who vacated the place before the large viewscreen and left the room. Trrk pulled up a recording and waved Eta'ak to the stool in front of the screen.

"This was broadcast a few minutes ago," he said and started the playback.

Eta'ak recognized the human female standing at a desk in front of a wall covered with replicas of aquatic fauna from Carico. The female with the yellow hair and ash-colored eyes was someone the envoy Lee considered an unfriend but who had been active in the search for the missing riders. Her tone was mostly lost in the electronic translation, but her face remained calm.

"Searchers today found the body of one of the missing Seven Wells riders. No cause of death has been released at this time, but the death is considered suspicious. The Marshal's Office has taken over the search.

"We are very concerned for the well-being of the other two riders. This appears to be a carefully orchestrated disappearance uncharacteristic of their normal behavior. Both have a history of stress-induced trauma reactions. If you have any information on their whereabouts, please do not approach them but immediately contact your nearest Marshal's Office so that they may receive the help they need."

Trrk stopped the replay. Eta'ak stared at the frozen image on the screen and said, "She damages the credibility of the envoy."

"Prime must be told." Trrk's crest clamped down flat against the back of his neck.

Yrrlt stepped into the room. "Indeed she must."

"Yrrlt." Eta'ak smoothed her face feathers. "This is not the first time that First-Comer has spoken so." She wished they had used the hearing facilitation devices rather than allowing broadcast of the translation for others to overhear. "The elder died from injuries suffered in a tarbh stampede. Not so suspicious." Except, of course, for the disappearance of the two taken by Trrk and his hunters, the two the First-Comers now searched for. Without turning her eyes from the screen, Eta'ak said, "Yrrlt, ask one of Trrk's brother-spouses to come to me here. I will send a messenger to Prime."

Yrrlt hesitated.

Eta'ak gave her a sharp look. "Now, please."

When Yrrlt had left, Trrk said, "Why not send a comm message?"

"Listen well," Eta'ak said. "You know Prime will rescind her approval of the strategy when she hears this, using the damaged credibility of the envoys as reason. And other councilors will follow her lead."

"Then I will be required to send our hunters to recall the envoys before they are found by the First-Comers who search for them." Trrk's crest flicked up and down uneasily.

Eta'ak lowered her voice to the softest whisper. "As long as the envoys are not recalled, the strategy stands."

Trrk bowed his head. "The envoys are anticipated to travel south. I will give orders for the hunters to go after them once word comes from Second." Looking her in the eye, he added, "But they will go another way. I will see to it."

"Quickly, before Yrrlt returns." She took a basket from the shelf. "You must have the hearing facilitators for the envoys so that they can understand what you tell them." He already wore one, a choker of braided rawhide with translucent green beads, as he often did to monitor the broadcasts. But to take them from the village for use by the humans without permission of the council bore severe consequences. "Are you sure you want to take this risk?" she asked.

"For the good of all our people." He transferred the two chokers into the satchel that hung across his body.

She set the basket back in its place and twined her tail with his tightly. Her fierce, loyal Trrk. "Be swift; be safe."

He stroked his hooked beak down her cheek and left her wondering if she had the strength to face Prime's inevitable punishment with dignity.

Chapter 4

Lee

Lee caught up to Seth when he stopped to check the horses' picket pins to be sure they were secure. Together they wound their way through the brush. Trrk waited where the hill began to rise, well-screened from the horses by the brush.

His hawk-beaked head sat on narrow shoulders. When he ran like some reborn dinosaur, his head and torso stretched down, balanced by his long, sinuous tail. Right now, he stood upright, just Lee's height if she didn't include the crest of crimson feathers flared up above his head. Not a good sign in her experience. Neither was the switching tail or the shifting dun colors of his fine down.

"What happened?" Seth asked. Lee stood back and let him handle it. Trrk was more comfortable dealing with another male than with her.

Trrk rasped something in response. Lee put her hand to her throat. They no longer wore the hearing facilitation devices like the one Trrk wore that let them understand the alien speech. Trrk held up a web of woven rawhide dotted with translucent green beads and offered it to Lee first. She turned around so the Kelok could fasten the choker around her neck and waited impatiently for him to repeat the action with Seth.

"Why are you here?" Seth asked.

"Trouble," Trrk responded. This time Lee understood the harsh statement clearly.

"I guessed that much," Seth answered.

"The Ranger female questions your stability." Trrk lashed his tail. "We believe that Prime will declare you unfit to act as envoys."

"Unfit? Scorch that woman!" Lee wished, just for a moment, that she could get her hands on Adel Verlane. Years ago, as roommates at the Ranger academy, Lee had learned not to trust Adel. Nothing had changed.

"For what reason does she damage your credibility?" Trrk asked.

"It can't have anything to do with your people," Seth said. "She doesn't even know you exist."

"The survey," Lee decided. "It must have something to do with the satellite survey and the settlement plan review. Some scheme she's working on. She's always got a scheme."

Seth gave her a look that said to leave it. He turned back to Trrk. "I guess you aren't here just to cancel the plan and collect the pouch to return it."

"Prime will send hunters to intercept you. She is sworn to protect the secret of our villages and only allowed you to leave to carry her invitation to your administrator."

"And will Second support wiping our memories now?" Seth asked.

Lee shivered. That was the Kelok alternative to simply killing intruders. But the lead male had unexpectedly defended them once. He might again.

"I do not know." Trrk's crest ruffled. "But you must turn to the north and west now. Among us only Eta'ak knows your clan lives in that direction. The hunters will expect you to return south, where you were when we captured you."

Their clan, Lee thought. Well, they did both have family in Under Rim, which lay somewhere to the northwest. And it was probably no further than the nearest communications site to the south. But Lee shook her head. "I don't know if Under Rim is a good idea, Seth. As a marshal, your father will have a lot of questions. How do we get to the PAO without giving away the villages?"

"He might be able to arrange that meeting." Seth pulled her close. "You know we can trust him."

"I know," she agreed.

"Bigger question is if we can get through that country with the horses," Seth said. "I hear it's pretty rough. Trrk, what do you think?"

Trrk hesitated. "I will show you paths."

"Can we really outrun your hunters?" Seth voiced Lee's own thought.

"You will have a day while they hunt elsewhere. And there is a boundary beyond which we do not normally go."

"Will that stop them?" Seth looked skeptical.

"I cannot say."

"How far?" Lee asked.

"It is possible for you to reach it ahead of them," Trrk replied.

Oh, good, Lee thought but kept her sarcasm to herself. A chance they could reach this imaginary boundary before the Keloks did; a chance the hunters wouldn't cross it; a chance that if Prime said bring the two humans back, the hunters would do exactly that.

Trrk drew himself up to his tallest and settled his crest down on the back of his neck. "Unless official word reaches you, you remain Prime's messengers. I will do all I can to help you vanish from the hunters. After that, I will return to my people, and you must decide for yourselves how to best complete your mission."

Trrk gave them directions for where to meet him, then went ahead, out of sight of horses who had yet to learn he wasn't a horse-eating monster.

"So much for just the two of us," Lee said as she helped Seth pack up what little they had unpacked the evening before.

"For a little while," he replied. "Trrk seems anxious to get back to his village."

She stopped what she was doing. "Not surprising.

He's helping us do something Prime's about to prohibit." She put her hand to her throat. "And he brought these. Remember all the effort they went to before they could let us use them in the village."

"Capture, initiation, adoption. Yeah, the sooner he gets home with these in hand the better." Seth laid his hand on her face, caressing her cheek.

She leaned into his touch. "You think we can evade Kelok hunters, even with Trrk's help?"

"At least he's giving us a chance."

Lee tore herself away and went to bring over the horses while Seth finished readying the packs. In silence, they saddled and loaded up their gear.

Seth gave her a leg up onto Clown and handed her Creamy's lead. He paused with his hand on her knee. "I don't know about you, but I'm not getting hauled back to Prime so she can wipe our memories to protect their secret."

She shared his desire to avoid anyone messing with her memories. Especially for a secret that the satellite survey would reveal in a few weeks anyway. She leaned down and kissed him. "Then I guess we'd better vanish."

Chapter 5

Lee

They followed Trrk north along the foot of the hills. His plumage, little more than down except his crest and the backs of his arms, proved good camouflage in the moonlight. Once the sun came up, his adobe and rust wouldn't blend so well with the chartreuse vegetation and verdigris soil. Lee wondered again how she had ever thought he and his kind were native to Carico where the large animals all had scales, four eyes, and bluish copper-based blood.

Not long before dawn he must have found what he was looking for because he turned up a draw and began climbing deeper into the hills. Sunrise found them scrambling up onto a ridge. Trrk trotted rapidly ahead, waving them on. They reached the top and faced a nightmare expanse of towering verdigris walls across their path.

"Elements and All," Seth breathed. "The Fins."

Lee had seen the name on maps but never looked closer. Now the name made perfect sense. Millions of years of ancient sea-floor turned on edge with the softer layers eroded away, leaving upright slabs of harder strata running across their line of travel. "Go into that?" Lee swept a hand across the barriers in front of them. "With horses? Trrk must be crazy. You must be crazy."

"Void! What a mess," Seth said.

"How far across?"

"About fifteen miles."

"If we could go straight, which we can't." She studied the fantastical terrain. "There has to be a better way."

"Stay here with the horses," Seth said. "I'll go talk to Trrk." He handed her his reins.

Lee led the horses to a clump of scraggly copper trees and tied them. She knew what the answer would be. They had to trust Trrk's judgment. He knew the country and the ones who would come after them. So they were headed into a mess of bad footing and narrow slits. She adjusted the saddles and tightened the lashings on the packs in preparation. Creamy was an experienced pack horse, accustomed to maneuvering the additional width of packs around obstacles. Tinker, on the other hand, was more used to being ridden. He had been Ike's saddle horse. Ike Allred, her riding partner from Seven Wells, who had died in the tarbh stampede when the Keloks had captured her.

If she and Ike had never left Seven Wells to scout a new area for JT Land and Livestock to expand its holdings, they would be at some outlying camp for the summer watching over recalcitrant tarbh while he criticized her life choices. Annoying, interfering old man never brought himself to tell her he was her great uncle. She'd found that out by reading his journal after his death. What she wouldn't give to have him here grumbling at her now.

She brought her mind back to the present, to a pack saddle, previously fit to another horse, that wasn't adjusted on Tinker to her satisfaction. And focusing on that kept her from thinking about all the things that could go wrong getting through the jumble before them.

Seth came back with a determined stride. "Trrk says it's doable. There are breaks between the fins that will get us where we need to go."

"Okay, but won't the hunters just track us into that maze?" she asked. She had developed a strong respect for the Kelok males. They were hunters by nature, fast, focused, and experienced.

"Trrk says no. *Unmotivated* was the word he used."

"So they still support Eta'ak's plan?"

"Unless Second says otherwise."

Second was the highest ranked male among the castaways. He had taken Lee's side once. But she wasn't sure if it was only that one situation or if he would keep nudging Prime to follow through with contacting the PAO. The Kelok females planned; the males carried out the plans A delicate balance. All she and Seth could do was hope, and put distance between themselves and where Trrk said the hunters would look first.

Lee followed Seth into the passage between the verdigris walls of the Fins. He led Tinker so he could help the inexperienced pack horse get past whatever obstacles they found. Lee led Creamy. The early morning sun only brushed the tops of the walls. Lee told herself to enjoy the shade while it lasted. These passages would be an oven later on.

The walls closed in like a back street in a city, except the urban buildings she knew were draped in vegetation and curved and folded like origami to catch the breezes and manage the heat. This wasn't Portside or far away Kasba-on-Oasis at the heart of the Interstellar Coalition. Here the walls ran straight and bare. But the floor was littered with brush and rocks they had to maneuver around.

Trrk said they had a day before the hunters would come here. Pursuit felt closer, its breath hot on the back of her neck. The horses felt it too. Tinker was nervous at best and hugged the roan's rump. Even placid Creamy kept crowding up on Clown's heels, unwilling to let the lead horse do the worrying as he usually would.

They came to the first break in the wall leading the way they wanted to go, a slit over a slickrock hump leading deeper into the maze. Seth looked back at her before turning the roan into the notch, keeping Tinker in line behind. One pack barely brushed the rock. Tinker leaped forward but the roan blocked his way. In another few steps they were clear.

Lee entered the space and stopped, drawn to lay a hand on the sandpaper roughness of the rock, so ungiving yet wearing away under wind and rain and ice. At the feel of its substance, the eeriness withdrew. The rock held the world at bay. She wanted to pull it in behind her like a protecting door. But the horses didn't share her new-found sense of safety. They still watched for scary somethings.

She lost track of the number of times they passed through such notches, sometimes one way, sometimes the other. At each one she caught a glimpse of Trrk ahead of them, guiding them. She could only trust that they were making progress in the right direction. The sun climbed; the rock soaked up heat; she and Seth and the horses sweated. No breeze penetrated the maze.

They found a slice of shade from a lone vine tree struggling up a rock face, and Seth stopped. Lee slid to the ground and stretched before checking Creamy's packs. "What about water?" she asked. "This doesn't look like a place to find springs."

"With the rain we've had, Trrk says we'll find pools," Seth said. "He'll wait for us at the first one he gets to."

"Trrk says … Have you wondered if we should be changing plans on his say-so?" she asked. Trrk might share Eta'ak's commitment to bringing their two peoples together peacefully, but she didn't delude herself into thinking they were more than uneasy allies.

Seth shrugged. "I think this is less risky than ignoring him and discovering he was right."

"True." The thought of being taken back and having their memories wiped so they couldn't reveal the secret villages made her stomach churn. Eta'ak had said a person wouldn't remember specific events or places or individuals, leaving blanks in the mind. But it didn't prevent a person from reacting based on the forgotten experiences without understanding why. Lee had had a false persona overlain with hypnosis for an undercover assignment. In spite of de-conditioning, elements of that other person surfaced at times. And decisions she'd made in that persona still haunted her.

"This shouldn't be so hard. I just want to deliver the message," she said. "Do what we can to help the first official meeting go smoothly, and then leave it in the hands of the authorities."

"We can do that as well by going to Under Rim as back to the south. Maybe better. With luck your friend Adel will be looking there, where she thinks we are. What's she got against you anyway?"

"I wish I knew," Lee said. She got a you-can-do-better-than-that look from him. "Okay, it goes back to school, the Ranger academy. I helped her out of a jam, let her into the dorm after hours."

"And?"

"She was involved in something that could have gotten her expelled. Helping her could have gotten me expelled."

"So you helped her, and she blamed you?"

"Afraid I'd give her away, maybe. She never let me forget that night. It set the tone for our relationship ever since."

"That was a long time ago."

"Yeah, but now what's she up to that she's afraid I'll

interfere with?"

He reached out and ran his thumb across her cheek. "We can worry about Adel later. Let's get through the Fins first."

"Yeah, the Fins." Lee muttered. But the terrain and Adel worried her less than the thought of who would be following them. She kissed his palm and turned to her horse. Seth mounted and brought Tinker in line. She swung into the saddle and urged Clown after him.

Chapter 6

Seth

Seth rode deeper and deeper into the maze of the Fins, drawn on by glimpses of Trrk showing the way, then vanishing through another gash in the sandstone. But Trrk didn't always have a good understanding of what a pack horse could negotiate.

Seth stopped in a wide spot and eyed a gap where a fallen slab blocked half the bottom. He gauged it against the width of the packs on the brown gelding.

"Can we make it?" Lee asked.

"It'll be close," he said. If the pack horses were careful. Tinker couldn't be trusted to judge the clearances the way Creamy could. Not his fault that he was more used to carrying a rider.

Seth dismounted and moved the roan over against the wall. He brought Tinker to the other side until he could back the roan past him. Looping the reins up so the roan wouldn't drag them, he left the horse to follow Tinker.

"Let me get through before you come," he told Lee. She nodded. He took a short hold on Tinker, squared him up to the opening, and led him forward. Tinker didn't like the idea of being out front. Seth used gentle tugs on the lead rope to keep the horse's attention while he kept a watchful eye over his shoulder to be sure the packs had clearance.

A mile later, or maybe only ten feet, they passed the slab. "Good boys, good boys." Seth moved Tinker over, and let the roan come up beside him.

He led them forward to give Lee room and watched her as she rode toward him, turning in the saddle to give Creamy a little guidance, talking calmly to the horse even when he could see the tension in her shoulders.

"This is getting old," she said.

"Hey, we haven't had to unload to get through anything yet," he said. But every one of these narrow spots slowed them down when he wanted to be moving.

Not much farther along, they came to a series of small pools where rainfall had collected in shallow hollows in the bedrock. They filled their water bottles and let the horses drink. The pools would have to wait on another rain to refill.

"Trrk said he would meet us here," Seth said.

"Good. Maybe you can explain how wide these packs are."

They loosened cinches and tied the animals to a pair of copper trees whose roots had penetrated fissures in the stone. Instead of cocking their hips and dozing, the horses were watchful.

"They really don't like this country," Lee said. "Even Creamy's uneasy."

"Maybe they're getting it from us." He rubbed at the back of his neck.

"Not me," she said. "There's something protective about these walls."

"Not for me." The walls closed in. The air was still, like a wind never freshened it. The midday sun beat away any hope of shade. Void of a place to be hunted.

He was glad when he heard Trrk's whistle from somewhere ahead of them. He left Lee with the horses and found Trrk waiting at a break in the fin, his dun plumage bright against the blue-green rock.

"The horses had no difficulty reaching here?" Trrk asked.

"We managed," Seth said, "but try and find wider places. It's been tight with the packs."

"I will do my best to select a passable route. We have this day, while my fellows hunt southward, to gain distance. But when they find no sign of you, they will search other ways."

"We can't outrun them."

"No, but it is forbidden to go beyond the Fins. One can hope they would abide by that even in pursuit."

"So it's a race."

"One could say so."

Seth used the break in the fin before them to explain

to Trrk what the horses needed, the width, how steep a scramble up and down. Then the Kelok was gone through the opening and off to scout for the next one.

A slow race, a distance race, a race with no end in sight, just another wall of rock beyond each breach. The horses lost their anxiety and plodded on as the sun heated the oven they passed through. Seth's sense of urgency faded. What mattered was each obstacle to get the horses around, each success soon pushed aside by the next challenge. One by one by one.

The frequent pools of water from the recent rains were a small blessing. Even the desert-raised roan, who never passed up water, quit drinking at every one even if he wanted to splash vigorously. Seth appreciated the cooling spray but stopped the antics short before the horse decided to lie down and roll in the water.

No thunderstorms threatened them. Seth couldn't decide if that was a blessing or not. No risk of flash floods, not that this terrain showed signs of that, but no cooling clouds and rain either. Just heat and another narrow passage or jumble of rocks in their way.

Slowly, slowly the shadows began to lengthen. Where was Trrk? He hadn't appeared for a while. They needed to take a break, let the horses rest, rest themselves. Just for a little while. Could they hope to get out of the Fins before dark? Lander would be nearly full, but Seth still didn't like the thought of trying to get through the tangle after sunset.

The roan's head came up, ears pricked forward. Seth saw a flash of dun up ahead at a break in the wall on his right. Trrk. The roan relaxed a little. The horse was getting used to the strange creature appearing in the distance.

Seth dismounted and tied the two horses to a couple scrubby bushes. "Wait here," he said. "I want to talk to Trrk."

"Good," Lee answered. She got off. "I feel like we've been chasing a wisp all day. I would like some idea of when we'll get out of this."

"Yeah." He headed for the opening Trrk had gone through without saying what he knew they were both thinking. Even out in the open they couldn't hope to outrun Kelok hunters. They could only hope Trrk was right and the hunters wouldn't go beyond the Fins.

Trrk was waiting for him in a wider opening than most they had gone through. "Is all well?" the Kelok asked.

"We're okay," Seth said, "but we need to rest the horses. How far to water?"

"There is a place just through here, a larger opening with water and grass. But we cannot stay long."

"This isn't good country to go through at night."

"You should give more credit to your horse animals. I have observed that they move well in the dark." Trrk's crest rippled. "But the way becomes easier beyond here."

"Good." Seth wondered what *easier* looked like to Trrk.

"Come then."

Seth went back to Lee and the horses. "He says there's a place to rest just ahead but not for long."

"How far to the edge of the Fins?"

"Not sure." He gave her a leg up onto Clown. "He says it gets easier from here on."

She gave him a crooked grin. "Ever wish you hadn't loaned me a horse back before this all started?"

"Never," he replied. "Or often. Depends on the moment." He'd still be at his place, only now beginning to wonder where she and Ike were if his horse Jester hadn't escaped and come home when the Keloks took her captive. "You do have a way of livening things up."

"I do my best."

He mounted the roan and led the way through the notch into a broad thoroughfare. The next fin was lower and broken into towers. Maybe they were getting near the end.

Trrk waved and disappeared again. Seth marked an odd colored rock as a guide to which slot Trrk had gone through and urged his hot, tired horses on. A glance told him Lee was following. He turned through the low, wide opening and brought the roan to a stop.

"Flaming frog-eels," he said under his breath. He sat in the gateway to a forest of lichens, the biggest, strangest lichens he had ever seen. They clung to the broken surface of every notch and slot along the base of the towers wherever a greenish-black ledge was exposed. They glowed in the sunlight — shoulder-high bugles with pale green tubes widening at the top into bright green bells with ruffled edges. Between the bugles, leaf-like growths encrusted the rock. Here and there beard-like clumps of filaments dangled, some bluish and some vivid yellow. Like nothing he had ever seen before.

"What's the hold up?" Lee asked.

"See for yourself." He rode forward, clearing the way for her, and watched to see her reaction.

She stopped just where he had. "What in the ... Now that is bizarre. I didn't know lichens could grow that big. They must be ancient."

"If they are lichens," he said, "not weird plants of some kind."

"There's Trrk," she said. "Let's go."

Seth rode by the strange growths, resisting the temptation to reach out and break off a piece. He could see gaps between them and trimmed edges on some that suggested harvest. Something the Keloks collected?

The growths extended for hundreds of feet to the point where the dark rock disappeared. It must have been a vertical inclusion in the sea-floor millions of years earlier. He couldn't think how else it could be a horizontal seam through the fins now.

He rounded the tower where he had seen Trrk go and found a series of deep pools surrounded by a grassy meadow. Vine trees clung to the towers. A tiny oasis in the rocks. He was about to swing his leg over to dismount when the roan's head flew up.

Chapter 7

Seth

The roan froze. Seth looked around, expecting to see Trrk. He did, along with five other Kelok hunters clustered at the base of a tower next to a pool of water. They were too far away to hear what they were saying, and they didn't seem to have noticed him and Lee yet.

"Scorch it," Lee muttered as she rode up next to him.

"Think we can talk our way out of this?" he asked.

"Depends on how Second feels about us as envoys. I'll go talk to them."

"You? You don't think this is male territory?"

"Prime designated me as her representative."

He studied the group of hunters. "Give Trrk a minute. See, the others all have their backs to us."

"He has them distracted?"

"Or they don't want to see us. Let's make that easy." He turned the roan and rode back behind the broken fin next to them. Lee followed. He dismounted and handed her his reins. "I'll get where I can see what's going on."

"Careful."

"Always."

Seth slipped around the tower of rock and lay down before inching ahead to where he could see the gathered Kelok hunters. Trrk and Second were talking together while four others hung back and waited. He could barely make out the voices, but they weren't loud enough for the hearing facilitator to translate.

Lee belly-crawled into place next to him. "Can you tell what's going on?"

"Not really." He could read impatience and irritation in the crests and twitching tails of the observers. Both Trrk and Second were more controlled. Trrk kept his eyes down, submissive to his superior.

"Poor Trrk," Lee said.

Seth put his finger to his lips. The Keloks had very good hearing.

Second said something to his companions and pointed them away with his beak. The four walked away to settle in a cluster by the farthest pool. Then he turned and led Trrk straight toward Seth and Lee.

Seth put his hand between Lee's shoulders to keep her still and moved closer to get behind the bush that screened her. Second hadn't given any sign that he was aware of them, so they still had a chance.

The two Keloks came almost to the base of the

tower the horses were behind. Second stopped a couple horse lengths from where Lee and Seth lay, glanced around, and put his back to their hiding spot.

Did Second know they were there? Seth lay still, keeping his breath shallow, resisting the urge to move off a rock under his hip. He could feel Lee against him, dead still.

Second faced Trrk. Seth didn't know them well enough to be able to figure out how much trouble Trrk was in. Second stood tall with his crest and arm feathers in full display. "Since you chose to look in an unexpected place," he said, "I charge you to stay here and watch for the First-Comers for two more days. You will then return to your village."

"As you wish," Trrk answered with his head bowed.

Second looked away, watched the other hunters. "I cannot speak to what will happen upon your return, to you or your spouses."

"Do not blame others for my actions," Trrk said.

"I know full well that you and your female are tight-knotted. And the strategy she devised was good." Second let his crest lower. "It *is* good. But only if the one selected as envoy can speak credibly to the First-Comer administrator."

"I have no reason to believe otherwise," Trrk said.

"Broadcasts question that."

"The envoy will dispel doubts when she can speak for herself."

"Then perhaps failing to find that one and recall her will prove to be in our favor in the end."

Trrk bobbed his head in silent answer.

"If she is not found." Second ruffled his crest. "Now we will go northward toward the Rim and see if they have gone that way. Bring a net of the tendril lichens back with you when you come. In case the healers have need of it."

"They will not," Trrk said, "but I will bring it."

Second bobbed his head once and stalked off to join the others at the far pool. They wasted no time shedding their satchels and net-bound packs and jumping in the water. Second joined them, a quick dip in and out, shaking his down dry. In a matter of minutes, he and his hunters were jogging away along the broken line of fins.

Chapter 8

Seth

"You may come out now," Trrk said.

So the Keloks had known they were there. Seth looked at Lee with a shrug. They got to their feet and came around the tower.

Trrk looked after the vanished hunters. "It would be best to wait until they are well away before bringing the horse animals out."

"Okay."

"They did not lay eyes upon you," Trrk said. "Their message was not delivered." He settled his crest into place. "It would be good if the envoy completes her task quickly."

"Yeah."

"Now we should not go the way I had intended. I will

show you another way out of the Fins." He paused. "Would your spouse wait here alone to rest the animals while we seek a path?"

Unlike Lee, the Kelok women were rarely by themselves. But spouse? Seth kind of liked the sound of that but didn't know how she would react.

Lee fidgeted with the rawhide bracelet she wore, a match to one on his wrist, with a hint of a grin. "I'll be fine." She ran her hand down his arm, squeezed his hand, and turned away, going around the rock toward the horses.

"Be right back," Seth told Trrk and followed her.

She stopped out of sight of the Kelok. "We are going to rest here for a while, aren't we?"

"The horses need a chance to graze."

"I'll unsaddle then."

"I don't know how long we'll be." He resisted the urge to put his arms around her and hold on, settling for a hand on her arm. "Once we are out of this tangle, we can make good time. Two days home, a day and a half if we push it."

"I know. Now get on with finding the way out of this maze."

He kissed her lightly and stepped away to get a flashlight and water bottle from his saddlebags. "I'm expecting a big dinner when we get back."

"Yeah, right." She said it with a grin. He left her there with the horses.

Trrk led him back past the lichens. "Why does Second want you to bring these?" Seth asked.

Trrk paused. "These," he said, pointing out a beard-like clump hanging from the wall. "The blue, not the yellow. Our healers use them to treat wounds."

"Oh." Seth thought about the implications of that. On one level he knew that the Keloks were fighters. He hadn't thought how that might play out if they couldn't set up a peaceful meeting.

"It will be all right," Trrk said. "You will be successful."

They stayed in the bottom, going beyond the notch they had come through into this aisle. He was hard-pressed to keep up with the Kelok. Not only was Seth more used to riding than walking, but Trrk was built to run. They passed several openings and got back into an area where the fins were unbroken. Finally, Trrk stopped and waited for him.

"There. Will the horses go over this place?"

They had reached a narrow break in the fin. A faint path, barely a hoof wide, traced up a steep climb to vanish through an opening. Tracks showed in the dust, swine-deer, Seth guessed, omnivores small enough to walk under a horse's belly. Or the more agile cliff dancers that could bounce up and down these blocks of rock like their name suggested.

"Maybe," he said. "Depends on what the other side looks like."

"I will leave you to assess it while I see how far it is to the next possibility. Go over and continue the way we have been going until I meet you."

"Why not use one of the earlier breaks?" Seth asked.

"There is a rock fall blocking the passageway on the other side between here and there."

Trrk trotted off, leaving Seth to scramble up through

the narrow opening. Getting up wasn't as bad as he had thought. On the other side was a steep but short slide down. Nothing the horses couldn't handle. But the passage it led to looked tricky. Broken slabs leaned against the walls creating tiny rockshelters just big enough to crawl into and rest out of the sun. But there was a path that looked wide enough for the pack horses, barely.

Seth followed it, winding between boulders where scraggly brush clung tenaciously. Something bigger than a cliff dancer, something with broad feet, had left vague marks in the sand. More than one animal or one animal several times.

The tracks might be indecipherable but the faint whiff drifting on the breeze had to be stink bear. The animal must be close. He had seen pictures but never actually run into one. They were secretive hunters, short-legged, stout, and unexpectedly fast, armored with large, overlapping, triangular scales, and fueled by a no-quit attitude. He'd heard that their stink, used to confuse prey, didn't last long.

Seth looked around. Another putrid whiff drifted to him. His eyes burned; he nearly gagged. He blinked away tears, saw something move. It rose on stubby legs, sprouted pine-cone scales, and charged at him.

He froze. Nowhere to run to. And the fumes — his eyes closed; he blinked furiously, began coughing. He dropped to the ground, curled into a ball with his hands locked behind his neck, held his breath, and tried to be a rock.

He could taste the stink bear's stench. Shnuffling

breath ruffled his hair; a broad muzzle pushed his shoulder. He did his best to be dead weight. No reaction. Don't breathe. If he did, he would gag. Through watery eyes, he could see short, sharp claws in front of his face. The muzzle shoved again; the mouth yawned wide above his head; razor plates lined the jaw. Seth closed his eyes and waited for the bite.

Something thudded into the stink bear. He heard Trrk yell, "Run!" He rolled away and stumbled for the highest pile of boulders he could see. He bounded up to balance on top.

Below him Trrk danced in front of the stink bear. The animal was smaller than Seth had thought, low enough to run under Trrk's raised tail, but stout. It kept one paw tucked up against its chest but that didn't slow it as it charged the Kelok. Seth expected Trrk to run, but he skipped aside, slapped it in the face with his tail, leaped over and around it, keeping it confused. Seth's eyes watered from the reek. How could Trrk stay so close?

Relentlessly Trrk struck with his strong, clawed feet, trying to come up under the bear's chin or into its belly. A scale tore loose; bluish blood stained Trrk's foot. The bear flattened the rest of the big, triangular scales tight to its body and curled into a ball. Trrk kicked it; it rolled over twice. Trrk pursued, swung his tail, knocked the balled bear into a rock. It unrolled and ran down the canyon, disappearing into the brush, leaving behind eye-burning fumes.

Trrk watched, swishing his tail across the ground, crest and arm feathers standing up, until the animal was out of sight. He whistled to Seth. "Let us go quickly.

Before it returns."

Seth scrambled down and followed Trrk at a run. He kept going until he was gasping for breath. Trrk stopped and waited for him, shaking himself to settle his feathers.

"Crippled," Trrk said. "The front leg."

"That might explain why it attacked me instead of running." Seth's heart still pounded.

"Are you hurt?"

"No," Seth said.

"Why did you not run?"

"To where?"

"But to lie as if dead?"

"It was either that or charge at it." The adrenaline seeped away, leaving him shaky. Seth brushed dirt from his clothes to cover his unsteady hands.

Trrk flared his crest in laughter. "You humans are very strange."

"How did you get that close with the stench? I could hardly see or breathe."

"Built in protection," Trrk said. Translucent membranes flicked across his eyes and flaps closed his nostrils briefly.

"I need to get away from the stink so I can breathe," Seth said. The odor was fading rapidly, but even the thought of it made his eyes water again.

"Yes, we need to go." Trrk draped his tail over his arm, something Seth had never seen him do before.

Seth looked closer and saw a bloody bite. The last third of the tail hung limp. "Let me see," he said.

"Later. Now more distance is advisable." Trrk moved

off, heading for the notch Seth had climbed through.

Once on the other side and headed back toward the lichens, Seth had no trouble keeping up with him. Not a good sign, but the Kelok plodded along steadily.

When they reached the lichens, Trrk stopped, leaning against a rock. "Pluck some of the bluish lichen," he said. "I will need it." He stumbled on, leaving Seth to collect the tendrils.

They approached the series of pools. Trrk barely looked up. The horses grazed in the little meadow with the roan and Clown staked on picket lines. The roan threw up his head and gave a trumpeting snort. Lee was on her feet, coming to meet them.

"Wait here," Seth told Trrk. "We'll move the horses."

Trrk nodded in response but didn't answer. How badly was he hurt?

Lee beat Seth to the horses. The animals snorted at the scent he carried. Their attention flicked back and forth between him and Trrk, ready to run.

Lee waved him away. "What is that smell?"

So much for it going away. "Stink bear," he answered.

"Does it wash off?" She took an exaggerated step away from him.

"No idea. Trrk's hurt."

"I thought he moved awfully slow."

"He hasn't even let me look at it yet. Tough and stubborn."

"Not like anyone else we know." She pointed at both of them.

"Move the horses away and we'll see how bad it is."

Chapter 9

Eta'ak

Eta'ak sat alone in the communications center with the broadcasts hushed. It was the third morning since Trrk had followed the envoys. The hunters came back a day ago, but he had not returned.

As planned, he had instructed his hunters to wait for orders from Second before pursuing the envoys. Then he had gone, telling them he would scout ahead. Not saying that he would divert the envoys from their planned course. Once that was done, he had intended to intercept the hunters.

But Trrk had not returned with them, and Second prohibited any search for him. Eta'ak was not privy to why. She longed to have them go and bring Trrk back.

She feared the consequences if they did.

She told herself that he must have accompanied the envoys, setting them safely on a different path, before coming back to her. That he would return at any time.

The males stayed close to the village, repairing nets and indulging in sparring matches. Releasing nervous energy.

The females also stayed, working at their looms, instructing the girls, watching the males uneasily.

No one spoke to her.

She set the communications equipment to monitor and record. She would scan later for any references of interest. She slipped out of the cavern, along the cliff, and into the slot canyon leading to the bathing area. She passed the pool and the showers and continued to her favorite place, a spur off the main canyon with overreaching walls that sheltered a garden of fungi from the sun. Carefully irrigated, it had first priority for the precious water they collected and stored. Racks and shelves built of cane lined the walls, supporting a profusion of growths that cascaded down. More grew in an artful pattern across the floor in substrates brought in for them. Reds, purples, shades of green, flaps, flags, mushroom caps. The room smelled of earth and spice. She breathed it in and focused on attending to the fungi.

Yrrlt interrupted her peace. "I thought you would come here."

"Do you need something?" Eta'ak asked.

"To be sure you are well. So much is uncertain now."

"For you perhaps." Eta'ak added a growth to the pile she had collected.

"So you still believe your pets will complete the task you gave them?"

"Is it our way to be disrespectful of clan mates?"

"They are weak. Our males can squash them as easily as —"

Eta'ak drew herself up tall. "They are thousands to our hundred. This is their territory. We have no battle forces to call. We cannot even lift from the surface of this planet. And we will be discovered before winter; interlopers to be offered assistance, to be refugees."

"Never. We will defend ourselves."

"Yrrlt, it is decided. Prime will meet with their planetary administrative officer as an equal and negotiate for us to hold what we have built here. And one day we will return to the starlanes and give our children the future they deserve."

"With the help of the two your spouse went to find?"

Eta'ak knew she shouldn't be surprised at Yrrlt's conclusion about Trrk's absence. She didn't answer, just waited.

Yrrlt continued. "He has not returned. And you have violated our trust. I am the new leader for Village of Canes."

Eta'ak lifted her beak and raised her epaulet feathers. "You may wish to be."

Yrrlt held out a multi-colored swatch of fabric. "By the council's decision, you have been unseated and rejected."

"No." Eta'ak took the cloth and read the colors that declared her spurned. Not banished but to remain within the bounds of the village as less than the pack of notalions that kept vermin at bay.

"Our clan-sisters have chosen me to replace you." Yrrlt paused.

Spurned. Of no account. Eta'ak used every measure of control she had learned over the years not to challenge Yrrlt. Of her clan sisters at Village of Canes, only Yrrlt aspired to leadership. Of course the others allowed her the responsibility.

Yrrlt's face flashed purple. "I will allow you time to consider your change in status. Then return to your communications room. You will remain there watching your precious First-Comers, keeping the translator operating so that any may hear what you hear."

Eta'ak tucked the swatch into her satchel and lowered her eyes. Apparent submission, but it hid the fire she felt.

"Good," Yrrlt said. "Appreciate that you are allowed to remain at Canes and not sent to Lichens under Prime's oversight."

The threat. Her future. She kept her eyes down until she heard Yrrlt's footsteps in the passage leading to the bathing room.

With Yrrlt gone, she was alone. Absolutely alone as she had never been in her life. Severed from the camaraderie of her clan-sisters, the support of the males. She had a new respect for the human Lee who had maintained such control through her apparent imprisonment.

Eta'ak stumbled from the garden. Dropping her satchel to the floor of the bathing chamber, she stepped into the pool and sank beneath the cool water, away from the summer heat, from reality. If she never came up, she would never have to face the eyes of the children unable to understand why she no longer told them stories. Selfish.

She raised her head above the surface, shook off water. Her personal status meant nothing against the future of their colony. She must take comfort in being among her clan, not banished into the wilds, even if it was a silent existence.

Chapter 10

Lee

Lee did her best to keep her emotions off her face. Looming cliffs all around, animals big and bad enough to injure a Kelok hunter, and no way out, yet. First things first. "Let's see what we can do for Trrk."

They found him at one of the pools with his tail in the water. The aroma of stink bear was distinct but fading. Lee was glad she hadn't experienced it fresh.

"May I help?" she asked.

"That will be necessary," he replied. "The injured area must be stabilized. My clan-brother has brought herbs for healing."

She took the beard of lichen from Seth. "Tell me

what to do."

"You will need to boil them."

"Okay, I'll get some things unpacked."

"I'll start a fire," Seth said.

"Thanks." She pinched her nose. "And thanks for not contaminating all our gear."

"I know. I'll wash as soon as we deal with Trrk." He started toward a clump of vine trees in search of wood.

"Seth," she said. He looked back. "I'm glad you're okay."

He nodded. "Me too."

She found the aid kit and set it next to Trrk. He was having trouble lifting his tail out of the water, at least the part below the bite. "Wait," Lee said. "Let me help." She fished a length of fabric out of the packs. It was almost as long as she was tall and two-thirds that wide, one of several she used as wrap dresses, ground cloths, blankets, and a dozen other things. This one had a gaudy yellow and bright blue abstract pattern with a spatter of blood stains from its last use as a blindfold to keep a man named Whip Willemsen from learning about the Keloks. He, his broken nose, and his bad attitude should be miles away, hiding out from the authorities.

More blood stains for the cloth now. She slid it under Trrk's injured tail and lifted it out of the water onto the bank. "Youch," Lee said. "That bear has one nasty bite." The tail looked like it had been slashed by knives from both sides. Apparently stink bears, like wolf lizards, the other large predator in the region, had shearing plates instead of teeth.

"Is it broken?" Lee carefully took the tail in both her

hands, feeling for fractures. "What?" No broken bones. No bones at all that she could tell.

"Broken?" Trrk asked. "The injury hinders its function. Is that broken?"

"No, I ... the anatomy is not what I expected. I thought there would be bones, an extension of the spinal column."

"No bones. Many, many muscles, like the nose of your mythical elephant."

"Not mythical," she said. "A living creature on the human home world." No wonder his tail was so prehensile. She looked closer. The cuts were deep. "With a human these would be bleeding badly."

"The vessels have closed to prevent that. The cuts must be drawn together soon to bring the flesh back in contact if it is to heal correctly."

"You mean like sewing them together?" She shivered at the thought, but it was the only reliable method she could think of to use in the wilds. They didn't have access to regeneration treatment so far from Portside. "We have temp skin. Maybe that will hold it."

Trrk clicked his beak. "Lichens first. Crumble them into water, enough to cover them. Simmer the mixture until it is thick. Coat the injury with it when it is still warm but cool enough to touch."

Lee studied the tail. "Okay. Lichens first."

Trrk eased himself down from his characteristic squat to sprawl on the ground. "I must sleep to heal. A full day, maybe more." Before she could ask him about that, his eyes closed and all the tension drained out of his body. He lay limp with only the slight rise and fall of his ribs to tell her he was alive.

"What happened?" Seth asked as he dropped an armload of wood.

"He said he has to sleep."

"That might make treating his tail easier."

"There's that." She stood up and shook the knots out of her shoulders. "We'd better get on with it. We're running out of daylight."

They cleared out a little pocket surrounded by rocks and brush where the flames would be hidden. Second already knew where they were, but Lee felt safer staying out of sight. While the blaze gathered strength, Seth got out a pot and filled it at a pool. While the first pot began heating, he got out a second and filled it.

"Might as well fix a hot dinner while we're at it," he said.

As the lichens simmered, they put off an odor that made Lee rethink cooking dinner at the same time. They set the second pot aside for the moment. The lichens must have contained a natural thickener; the concoction jellied rapidly. Lee took it off the heat.

"What now?" Seth asked.

"Trrk said to smear it on as soon as it's cool enough to touch."

Seth held the light while she spread the warm goo onto Trrk's tail. The two deep cuts from the bite were swollen and pale. The pungent smell of the lichens mingled with the lingering stink bear odor and made her eyes water.

"Come hold the edges together for me," she said.

"I'll see if I can get the temp skin to hold it." With Seth's help, she gave the tail a liberal coating. She wasn't happy with the result, but the temp skin would keep the wound clean and protected. She finished off by sliding an inflatable splint over the injury to stabilize it.

"Not much more we can do," she said.

"Do you know how long he's going to sleep?"

"A day, maybe more, he said."

"A day! We can't leave him like this," he said. "And it didn't sound like Second and the others planned to come back this way."

"I hope they don't. But you're right. We can't just leave him." She picked up the wrap she'd used to move his tail. "Right now, let's get dinner. I'll cook while you wash and change clothes."

The fire had nearly gone out while they worked on Trrk's tail. Lee built it up and heated water to boiling. She stirred it into a pouch of trail food and sucked in the aroma. Much better without the competing smells.

It was dark down among the fins. The larger moon hadn't climbed above the rocks yet but gave enough light that she could make out Seth doing his best to wash off stink bear in the smallest of the pools, too desert-conscious to spoil more water than necessary. "Tarbh stew," she called to him. "It'll be reconstituted in a minute. I'm hungry."

Seth checked on the horses and then joined her by the fire. Not that they needed it. The rocks radiated the day's heat.

"One of us could make it back to Trrk's village in a day," he said, shoving his stew around with a spoon.

Lee refrained from wondering if either of them could even find their way back through the Fins. Or mentioning the little matter of getting their memories wiped. "He'd never forgive us," she said. "He's totally committed to making this meeting between the PAO and Prime happen."

"I have to admire that about him. In fact, I'm kinda getting to like him, even if he is a cocky rooster."

Lee wasn't so sure, but she hadn't spent as much time with him as Seth had. "You figure we're what? Three days from Under Rim?

"Less. But isn't the whole idea to keep rumors about aliens from reaching the PAO before she gets a firsthand account?"

"It was," Lee said. Villages of castaway aliens seemed like something the top officials needed to hear about first, no matter how bottom-up Carico's government might be.

"I'm too tired to sort it out tonight."

"Me too," she agreed. "Do we need to stand watch?"

"Let the horses do it for us," he said.

They cleaned up camp, made sure the fire was out, and checked on the horses. Seth made a good story of the stink bear attack. Neither of them voiced their concerns over Trrk's condition. That didn't need saying. She enjoyed the feel of lying against Seth in spite of the night's heat while he made it clear he didn't mind in the slightest. Decisions could wait until morning.

Chapter 11

Seth

Seth held the roan's hind foot and eyed it for level. Satisfied, he let the horse set the foot down. He had one more horse to trim and give new coatings of protective palm pine sap. They were overdue for that, and their feet showed it after yesterday's tromp through the rocks. And it gave him something to do while they waited.

It was getting hot in the little oasis among the Fins. Trrk slept unmoving under the shade they had rigged for him. Lee was off looking for a way out of the Fins, unable to sit around camp. He knew how she felt — the urgency to be gone in case Second changed his mind and came back; to deliver the message and pass the responsibility for contact between the Keloks and humans to someone else; to do something to help Trrk.

Midday. The only thing they had decided was to give Trrk a day of sleep. At sundown, what? Seth moved along the highline under the vine trees from the roan to Tinker, to something useful he could do. He picked up the brown gelding's left front foot and went to work on it.

He finished before Lee got back. From the bounce in her step, he expected good news. "You found the way?"

"I did." She pointed the way that Second and his hunters had gone the day before. "It's a ways, but a straight shot along this passage will get us out onto a rocky tableland. I could see hints of a forest to the north."

"Sounds promising." If they were heading for Under Rim. But he didn't voice that. "I don't know about you, but I'm hot. What do you say to a good soak in a cool pool?"

The sun dropped behind the fins and cooled the day. Seth hobbled the horses and turned them loose to graze for the evening. Lee dropped an armload of firewood and went to Trrk. The Kelok still slept, rarely shifting, as he had since they had treated his wound the night before.

"I don't like the way he looks," Lee said. "His respiration is barely noticeable, and he's so pale."

Seth joined her. "He said it would be a day." He didn't like Trrk's condition any more than she did, but what did they know about Kelok healing trances? "I'll start dinner. We should have something ready when he wakes up."

"What do we do if he doesn't?"

"He will." Seth tried to believe that.

"I think he needs a doctor."

"Got one in mind?" he asked.

"Uh ..."

He could see the thoughts running behind her eyes. He took her hand, pulled her closer. "Look, I'm worried too, but let's not panic until he's had at least a full day's sleep."

She leaned in. He hugged her, then took her by the shoulders and looked her in the eye. "We'll work it out."

She nodded. "It's just ... We have to get the invitation to the PAO before the satellites start transmitting data or risk the villages being found first."

"I know that."

"And our best chance of reaching the PAO without a formal appointment might be Settlement Day when she'll be out among the celebrations."

"Okay." He counted it out in his head. "That's what? Five days?" That should give them enough time to get to Under Rim and find a likely spot to cross paths with the PAO.

"If Trrk wakes up in good enough shape to leave on his own. If we get out of the Fins without Second and his friends coming back. If we can avoid Adel's interference." She looked over at Trrk. "In any case, we can't wait long enough for him to recuperate. Maybe I should go on ahead and bring Doc here."

"No," he said. "No."

"Why not?"

"I just think we need to stick together." He reached out, stroked his thumb along her cheek. "Maybe we could take him back toward Canes and leave him for them to find." Bad idea but did they have a better?

"And risk them finding us too?" She shook her head. "We can't stay here; we can't go back; you don't want me to go on alone. Then we'll have to take him with us."

"To Under Rim? Are you crazy?"

She looked at him steadily without a word.

"And have people see him before we get to the PAO?" He shook his head. "Besides, what kind of welcome do you think he'd get?"

She looked puzzled. "What do you mean?"

"Where you come from non-humans may be common, but I'll give you odds that most people in Under Rim have never seen one face-to-face."

"What about your father and Kiri? And Doc Legat?"

"Okay, I didn't say there weren't exceptions. My point is if we take Trrk to Under Rim, word's going to spread like fire."

"So we take him someplace away from town where we can get him help without everybody knowing about him."

He knew that stubborn look, jaw set, shoulders tense, eyes narrowed. "You're right. We could. But how would we get him there? Put him up on Creamy? Unconscious?" He stepped back from her. "Let's give him a little time."

"And hope everything works out?"

"For the moment."

"What if we wait too long? For him, I mean."

He looked at the slack lump that was Trrk. "If he isn't awake by the time Lander rises, we'll talk about it again."

They fixed dinner and waited. At last, the moon, nearing full, lit the tips of the fins. Trrk showed no sign of waking up. And Seth was no closer to figuring out what to do about it. In many ways, Lee going on alone made the most sense. But the tightness in his chest at the thought of separating had nothing to do with sense. Or with knowing she was more than capable.

"He's no better." Lee straightened from inspecting Trrk.

"I know. Void! We can't stay; we can't go. I wish I had a good answer."

"We need to go and take him with us," she said. "To Doc. You know Doc will keep him secret. He'd never violate a patient's confidentiality."

"How about bringing Doc to him? Someplace like Fallen Pine Cabin?" Her parents' seldom-used place clear up against the foot of the Rim.

"Or someplace no one would think to look for us," she said. "One of the outlying camps like Tobin Canyon." Used twice a year during the tarbh migration to trap the half-wild animals. "Or Ike's cabin. Is it still standing?"

He nodded. "That would work if it is. And if we can find it." Seth wasn't sure where the place was. He didn't recall hearing about the man when he was growing up even though his pa had to have known him. There were too many family connections.

"There's a sketch map in the journal we found in Ike's things," Lee said.

"There's still the problem of getting Trrk there."

Lee grinned. "You convince Creamy to get close to Trrk. I think I can take care of the rest." Before she finished what she was saying, she was headed for the vine trees where the horses were tied.

What did she have in mind? He shook his head. At least one of them had a plan.

Getting the horses to accept Trrk was a matter of familiarization. Not difficult. It just took time they hadn't taken.

Seth led the horse from the highline to a pool for a drink, passing within a few feet of Trrk. He let the horse stop and get a good look and smell before encouraging the animal to walk on. He led him back by again after Creamy drank. Then back again to the grass where he let the horse graze. Creamy paid little attention to the Kelok. Trrk was not very threatening in his current state — more an object than a potential rider, and Creamy had packed a lot of objects.

Lee rejoined him. "Good. Step one. I need Creamy for step two."

"What are you up to?" Seth asked.

"You'll see."

He followed her back to the highline. She took Creamy's lead from him. "You'll have to put Creamy's pack saddle and packs on Clown," she said. "I'll use my saddle on Creamy."

With a shrug, he did as he was told. It took a while. Clown was much lighter built than Creamy. He was only half done when Lee led Creamy out into the sandy bottom above the pools. She took the horse to something lying on the ground. He couldn't resist going to see.

"It's a travois," she said. "A drag sled. For hauling loads."

She'd taken two long poles, almost straight as vine trees went, and lashed shorter branches between them at one end, making a platform of sorts on about a third of the length. At the other end, she'd used spare rope to make a harness. "See. This fastens to the saddle. One pole on each side. The other ends of the poles drag on the ground. And Trrk rides on it."

He studied the contraption. "It might just work. If Creamy will pull it."

"Let's find out."

Creamy didn't object to having the frame dragged along next to him or behind him. He was only mildly uneasy about having it attached to him and pulling it. But with Lee on it, he hesitated. Seth coaxed him into a few steps. Once the horse got comfortable with the feel, he steadied and plodded along at Seth's side.

"Guess you're walking," he said.

"Guess I might perch on the saddle even with the poles along the sides." She disconnected the drag and hobbled Creamy on the grass. "Let's get packed up."

While he finished adjusting the pack saddle on Clown, she disappeared and returned with a bundle of the lichen they had used on Trrk's tail. "Just in case," she said.

It didn't take long to pack. It was a familiar routine. Lee fussed with the adjustments on Clown's saddle while Seth checked weights to be sure the packs were balanced. He took care to be sure everything was secure. Clown rolled his eyes at the unfamiliar load on his back. Lee rubbed his neck and led him around to get him used to the sight and feel. Once he relaxed, she tied him behind Tinker.

"Let's do this," she said and led Creamy over so the drag was next to Trrk. They used a blanket as a sling to hoist him onto it. Trrk never moved. Seth laid a hand on the Kelok's chest and was relieved to feel the slow rise and fall of his breath.

"Better tie him on," Lee said.

Seth freed a net from the outside of Trrk's satchel and stretched it over the Kelok, tying the corners to the drag frame. "That ought to do it."

Lee walked, leading Creamy and trying to pick a path the drag could get through. Seth rode behind, keeping an eye on Trrk and leading the pack horses. Luckily the passage was one of the wider they had seen. But not ideal for the drag. Too many obstacles. It was slow going. The moon passed overhead and sank westward. They still hadn't reached the end of the Fins.

"Stop," he called out for the umpteenth time. He dismounted and lifted the drag off the rock it was hung up on. "Okay." Lee went on. Seth gave up and walked, tucking his horse's reins under his belt to leave his hands free.

"Getting narrower," Lee called back. Lander had dropped until it just brushed the top of the fins with silver, giving some light. The walls closed in.

Creamy stopped. "Come look at this," Lee said.

Seth wrapped the roan's reins around a bush and stepped around the drag with its unmoving load. "Void!" A pool of water filled the bottom of the cleft in front of them from wall to wall. "You didn't mention this earlier."

"I wasn't thinking about getting a drag through it. How deep do you think it is?" Lee asked.

In second-hand moonlight off the rock wall, the dark surface was a mirror. He broke off a dead whipbrush stem and tested the depth. "Only knee deep."

"Yeah, two feet in front of you. How about in the middle?"

"I'll ride the roan through and find out." The whole pool only ran a couple horse-lengths.

"How do you plan to get him past Creamy and the drag?"

He shrugged and walked into the water, feeling out each step before committing. What kind of traps waited out of sight? But the footing wasn't bad and the water, at the deepest, barely came above his knees. No problem for the horses.

He came back through. "Looks like this opens up not far ahead."

"The end of the Fins. All we have to do is get there." She looked back at Trrk. "Can you carry the end of the drag alone?"

"Just like one end of a stretcher." It might be easier than all the bending and lifting he'd done so far. He scrambled past Creamy and picked up the ends of the poles.

She urged the horse forward. Creamy moved steadily into the pool. Seth lifted the drag as high as he could, keeping Trrk above the water. At the deepest point, Seth's foot slipped on a rock, and he jostled the drag. One of Trrk's hands reached out and grasped the drag frame.

"He moved. Trrk moved."

Creamy stopped, and Lee looked over her shoulder.

"Keep going," he said. "Get out of the water."

"Right." She moved Creamy forward until Seth was on dry ground before jumping off. "You're sure?"

Trrk pushed against the net and opened his eyes.

"Easy," Seth said. "Lie still."

The big eyes focused on him, then closed. Trrk settled back but one hand found a new grip on the poles under him.

Lee looked at Seth. "What now?"

"Go on. See if we can find a decent place to camp."

She led Creamy ahead while he went back through the pool and got the other horses. He caught up with her before she reached the end of the fin where it sloped into a sandy hill. Without the towering fin to block it, moonlight showed scattered clumps of grass and low brush, and lots of exposed rock. Still not easy ground for the drag.

Lee stopped at the top of the first rise. They unhitched the drag and laid it flat. Trrk hissed softly and shifted but didn't open his eyes again.

"At least he's responding," Seth said. "That's good,

right?"

"It's a change. Are we stopping here?"

Seth looked around. A clump of copper trees promised shade when morning, and the heat, came. The graying sky told him that wasn't too far off. "For a while." How long remained to be seen.

Chapter 12

Eta'ak

A night passed and most of a day since her spurning. Eta'ak's two spouses occupied the communications room. In the back of the space, separated from them by a mat wall, Eta'ak schooled herself to be patient, pouring her tension through her drop spindle as she turned fiber to thread. While she listened to their familiar voices.

Bless them. They honored the spurning to the point of not directly addressing her, but had seen to it that she had a place of her own, out of sight but not hearing. And when Yrrlt had removed her chaise bed from the women's quarters, they had 'disposed of it' in her new space.

"No word and no word and still no word," one of them said. "Not of missing riders being found; not of the appearance of an alien among them. What has become of our brother?"

"Better that he be helping the envoys than be here yet not here like ..." The voice trailed off.

"You believe that is what he is doing?"

"Assuredly."

"They have little time to complete their mission. The ship bringing the satellite arrays will arrive any day now."

"Prime will not wait or trust."

Silence. They kept the volume of the broadcasts too low for her or others outside that room to hear the words. But she heard the tone signaling a communication from Second.

"It is as we feared," one of her spouses said.

Eta'ak rose and peeked around the mat. She had been avoiding facing them openly, not wishing to put them in an awkward position. They were under enough threat by being her spouses. But she had to hear this.

"Yes. Second calls for relocation of critical equipment to the Village of Lichens. He is sending runners to collect the communications apparatus. We are to dismantle it in preparation."

Eta'ak bowed her head. She had expected this. Gathering irreplaceable technology in one place to defend it was part of a long-established plan in case they were discovered. What would she do now with her sole responsibility taken away? How could she know if the envoys succeeded? She had no answers.

She brought out baskets stored in the space she occupied. Without a word to her spouses, she helped them pack. They left a single voice-only link to the other villages. The equipment to monitor the human broadcasts, the holographic conferencing, the big viewscreen were all packed away. Eta'ak made sure the empty basket that should hold the hearing facilitation devices was deep in the bottom of a larger basket where it might go unnoticed for a time.

Her spouses muttered to each other, telling Eta'ak without openly speaking to her, about the plan Prime had ordered implemented, about the council supporting her in this emergency, reverting to the old command structure from their shipboard days. About their fool of a brother who was no doubt helping the tailless ones when he should be back at Canes. For her part, Eta'ak did her best to protect them from her disgrace with the pretense of not hearing, of being alone in the space.

Eta'ak clung to the hope that the envoys would achieve their goal and deliver the invitation to the planetary administrative officer. Should word of that reach the villages, honor would demand that Prime carry through with the meeting. If Prime refused to attend, it would only delay contact with the First-Comers and put the Keloks on the defensive. Eta'ak needed a strategy to persuade Prime to place honor over fear. But with no one monitoring the broadcasts, how would they even know?

Chapter 13

Seth

Seth found a seat against the base of a copper tree. The horses were hobbled and grazing. Their minimal camp was set up. Just the basics — bedding, a highline to tie the horses to later, and Trrk. They couldn't help Trrk if they didn't get some rest themselves after that trip through the Fins.

Lee leaned over Trrk. "I don't like this. The end of his tail is cold. I think we should rest for a couple hours and then go on."

He couldn't argue. "If we go up into the palm-pines, we should have good ground all the way to Under Rim."

"So you're all right with taking him there?"

Seth shook his head. "Not town. Ike's old cabin, I think. His journal shows it's on our way, and Doc can come there."

"Adel will be watching Under Rim."

"You think so?"

"She's not stupid." Lee paced. "Trrk and the hunters didn't leave any clues. If ... when ... your father and Dougherty give up trying to find us, she'll follow their lead. And wait to see what they do."

"One more reason not to show up in town."

"Just to get Doc, then. You're right. He'll keep a patient confidential."

"No," Trrk rasped. Seth got to his feet. Lee beat him to the Kelok.

"You're awake." She knelt by him.

"I will not go to your medical person," Trrk said, his voice weak. "You must focus on your task."

"We'll deliver the message," she said. "We can do that and see that you get the care you need."

"I am ..." He trailed off, looking around. "Where have you brought me?"

"We're just outside the Fins." Seth dropped down next to Lee.

"How long have I slept?" Trrk asked.

Lee reached out to smooth his feathers. "Since you went into your trance or whatever it was? A day and a half."

"Then you may go on your way." He pushed himself into his characteristic squat. "I will rest. Then I will return home."

"We need rest too," Seth said. "We took all night

getting you this far. We'll talk later about what to do next."

"No need to talk. You will carry out your mission. I will go home."

"You can't," Lee said. "You aren't fit to go anywhere on your own."

Seth read the stubbornness in Trrk's look. "Later," he said, taking Lee by the arm and pulling her to her feet. "Let's get him something to eat."

"But ..."

He drew her away. "Let it go for now," he said. "He needs food and water."

"Okay, you're right. But we can't leave him in his condition."

"I'm not saying we should. But don't push him." Trrk was already lying down again.

"All right," Lee said. "Get him some water. I'll find him something to eat."

They moved Trrk under the copper trees where he'd be in the shade when the sun came up. He drank eagerly and barely nibbled at the food. He refused to let them look at his injury. When they left him alone, he soon fell asleep.

"You get some rest," Seth told her. "I'll keep watch."

"For what? If the Keloks come back, they come back." She leaned against him. "I'll join you in a minute."

"Do that." He watched as she walked away. She checked the horses, then took water bottles back to the last pool they had come through. The sun wasn't above the hills yet, but it already warmed the air. As she trudged back to him, Seth could see she was as tired as he was. How much more tangled could this get? A diplomatic mission; Adel undermining them; now Trrk's injury.

Lee came back and stretched out next to him. "It's going to be hot once the sun comes up."

He pulled her against him. Having her with him again and not having time to enjoy it might be the worst part of all of this. "How tired are you?" he whispered.

"Exhausted," she said, but she didn't act like it.

Sometime later — he wasn't sure how long — Seth disentangled himself from her, trying not to wake her in the process.

"What is it?" she asked.

"Not sure. I heard something." He stood up.

She joined him. "Trrk." She pointed to where they had left the Kelok. He was gone.

"Taking the decision out of our hands." Seth shook his head. "Stubborn."

"Well, he's not going far in his condition," Lee said and began pulling on clothes.

She was right. They found him where he had crawled into a thick clump of thousand-seed plants, not quite far enough to hide the end of his tail in its splint. When Seth pushed aside the stems, Trrk opened his eyes and lifted his head.

"Go," he said.

"Okay," Seth replied. "We'll go back to camp." He offered Trrk a hand. The Kelok refused to take it. "Get the drag," Seth told Lee.

Trrk pushed himself to his feet and wobbled into the open. "Why will you not leave me?"

"You got hurt helping me," Seth said.

"And we are of the clan, aren't we?" Lee asked.

"But I am not." His head dropped. "Not anymore."

Oh. Well, they figured Trrk had violated Kelok rules by coming after them. "You are part of our clan," Seth said. "Now come back to camp." He took Trrk's arm and urged him forward. Trrk accepted the help.

Seth settled Trrk onto the bedding. Lee rummaged in the packs, brought out a shallow pan, and put one of the trail bars in it to soak in water.

"What did you mean about not being part of the clan?" she asked.

Trrk hesitated.

"Is it because you came to warn us?" Seth asked.

Trrk bobbed his head. "In part."

"And your tail?" Lee asked.

"If it does not heal properly ... I do not wish to talk about it."

"Then we'll have to make sure it heals," Seth said. "You come with us. I know a doctor who can help. You can help us deliver the invitation to the PAO."

"I cannot be seen, not until your PAO meets with Prime."

"Doc can't tell anyone about his patients," Seth said. "He took an oath."

"If we need to, we can let people think you are alone until after the message is delivered. The only one of your kind on Carico." Lee brought him the pan of food. "Now let that soak a while, then drink the broth off it. Do you want it heated?"

"Cold will suffice." He looked at Seth. "I must accept

your assistance. If I can no longer prevail in the arena ..." He paused, ruffled his crest. "I would lose the right to be spouse to Eta'ak."

"She might have something to say about that," Seth said. "I don't know how things work with your people, but I've seen the way she looks at you."

Trrk eased down onto the bedding and closed his eyes without answering.

"What now?" Lee asked.

"Let him sleep a while." Seth checked the angle of the sun. Nearing midday. "We should try to get through this rocky ground before dark."

"How far do you think?"

"I don't really know." This was new country to him. He had seen the Fins on maps but never paid much attention. Maps! "Where's the map you and Ike had?"

She shook her head. "In the packs, but it didn't include anything north of the hills by Stampede Spring. We hadn't planned to come up here."

"Oh, well." He tried to picture the maps he had seen in the past. "The Rim can't be too far north of us, a day at the most. And there's a wide band of pines below it, at least around Under Rim." He looked at Trrk, already deeply asleep. "Wait a couple hours and then move on?"

"Should we tie the horses?" she asked.

"I hate to. They need time to graze."

"Trustworthy bunch," She grinned. "Even that nameless roan."

Seth kept a straight face. "He's not nameless."

"Oh? Then what's his name?"

"RC," he said. Just because he never used it didn't

mean it hadn't been in his head all along.

"Arsy?"

"R. C. for Roan Colt."

"Roan for short." She shook her head with a laugh.

"Roan for short." He didn't mention that those were also her father's initials. Ran Cory had been almost as instrumental in his recovery from Jerdix's torture as the horse had been.

The look in her eyes told him she hadn't missed that connection. "Okay. If you say so." She pillowed her head on his shoulder. "Roan and the others can graze while we rest."

Chapter 14

Seth

Seth stopped walking and looked ahead. Palm-pines at last. Good. Maybe there he could ride, and Creamy could go faster. Or they could call it good for the day. They were running out of daylight, and energy, anyway.

He stopped at the first big tree they came to and brushed a hand across the bark. Palm-pines. Carico's all-purpose tree – wood, sweetener and protective coatings from the sap, and shade. He had never been so glad to see the straight trunks towering skyward with the open understory, kept clear of brush by regular wildfires. And dirt, not rock, for the drag.

They didn't go far before Lee stopped. "Time for a

break," she said. Seth was more than happy to rest. He had walked most of the afternoon, wrestling the drag over the rocky ground. Trrk had tried to walk for a while, but that slowed them down even more.

They freed the drag from Creamy, leaving Trrk to settle himself in a bed of fallen pine leaves while they pulled the packs and saddles off. With the horses hobbled and grazing, Seth stretched out in the shade with a groan. His back hurt for bending to lift the drag over obstacles. His feet hurt from walking. His boots, already worn when he had left home to find Lee, had more hole than sole now.

"Hungry?" Lee asked.

"No. Yes." He didn't want to move, but his stomach had other ideas. He sat up. "Kelok trail bars just never get old."

She laughed. "I can dig into the packs. We have a couple pouches left from what Ike and I packed."

"That would be good." He took a drink from his water bottle. "How about you? How's riding with the drag working out?"

"Okay." She rubbed at her neck. "Too much looking over my shoulder though."

"It'll be easier now. We'll let the horses graze a while and then go on." Lander would be full when it rose soon. Plenty of light to travel by. If the clouds from the afternoon storms cleared. A rumble in the distance told him they weren't done yet.

Trrk refused the human food but nibbled at a trail bar, washing it down with a bottle of water. Seth took that as a sign that he was feeling better.

Water was another thing. Up near the Rim there were lots of streams and springs, but they came together into a few major drainages before reaching the open tableland below the palm-pine forest. Going west, Seth had no idea how far they would have to go to find one.

They could go farther toward the Rim before turning west. Better chance for water but more drainages to cross meant tougher ground for the drag. And Trrk still needed the drag to ride on. Trade-offs.

He didn't bring up any of that. Let Trrk and Lee rest without those worries. They could talk about it when they got ready to move on. He stretched out, tried to ease sore muscles, and dozed a little, aware that his companions had no problem sleeping. Truth was that the farther they got from Blue Canyon and the closer to Under Rim, the more he felt like the one who was supposed to have the answers.

So he watched Lander's bright disk climb higher into the sky, listening to the quiet munch of horses grazing until they had their fill and dozed together in the moonlight, hips cocked. Thunder rumbled in the distance and clouds passed over the moon. They could wait a little longer to move on.

A quick evaluation of Trrk's condition changed his mind. Trrk, who had refused to let them look at his injury earlier, moved restlessly in his sleep, his tail twitching and jerking. And rasping deep in his throat each time it moved. It had to hurt; it needed care. Stubborn Kelok.

Seth got up and went to get his roan. When his horse

was brushed off, saddled, and ready to go, he got Tinker. The other two followed him to camp, hobble chains clinking. Enough to wake Lee. Without a word, she joined him and began to brush and saddle Clown. He loaded the packs on Tinker and Clown while she got Creamy ready to go and the drag in place.

She went to Trrk while Seth settled the last pack on Clown. The little gelding didn't think much of being a pack horse, twitching his ears and switching his tail. But he stood.

Trrk was on his feet. Lee dropped the bedding on the drag and came over to Seth. "You go talk to him," she said. "He won't listen to me."

"What?"

"He refuses to get on the drag or let me look at his tail. In fact, he didn't seem to want to talk to me at all."

"Okay." Seth laid his hand on her shoulder lightly. Feeling her tension, he resisted the urge to hug her. "Get the pack horses lined out. I'll see what I can do."

She patted his hand and stepped away. He watched her for a moment. So tough; she just kept going. One of these days, they were going to have time just to be together. Someday.

"I will walk," Trrk said, then added, "for a while."

"You should let Lee check your tail."

"It would not be right."

"Ah." Apparently the Kelok male-female boundaries were back in place. "Would it be okay for me to look at it, make sure the splint is not too tight?"

"You may do that."

"You let her treat it before," Seth said. "Why not

now?"

"That was ..." Trrk's crest ruffled. "That was the first, the evaluation to establish what is needed. Now is to carry out treatment."

"A male responsibility."

"My brothers' responsibility."

"Just say so," Seth said. "We don't understand how you do things. You have to tell us."

"Instructing a female is uncomfortable for me."

Seth checked the splint. It was snug but not tight. Still, the end of the tail felt cold. Seth loosened the splint. "Are you sure you won't ride on the drag? We'll travel faster that way."

"I ... yes, I will ride. For the sake of speed."

The horses eyed him suspiciously but let him approach and settle onto the drag. Once he was still, they relaxed.

"A male thing?" Lee asked when Seth went to offer her a leg up onto Creamy.

"Yeah."

"Better go with it." She brushed his cheek with her lips and turned to gather her reins. He cupped his hands and gave her a boost up.

"Lead off. I'll keep an eye on the drag."

"West?"

"West."

Chapter 15

Seth

Seth followed the drag. The horses were getting better about ambling along behind instead of trying to travel at their normal speed. And Lee was able to set a faster pace with the smoother ground. Trrk slept, or appeared to, with a grip on the poles of the drag and his tail carefully curled up so it didn't dangle off.

Moonlight trickled in through the broad leaves of the palm-pines, vanishing behind clouds to reappear, casting ever-shifting shadows on the forest floor. Time blurred into the soft hoofbeats, the creak of saddles, and rustling of leaves in the shifting breezes.

"Hold up." Seth stopped the roan. Lee looked back

and brought Creamy to a halt.

"What?"

"When did we turn north?" The moon had just dropped below the clouds and was off his left shoulder. How long had it been hidden?

She looked around. "No idea. Sorry."

They were going the wrong direction. For how long?

Trrk pushed himself up. "Difficulties?"

"Just a little turned around," Seth said.

"What now?" Lee asked.

"Southwest," he said. "If we want to go to Ike's old place."

"Since we're closer to the Rim now, we could go up to Fallen Pine." Lee sounded hopeful.

"Yeah. But will they be watching for us there?" It was a place they had used as a refuge before.

"Joe will, which means Adel could find out about it."

"Ike's then. If it's the place I think it is, it's a ruin. Not many would put it together with Ike, much less us."

"This is a place I will not be seen?" Trrk asked.

"That is the idea," Seth said. "We can bring Doc there."

"But can the message be delivered?"

Lee twisted around in her saddle to face him. "I will make sure of that."

Trrk pushed himself to his feet, facing Seth. "I am afraid you do not fully appreciate the urgency."

"I know how long we have." Lee glared at the Kelok. "I — no, *we* — got a little lost. In the woods, in the dark. A couple hours."

"Don't worry," Seth said. "We're all tired. But we

have time."

"I delay you. You should not have brought me with you."

Seth didn't want to go through that argument again. "Things have a way of working out." He let it go at that.

Lee took a careful look at the moon, turned her horse to the southwest, and moved out without a word. Trrk may not have realized it, but she was definitely feeling the pressure. Seth saw it in the set of her shoulders and the way she kept pushing the horse to walk faster. No wonder her temper was frayed.

And he was as much at fault as she was for getting off track. He hadn't been paying attention either. When the moon disappeared behind clouds, everything looked the same. At least now the sky had cleared. Besides, he told himself, how lost could you get when you didn't know where you were to start with?

Water. He could hear it. The horses moved faster. And they came to a draw. Not very deep but not something the drag could cross easily.

"Scorch it," Lee said, looking down into it.

"Trrk, you are going to have to walk," Seth said. "Can you do that?"

"I will walk."

"Wait here. Let us get the horses down."

Trrk climbed off the drag and moved aside to squat under a big palm-pine. The horses barely gave him a second look. Progress.

Seth got off the roan and helped Lee unhook the drag from Creamy. "Take the horses," he said. "I'll get this thing."

"Fine." She got back on Creamy and took the roan's reins.

"Camp here?" he suggested.

"Yeah." She rode down the slope with the string of horses behind her.

The ground wasn't that rough, just a little steep. Not bad for the drag by itself. He picked a path, glad the moon was still high enough to give him light, and pulled the contraption down.

Lee sat on Creamy, letting the horses drink. Before he got down to her, before the animals were satisfied, she pulled them away. He left the drag by the creek, jumped across, and helped her tie the horses.

He laid his hand over hers as she started to unpack Clown. "We're doing fine," he said.

She turned around. "I know." She leaned her forehead against his chest for a moment before pushing back. "I'll get this. You better go make sure Trrk makes it down okay."

He cupped her face with his hand and ran his thumb over her cheek. Then he headed back to get Trrk.

The Kelok refused help and made his way down the hill with careful, determined steps. When he reached the creek, he settled down on his belly in the water with his tail on the bank and sighed.

Seth left him there and went to help Lee unsaddle and hobble the horses so they could graze. They went through the routine of setting up a minimal camp and carried the drag over the water. Seth started a little fire in a sheltered spot.

The smell of food cooking brought Trrk from the

water. But he didn't eat much and avoided looking at Lee. He shifted his tail frequently.

"Want me to look at that?" Seth asked. "Maybe I can adjust the splint a little."

"If you wish."

Seth deflated and reset the splint. He didn't like the look of the tail below the bite but kept it to himself. Nothing they could do about it except get him to Doc.

"How long will we rest here?" Trrk asked.

"A while. The horses need to eat."

"How long before the ship with the satellites arrives?"

Seth looked at Lee. "Two days?" he asked. He was losing track of time.

She nodded. "Something like that."

"Before you will reach the PAO?" Trrk looked at Seth.

"Probably," Seth said.

"The ship will mean discovery is inevitable." Trrk's crest lifted tensely. "Prime will act to prepare to protect my people."

"Makes sense."

"You have barely glimpsed the technology we possess. Do not believe we are defenseless."

A niggle began in Seth's gut. They hadn't seen much technology but what they had seen — the hearing facilitators, holo-conferencing between the villages, even being able to monitor the humans' broadcasts — impressed him. What kind of weapons had these people salvaged from their failing starship?

Trrk looked him in the eye. "Our only hope is for your PAO to accept Prime's invitation and for Prime to honor that. If not, both our peoples will bleed and mine, ultimately, will die. We will not give up what has been paid for with the lives of the ones who did not survive the first years." He took a breath, folded his crest down, and lowered his eyes. "We must not fail."

Lee stood up. "We might not get to the PAO before the ship arrives, but we will before the satellites are deployed. And before your villages are revealed." She walked away toward the horses.

"We won't fail," Seth said.

"Go to your spouse," Trrk said. "I am afraid the healing sleep comes back on me. Do not let me delay you." He sagged onto the bedding, and his eyes closed.

"Frog-eels!" Seth turned away and went across the meadow to catch up to Lee. Damele had risen, its half-disk adding to the light from Lander in the west. It would be dawn soon.

Lee didn't say anything when he reached her. She wrapped her arms around him and kissed him. He gave himself to the moment, leaving it to her to draw back. "Mmm, you know how to distract me."

"Works both ways." She leaned against him. "How do we get through this?"

"Just like we have been. One step at a time."

"There's so much at risk."

"No more than there was yesterday or the day before."

She looked up at him. "Right. I've always known they would fight if pushed. It was just hearing him say it."

"I know." He kissed her again, keeping it light. "We go to the PAO; she meets with Prime. Like we planned.

Now, I need some sleep. What about you?"

"Does it show?" She pushed away from him and pulled herself up straight.

"Nah," he said. "But Trrk, well, he's going back into that healing sleep he does."

"I guess we might as well rest too."

Chapter 16

Seth

Seth got up when the sunlight hit him, leaving Lee sleeping. Trrk lay unmoving except for the very slow rise and fall of his breath. The horses grazed near the creek. He picked up the roan's halter.

"What are you doing?" Lee asked. She got to her feet.

"Going for Doc."

"Wait." She pulled her pants on. "I can't manage Trrk on my own."

"You'll be fine. I'll bring Doc here."

"No, I'll get Doc. You get Trrk to Ike's old place."

Seth rubbed at the back of his neck. She was right. She couldn't get Trrk on and off the drag by herself, aside from the Kelok's gender separation issues if he did wake up. And getting him to Ike's would mean they could work from there to reach the PAO. "Okay. Okay. You go."

"Good thing Doc is male." She picked up the rest of the halters. "Better get everything packed and loaded before I go."

"And get Trrk up out of this draw."

They brought the horses in and got them saddled. With Lee taking Clown, Seth put his riding saddle on Creamy to pull the drag. They packed Tinker and his roan. At least the roan would have open ground to figure out how to carry a pack.

Eyeing the way out of the bottom, he found a route that wasn't too steep or rough. "I think we can get the drag up there with Trrk on it," he said. "If you help."

"Let's do it."

They took hold of the bedding and lifted the Kelok onto the drag. Seth secured him with the net again. Lee led Creamy, and Seth followed behind to lift the drag over obstacles. In a matter of minutes, they were up on relatively level ground.

Leaving Creamy tied to a tree, they went back for the rest of the horses. He checked Lee's cinch for her. She brought her saddlebags over. He settled those in place, knowing she was there, inches away, and resisting the urge to hold on to her and refuse to let her go.

"Stay up in the palm-pines, out of the rocks," he said, securing the saddlebags, not looking at her. "Just keep going until you find the trail from Wide Ford to Under

Rim." He had no idea how long it would take her. He didn't know for sure where they were.

"I can't miss that."

"Not if you go west." He managed a grin at the glare she gave him. "Follow the trail to town but be careful."

"I'll stay out of sight."

Doc's was on the edge of town. But pretty much everything was. Easy to circle around through the forest and get to the clinic without being seen. "If you're lucky it'll be dark before you get there," he said. "You know where to find him?"

"The clinic or home or the inn, if it's dinnertime.

"If he's not out on a call somewhere."

"I'll track him down. And bring him to Ike's old stead."

"Tell him Lickskillet Canyon. He'll know where that is even if he doesn't know the place."

"Are you sure you can manage Trrk and three horses?"

He cupped her face in his palm. "Don't worry about me." He forced himself to step back and offer her a leg up onto her horse.

She accepted, then leaned down to kiss him. "Back together by this time tomorrow," she said, and she moved Clown away.

He turned his back and went to the two packed horses. "Come on, boys. Time to go back to work."

How was he going to manage three horses with the drag? He gave in to the only obvious solution. He got out one of the highline ropes to use as long reins so he could walk behind the drag.

"Sure hope you remember your colt days and

ground-driving lessons," he told Creamy. "Walk." He slapped the reins against the horse's broad rump. Creamy hesitated. Seth repeated the order, and the horse took a step and then another. "You got it," Seth said, encouraging the animal with the reins again.

Creamy walked, pulling the drag with Trrk. Seth followed behind with the roan's lead tucked through his belt. The roan and Tinker fell into line. And his little parade ambled off in the direction Lee had gone.

It worked, but it was slow even though the widely spaced trees and open ground between them were perfect for the drag. He found he could ride Creamy, with his legs dangling over the drag poles, and lead the pack horses alongside.

He followed the tracks Lee had left. They reassured him that she was doing okay. Not that he didn't trust her on her own. She had years of experience on Carico now and had proven herself a capable rider. That didn't keep him from worrying, from wanting to keep her safe, from feeling better when she was close by.

He took short breaks fairly often, letting the horses rest while he checked on Trrk. The Kelok remained unresponsive. On they went, through the morning, into the afternoon.

It was dry country. Much as he cussed the occasional drainage crossing his path and having to half-carry the drag to get through them, he took advantage of the ones that had water to soak one of Lee's wraps and drape it over Trrk to cool him. Luckily, he didn't come across one as deep as where they had camped earlier.

Thunder clouds built in the afternoon, rumbling

around him. Nothing to do but go on and hope the tree the lightning picked wasn't one he was passing under. A brief downpour cooled him off and brought dirty looks from the roan who hated facing into rain. But the shower didn't disturb Trrk.

It was dark before they came to what Seth thought was Lickskillet Canyon. It was deep even up this high but not steep-sided. According to the sketch map in his journal, Ike's old place had been down out of the palm-pines in the head of a side-drainage coming in from the far side. Seth managed to get Creamy and the drag down into the bottom and up the other side. He needed rest but with his goal so close he pushed on, turning down out of the pines into the slick rock and copper trees, walking and hoisting the back of the drag over and around brush and rough spots. With the roan's nose at his back, nudging him to quit walking so slowly.

Chapter 17

Lee

Lee sat on the ground, holding the reins while Clown grazed. Afternoon clouds blocked the sun. No shadows; flat terrain; no landmarks. A ten-minute nap and now she wasn't sure which way she was supposed to go. All turned around again.

She got to her feet and began a slow search for the tracks Clown had made reaching this point. Not too hard to find in the sandy soil and scatter of leaves. There. Coming from that way. She put her back to that line of tracks, picked out a tree with a distinctive crooked branch in the direction she needed to go, and led Clown toward it. She needed to walk awhile to stay alert. Heat and lack of sleep weighed on her like a pack on her back.

A thunderstorm whirled wind through the trees, whipping the tops of the tall, slender palm-pines around. Lee trudged on, turning her collar up against the spatter of rain, losing her direction again, backtracking, moving on. She was supposed to be the one making fast time to Doc's and here she was, wandering around.

A ray of sunlight leaked through the clouds, bringing heat and casting shadows. Lee climbed into the saddle and adjusted her course. She pushed Clown into a trot, taking advantage of the sun's guidance while it lasted.

Twilight found her at the main trail that ran from Wide Ford to Under Rim. It was unmistakable, a meandering swath through the forest for skimmers to follow; they were more efficient over ground than trees. Following it would guarantee she didn't get turned around in the dark, but there was the chance someone would see her. Settlement Day was only a couple days away, and people were moving, going to visit or to attend celebrations. With a shrug, she took that chance.

The trail angled to the northwest, winding among the tall palm-pines. If she remembered correctly, it would turn mostly west for a ways before swinging back northward a couple miles out of Under Rim. She had to be at least an hour or so away at a steady trot.

Daylight faded. Lander would be just past full when it rose in a couple hours but, with luck, she'd be at Doc's by that time. The forest closed in, denser as she gained elevation, leaving the trail brighter only by contrast. Clown trotted on, unconcerned.

And they seemed to get nowhere. Like they were on

a treadmill between unchanging walls. No time, no distance. Just the regular thud of hooves.

She counted steps to give herself some sense of progress. And thought about Seth and Trrk. Had they reached Ike's old stead? Was there anything left of it? Had the Kelok hunters changed their minds and come after them? Would Doc even be able to help Trrk without taking him to the well-equipped facilities in Portside? Unknown alien physiology. A tail without bones.

Clown's trot never faltered. One, two, one, two. Monotonous, meditative. She almost didn't notice when the trail curved to the left and took a new line. The turn to the west. She let Clown walk a while. Poor horse had hardly had a break since this time the night before. At least it was cooler with the sun down.

Clown picked up the trot again on his own. Did he remember the trail? Know that rest was not far ahead? He'd been this way before but not for three years. She settled into the one-two gait.

She was half asleep when Clown brought his head up and his easy trot turned jolting. She moved him off the trail into the trees and stopped him. He turned to look back, and she heard the faint hum of a skimmer coming. Scorch Clown's highly visible white patches. She moved him farther into the trees, putting a big trunk between them and the trail.

The skimmer slowed. Had its sensors picked them up? Foot traffic had the right of way. Skimmers were expected to move off over the trees and go around. But she wasn't on the trail.

The vehicle dropped lower and turned on a spotlight. Lee held her breath. The light turned away, lit the trail in front of the skimmer. With it out of her eyes, she could make out some kind of insignia on the side.

A Ranger vehicle. Adel? Lee fought the urge to slip farther into the trees. Movement would give her away.

But the skimmer went on, slowly, the spotlight trained ahead until it picked up a trail coming in from the side. It turned there and was gone.

Lee waited, but the skimmer didn't come back. She rode on, staying off to one side of the trail, not ready to expose herself. When she reached the junction where the skimmer had turned, she stopped.

She knew the trail. It led to a big stead once owned by a man named Jerdix. She had history with the place she would rather forget. But couldn't. The feel of those big, harsh hands grasping her, pushing her down. The sight of Seth hanging by his wrists from a hook in a stall in the barn, tormented. And now Adel sought out the place in the dark of the night. Lee turned Clown onto the main trail toward Under Rim and put him into a fast trot, more interested in distance than secrecy.

Her heart quit pounding. She slowed Clown to a walk. Jerdix was gone, three years dead. She didn't even know who might own the stead now. Or why Adel might be going there. She needed to reach Doc without being seen, get him to Trrk. Now. Quit thinking about what was past.

She rode off the trail as soon as she glimpsed the village ahead. It was laid out around a triangular plaza with the inn and tavern, cafe, and a few businesses along the street to the west, apartments and corrals to the northeast, and Service Row, including public safety, education, and the medical building, to the south closest to her. She stayed under the cover of the forest and made her way around the parking areas that lay behind the buildings.

Doc's house was a little prefab that had begun life as a transport container for medical equipment and then been converted to quarters when the clinic and hospital were established some forty years earlier. It sat against the forest. A single light showed in one window. Across the parking area, the little clinic and hospital were dark, but the outside lights would come on if she got too close. She tied Clown out of sight and slipped around to Doc's front door. She listened for a moment to be sure he was alone, then tapped.

"Coming." Sounds of movement. The outside light came on and the door opened. "What can I do for you?"

"Hi, Doc."

"Lee Vawn-Cory!"

"Can I come in?" she asked. She glanced over her shoulder to see if anyone might have noticed the light.

"Of course." He stepped aside and let her into the tiny front room. He turned out the porch light and shut the door. "Are you okay? You have a lot of people worried about you. You and young Seth."

"Long story."

"That you don't want to go into right now?"

Doc always was perceptive. "Medical emergency first," she said.

He looked her up and down. "Seth?"

"No. A friend of ours."

"Where?"

"Lickskillet Canyon. Ike Allred's old place." She hoped Seth had been able to get Trrk there.

"I hear Ike's dead."

"You knew him?"

"Long time ago. So who's my patient?"

"A stranger." She hesitated. How much to tell him now? "A beyonder. Seth's taking care of him. Waiting for you."

"What's the problem?"

"Stink bear bite."

"Broken bones?"

Lee shook her head. "No. Deep lacerations. Poor circulation to an extremity." How formal did that sound?

"How long ago?" he asked.

It took her a moment. The attack. A full day there, waiting for Trrk's trance to end. The night's trip out of the fins. And two more days. "Late afternoon, three days ago." It seemed longer.

"You treated it, of course."

"As well as we could. We sealed the cuts with temp skin."

"Good, good." He laid a hand on her shoulder. "You want to send a blip to Joe Reilly while I get ready?"

More than anything she wanted to call Joe and let him take over, relieve her and Seth of the responsibilities. "Not yet," she told Doc. "You'll understand when you meet your patient."

He raised an eyebrow. "Okay. Better turn your horse in with mine. The pasture's out back, out of sight.

Descriptions of your animals are all over the broadcasts."

"Thanks, Doc."

"It's refreshing not to be treating you for a change. And you will owe me the entire story when you are at liberty to share it."

"Absolutely."

"I'll go get a couple things from the clinic. Meet you at my skimmer."

"Doc, one more thing." No help for it. He needed to know. "The patient. He's non-human."

"And you're sure it's not the veterinarian you need?"

"No. Well, they might be just as well equipped. But no."

"What species? I need to know what to prepare for."

"None you've ever heard of."

"None I've ..." He shook his head. "You're telling me this is a non-human person of an unknown species."

"That's what I'm saying. But he eats what we do and uses some of the same herbs for things like bruises."

He studied her for a moment. "A new species?"

"Doc, I am not crazy, no matter what Adel Verlane has been saying."

"Whoa." He held up a hand. "I believe you. I'm just surprised."

"Sorry."

"Go take care of your horse. I'll be ready when you're done."

Lee did as she was told. Trust Doc. What else could she do? He had to protect patient confidentiality. Trrk's. But as for her suggested instability? Did he still consider her his patient? She'd been gone from Under Rim for almost three years.

She turned Clown in with Doc's mostly retired sorrel gelding, left her saddle in the shed behind his house, and slung her saddlebags over her shoulder. The bags with a diplomatic pouch from one species to another tucked away inside.

She sank into the seat of the skimmer as the adrenaline subsided. She'd made it to Doc's.

And found herself clutching the seat as the vehicle sped away from the village. Had she been in one since returning to Seven Wells from the conference in Portside back in the spring, a lifetime or two ago?

They passed the turn-off where she'd seen the Ranger skimmer. "Who has Jerdix's old place?" she asked.

"It's still held by the Emerging Territories Business Consortium. They're using it as a guest house these days."

She remembered then. In the aftermath of Jerdix's death, it had come out that he had been the manager, and everything actually belonged to an interstellar consortium. "On my way in, I thought I saw a Ranger skimmer turn in there."

"Here for Settlement Day, probably. Seems our Planetary Administrative Officer is ending her district tour in Under Rim this year. I heard she's renting the main house for her stay."

Lee couldn't help the shiver that ran through her. She'd been in that house, last time on the night Jerdix had raped her. Then what Doc said sank in. "Emmerling? She'll be here?" Finally. Something going right.

"So I hear. Your Ranger Principal Vinz will be joining her. And Adel too, I imagine. She's been here for a couple days already, hoping for word of you."

Too much information all at once. "Wait. Vinz will be here? Adel won't be acting anymore."

"That's the word."

"That's good news." She leaned her head against the seat back. Doc on his way to help Trrk; the PAO within reach; and Vinz present to rein in Adel.

"Vinz has been vacationing at Tobin Canyon Camp," Doc said. "You know his interest in the aquatic fauna."

Is that where Adel had been coming from when Lee had seen her? Talking to Vinz? Filling him full of her version of things, of an unstable Lee associated with Ike's death. "When's Settlement Day?" she asked. "I've lost track."

"Three days."

Plenty of time for Adel to spin her web. A quiver of anxiety filled Lee. She was going to have to get to Vinz, who she knew had a personal connection to Emmerling, and convince him to help her have a private conversation with the PAO. Without telling him about Trrk. In spite of Adel.

Chapter 18

Eta'ak

Eta'ak resettled the pack basket on her back and looked around in the night. Something rattled through the whipbrush ahead of her. Something small. Not one of the wolf lizards she could hear whistling in the distance. She choked down her anxiety and plodded on, trailing far behind the runners carrying the technology. They had ignored her all the way from Village of Canes but had never quite gotten out of sight, as if they would not leave her completely alone in the dark. Until now.

Dawn approached, bringing enough light to begin to color the world. The fifth day since the envoys and Trrk had left the Village of Canes. Eta'ak recognized the bean tree grove that concealed the narrow back way into the Village of Lichens. She had reached her destination. But would she be allowed into the refuge of the cavern? She hesitated between the unfamiliar isolation and the fear of rejection.

When the runners had come for the equipment, she had waited with her few possessions in a pack basket: her portable loom, her drop spindle, the Beulah ferment and the bread maker, and her personal essentials. No one had prevented her from leaving. Her two spouses, hers no longer, had followed at a distance before turning aside. Perhaps far enough to be confident the runners would not abandon her to the night. She hoped her going would free them from her disgrace.

She was spurned, not banished. Who else would be willing to monitor the First-Comers' broadcasts? She'd been allowed that much before Prime had recalled the equipment. She must continue to do so. She would claim that. She gathered her fragmented determination and climbed through the bean trees.

The Lichens cavern was low-ceilinged compared to Canes but with more floor space, a huge wedge behind three wide rock columns across its front that hid it from casual view and kept the interior dim. In spite of the early hour, Prime stood in front of the female quarters watching Second direct the stowing of the equipment from Canes. In the plaza, representatives of all the villages except Canes mixed with the residents of Lichens. Eta'ak schooled her face to remain unruffled, to not give away her concern that Canes was being excluded because of her actions.

Eta'ak halted at the edge of the plaza. Prime locked pale-gold eyes on her for a brief moment, then turned her back. The others followed her example. All of them. As was fitting, given her status.

Second passed Prime with his head bowed. He directed the runners to remove most of the equipment to the storage areas in the back of the village, except for that needed to monitor the human broadcasts. They set that up against the center rock pillar, in plain view of the plaza. "The broadcasts must be reviewed," he said to no one in particular before walking away.

Prime and the others all kept their backs turned. Eta'ak crossed to the monitoring station, set her pack basket against the rock, and took her place in front of the large viewscreen with her back to the cavern, to the villagers. She imagined their eyes on her, pricking into her. She drew a mental curtain to shield her and began to scan the recorded broadcasts she had missed in transit for any word of Trrk or the envoys. Alone. But not quite alone. At least there were others around her.

Chapter 19

Seth

Seth tried unsuccessfully to sleep. Trrk hadn't regained consciousness but shifted and turned. And rock rats rummaged around the shell of Ike's cabin, unhappy about the invasion of their home.

The cabin was a low building with enclosed rooms on both ends. The breezeway between was open to both the north and south. It had been the kitchen in its day. Seth had cleared out the years' accumulation of walking weed and dead grasses to make space for them to get out of thunderstorms that persisted after dark. When daylight came, it promised to have a fine view of the tableland running down to the lower desert. Now, in the middle of the night as Lander rose, a little past full, and he waited for Lee and Doc, it was lonely and sad.

He got up and walked outside. A creek, small enough to step across, ran past and watered a strip of meadow where the hobbled horses grazed. The water chuckled and gurgled through the rocks, sparkling in the moonlight. Must be a spring higher up. Once upon a time water had been piped into the kitchen.

He should check Trrk again. He didn't. Every time he did, he feared the Kelok would be dead. Only the faint rise and fall of Trrk's chest told him otherwise. And the occasional twitches of legs and arms. Was he dreaming?

Finally, the distant hum of a skimmer. Lights appeared to the north, a spotlight sweeping, searching for the little stead. He fetched the light from his saddlebags and flashed it. The skimmer turned slightly and aimed straight for him. If it wasn't Lee and Doc …

But he recognized Doc's old skimmer, and it was Lee who climbed out and came toward him. He resisted the urge to wrap her in his arms and reassure himself she was really there. Until that moment, he hadn't realized how worried he had been that Adel would hook her up under Ranger authority or she would vanish into the wilds again like she had when the Keloks had taken her.

She took his hand, squeezed it. "How's Trrk?" All business, almost.

"Alive," he said. "He's inside."

Doc joined them. "Good to see you, boy. Your family is worried about you."

"I know."

"Now, where's my patient?"

"This way." How much had Lee told Doc about Trrk? Did he know what to expect?

Trrk lay against the wall just inside the central breezeway. He didn't move when Doc shined a light on him. Neither did Doc for a long breath.

"Many years ago, in my school days, I treated non-human persons, but I don't believe that training prepared me for this one. Certainly new within Coalition territory." He knelt and looked without touching. "How did you come here, so far from wherever you call home?"

They should have settled on a story to explain the Kelok. But at first they had thought he'd be going home. Then they'd been too busy getting him here.

"Castaway," Lee said. "He said his ship wrecked on Carico."

Good thinking. Seth let her run with it.

"So you can communicate with him."

"When he's conscious." Lee fingered the choker she wore. "They... he has these hearing facilitation devices, translators."

"Helpful. If he was conscious." Doc looked up. "Seth, in my skimmer you'll find a light on a stand and a hard-sided equipment case. Bring them, please."

Seth went, leaving Lee explaining how they had treated Trrk's injury. He trusted the man who had healed a childhood of mishaps. Doc was there. Doc would fix it.

Doc scanned Trrk from head to toe before turning his attention to the injured tail. "One of you at his head, please. Be ready to hold him if he awakens. That beaked snout is a bit threatening."

"Right." Seth decided not to explain the cultural prohibition against attacking with the wickedly hooked beak. The more they said the more risk they ran of giving away five secret villages. He put himself between Trrk's head and Doc.

Lee helped Doc remove the inflatable splint from the damaged tail.

"Nice job but not quite what temp skin is designed for," Doc said. He studied his patient. "No spine in the lower tail? Interesting. And feathered. Did they never evolve flight, or give it up?"

"I don't know," Lee said.

"Not something that comes up in casual conversation." Doc pulled at the edge of the temp skin. It peeled off easily. "Ah, now let's see what this looks like." He frowned as he worked.

"Well?" Lee asked. Seth didn't need to. He could see that the wound wasn't closing.

"What did you use on it besides the temp skin?" Doc asked.

"A paste made out of some kind of lichen that he told us about." Lee leaned over, then backed out of the light again.

"I'm afraid the wounds weren't held closed adequately." Doc adjusted the light. "See here. This side looks good. It's healing over. But the end of the tail hasn't gotten enough blood flow. It's dying. I thought maybe the odor was natural to him, but it's this."

The smell of decay hit Seth. How could he not have noticed? Just used to it from being around Trrk all the time as the tail got worse?

"Can you do anything?" Lee asked.

"Possibly. But not here. I need him in my hospital."

"You want to take him into Under Rim?" Seth ran his hand through his hair. "You think that's a good idea?"

"I think whatever small chance I have of saving the end of the tail depends on it."

"We were planning to..." Lee began. "Well, to go to the PAO and tell her about him before rumors start flying."

"I can sequester him on medical grounds. Keep anyone from seeing him. For a while."

"Until Settlement Day?" Lee said. "You said Emmerling will be in Under Rim."

"Yes."

"That's good news," Seth said with relief. "Let's get him in your skimmer." Best to get into town while it was still dark.

"Lee, if you'll bring the gurney, I'll get the splint back on to keep this stable."

Seth watched Lee jog to the skimmer. "Can you really save his tail?" he asked.

"There's a chance. Not good. It depends on how much of it is necrotic. I'll need healthy tissue for it to grow together."

They got Trrk secured on the gurney float. Seth went to turn the horses loose while Lee stacked the packs inside one of the enclosed rooms. He hoped the animals would be satisfied to stay nearby where they had grazing and water. It might be a few days before he could get back to collect them.

Lee met him as he carried the hobbles back to the

cabin. "Need anything but your saddlebags?"

He shook his head. "How about you?"

"I've got the pouch. That's all that matters."

"So the PAO's coming here?"

"Her last stop on Settlement Day. We won't have to go to Portside. But Adel's around. At least, I saw a Ranger skimmer turning into Jerdix's old place. PAO headquarters for the visit."

One place Seth could do without ever seeing again. "It wasn't Vinz?"

"Doc says he's at Tobin Canyon."

"And probably in Under Rim for the PAO's visit?"

"Probably."

This was looking almost too easy. "Let's get Trrk to Doc's," he said. "Then maybe we can spend a day or two at home while we wait." Hot showers, clean clothes, and a real bed.

"Home? Where's that?"

"I meant Pa's."

"I know. And we need to let them know we're okay. But I don't want anyone keeping us from delivering the message to the PAO."

"And you're worried about Adel?"

"About what she's told people, convinced people, about me that will interfere."

"The Void take Adel Verlane. I'm here to vouch for your mental health." He pulled her close and cupped her face with his hand, running his thumb along her cheekbone. "Once this is over, we are going home, my home, Rock House, and we're going to spend some uninterrupted time together, just the two of us."

Her kiss was hungry, full of promise, and totally distracting. He forced himself back. "Trrk."

"Yeah, Trrk."

They walked back to the cabin, close but not quite touching. Seth hung the hobbles with the halters on pegs in the outer wall under the eaves, set there decades ago when Ike had built the place stone by stone. Good work. Still solid. But all the dreams that had gone into it had died with his wife. A caution to appreciate what you had. He climbed into the back compartment of the skimmer where Trrk sprawled on the gurney. From there he could see Lee, up front with Doc. Their goal was in reach. "Don't put a rope on something too big to handle," he silently warned Adel.

Chapter 20

Lee

Lee stared out of the skimmer at the two moons. The full disk of little Damele ran out ahead of Lander, waning gibbous, in their race across the sky. She settled into her seat with relief. They had Trrk in good hands. Emmerling was coming to them. They just had to avoid entanglements for a couple of days.

"A castaway, you said." Doc broke into her thoughts.

"That's what he told us," Lee said. It was the truth, if not all of it.

"And he uses some of the same botanicals we do?"

"He had a liniment salve that smelled familiar. But the lichens he had us use were new to me."

"Have you got any of those left? I'd rather use something proven safe on him than risk a bad reaction needlessly."

"Yes." Luckily the last handful was in her saddlebags, not left behind in the packs. "Is he going to be all right?"

"I can't answer that. I don't know enough yet. But I don't like the looks of that tail."

"You won't tell anyone?"

"About your friend? I can keep him confidential for now. I am trusting you would say so if he was a danger to the community."

"He's not. No." Not him alone. Prime and the rest? She hoped not. Not if Prime and the PAO met and talked. "Are you going to tell Joe about Seth and me?"

"You're going to do that yourself. They're half out of their minds with worry."

"In the morning. Once we have Trrk settled."

"You know the Marshal can be discreet."

"There's more at stake than you know."

"I guessed that. One injured castaway? For that you would have gone straight to Joe for help."

If only it was that easy. Maybe Seth could. "There's a medical suspension hanging over me, Doc. I can't have Adel Verlane snatching me up under that authority, not before we see the PAO."

"Verlane seems sincerely concerned."

"She can be very convincing."

They reached Under Rim well before daylight and brought Trrk into Doc's little hospital wing — two rooms on one side of the hall, one on the other, along with a tiny sitting area just inside the door opening to the parking. Doc installed Trrk in the room across from the sitting area, darkened the hall windows, and posted a Restricted Access sign on the room door.

"Still no full-time help?" Seth asked.

"On call, as needed. Same as always. The monitors let me know if I need to check on a patient. Although I have no idea what settings are normal for your friend."

Lee stroked Trrk's crest feathers into place. "If we can wake him, we can find out."

"Let me deal with his injury first." Doc engaged the restraint field and removed the splint from Trrk's tail. He shook his head. "See here? There is too much deterioration of the distal end. It is dead tissue. Even in Portside, they wouldn't be able to revive enough to reattach."

In the strong light, Lee could see the necrotic tissue where the blood flow had been cut off, the source of its own stench. The stink bear had bitten almost through the tail, clean shears by the plates that lined its mouth in place of teeth.

"Now this." Doc indicated the upper side of the wounds. "This is healing very nicely."

"You need to take off the dead tissue." Lee looked at Seth. "Will he have full use of his tail?"

"Of what's left of it?" Seth frowned.

"He's lucky the healthy tissue didn't become infected," Doc said.

Seth's shoulders sagged. "I get it. I just don't know what the loss will mean to him."

"We don't know much about his culture," Lee said. But they did. Status depended on ritualized, unarmed combat. Trrk had made repeated joking references to Seth's lack of a tail in relation to initiating the human into the clan. It hadn't disqualified him. Still ... "He uses the end of his tail like another hand," she added.

"Prehensile. Yes, I can see how it would be." Doc stepped away from the bed. "You did what you could under the circumstances. Nothing left now but for me to remove what can't be saved."

"What can we do to help?" Lee asked.

"Leave me to work. The restraint field is the same technology used to treat most non-human people and that veterinarians here use on everything from horses to spinxi. I should be able to find a setting that keeps him unconscious, meaning that his brain won't process information about what is happening."

"He won't feel it?"

"Or be responsive to anything. Now go. In the back room on the clinic side, you'll find tea and leftovers from my lunch yesterday. Ila makes sure I eat well, too well."

Ila owned the inn and tavern. Everyone knew to look at her place if Doc wasn't home, but nobody understood their relationship. Maybe they didn't know themselves or maybe they enjoyed the secrecy.

"Doc ..." Lee hesitated.

"Your secret and his are safe with me for the time being. But you need to talk to Joe soon."

"Thank you," Seth said. "Take good care of Trrk. He's a friend."

"I gathered that. As if it mattered when he's my patient."

They exited and closed the door behind them. Down

the short hall and through another door was the clinic waiting room. From there they could see across the esplanade where the public safety building sat dark with the first hint of gray sky behind it. Next to it was the Marshal's Office and then the livery stable along the east side of the plaza. The only light was showing around the stable door which was not quite closed tight. Someone leaving town early maybe.

A second hall opened off the waiting room, leading to the office, a couple of exam rooms, the mechanical room with the guts of the building, and the back room that served the clinic as a break room. Lee remembered the layout. She'd been in and out of Doc's too often in her first months on Carico, first for an injured shoulder and then in the aftermath of Jerdix.

She pushed memories aside and found the leftovers. "Ah, tarbh strips and roasted ball tubers. Real food." Not grubs, not raw, not dried. She put the food in the heating unit and waited, breathing in the aroma.

Seth sat down on the couch and ran a hand over the fabric. "Strange being here, inside, with furniture and lights. But it hasn't been that long ago that I moved back to Rock House after wintering at Pa's."

"Or since I left Seven Wells. But everything seems different. The skimmer ride was unnerving."

"Yeah."

She sat down next to him and perched the plate of food on her knee. Finger food. "Help yourself."

"I hate waiting. He got hurt saving me."

"I, for one, am glad he did that." She chewed on a strip of tarbh, tender and cooked just right. It gave her time to think. "Losing part of his tail isn't good, is it?"

Seth shook his head. "I think his status just crashed. If he had any left after coming to warn us."

"I wonder how Eta'ak is doing. Prime can't be happy with her right now."

"Trrk said Prime would have to honor the invitation once it's delivered to the PAO. If their meeting goes well, Eta'ak should be a hero."

"We can hope." She handed the plate to Seth. "Did you get some sleep?"

"A little, before you and Doc got there."

"Well, I didn't." She stretched out with her head pillowed in his lap. "Wake me up when Doc's done."

"Did you hear that?" he asked.

"Hear what?" But then she did. The door chime. Someone had come in the front door.

"Stay," he whispered. "I'll see who it is."

Chapter 21

Seth

Seth stopped in the door of the break room. The hall was dim and silent, but the waiting room lights were on. Booted feet crossed it toward the hospital wing.

"Hey, Doc. Everything okay?"

His pa's voice.

"Just a patient." Doc's voice came faintly from the far end of the other wing.

"I saw lights. Thought I'd better check."

Seth couldn't make out Doc's reply. Something about it being early.

"Not sleeping so well these days," Joe Reilly said. "Well, I'll leave you to your work."

Seth felt Lee's hand on his back. "Better do it," she whispered.

"Just me. Okay? Until I find out what your status is."

"I'll wait here."

Seth stepped into the hallway and hurried toward the waiting room. "Pa," he said.

Joe turned in the outer door. "Seth? Son?"

"Morning," Seth said. He had no idea what he was going to tell his pa about anything.

Joe took a couple steps toward him, staring, then wrapped him in a bear hug. "You're alive." He stepped back. "Doc's patient? It's not ..."

"No, it's not Lee. She's fine."

"Where? What have you two gotten yourselves into this time?"

"I'll tell you what I can," Seth said. "But first, what's going to happen to Lee when the Rangers know where she is?"

"A whole lot of questions, no doubt."

"Her medical suspension?"

"I can't say." Joe took him by the shoulders. "You are both really okay?"

"Yes. No truth to any suggestions about our mental well-being."

"I never thought there was, but you sure have a lot of explaining to do."

Lee came into the room. "We are sorry, Joe. But so much has happened, and we didn't have any way to communicate until we got here."

"And when was that?"

"Lee came in last night and got Doc. Our, uh, friend

was hurt. We just got back here with him a little while ago."

"We didn't want to scare you and Kiri with a blip in the middle of the night," Lee added.

Seth made a sudden decision. "There might be something else you need to know too." Lee gave him a puzzled look. "Better come see Doc's patient," he said.

"Before I hear your story?"

"It'll answer a lot."

Lee gave him a questioning look. Seth squeezed her hand. "We ran into someone," he told his pa. "He's a castaway. Been getting by back of beyond for quite a while now."

"That's who Doc's working on?"

"He got hurt saving me from a stink bear. This was the closest place to bring him. Come on." He led the way into the hospital wing and tapped at the room door.

Doc opened it. "Just finished. Oh, morning, Joe. I see my visitors found you."

"You might have called me."

"Medical care first."

"Doc, how is he?" Lee asked.

"Stable as far as I can tell. I used some of that lichen you brought on the wound. And now, if you'll stay with him, I'm going to Ila's for breakfast. Joe, we can talk later. And keep this door closed. Restricted access." He went past them and disappeared out the back door.

"Are you going to explain?" Joe asked.

"Let's go see Trrk first," Seth said. "Then we'll fill you in."

"Trrk? Unusual name."

"Non-human," Seth said. "Come on. See for yourself." He stood aside and let his pa see the patient on the bed.

Joe walked slowly around Trrk. "Never seen the like. He, you said?"

"He," Seth replied. "His name is Trrk. He calls his people the Kelok."

"Stranded here?"

"His ship crashed," Lee said. "Several years ago."

"Years? And where does he come from?"

She shook her head. "He can't answer that. It was a navigation malfunction that brought him here. He said we are off his charts."

"So you've been able to communicate with him."

"These." Seth hooked a finger under his choker. "He calls them hearing facilitation devices."

"Translators? The Coalition gave up on developing a universal translator a long time ago."

"They aren't universal," Lee said. "They have to be programmed with the languages. He monitored our broadcasts and studied our library files for a long time before he was able to get them ready to use."

"Oh, really." Joe walked around the bed. "Interesting body design. Bet he can run. Impressive beak on that snout. Feathers. And a tail. Ah, that's what got hurt."

"Look, Seth." Lee reached out but stopped short of touching the bandaged end. "Poor Trrk."

Seth nodded. "The bear bit most of the way through. Doc couldn't save the end. It had gone necrotic."

"When did it happen?" Joe asked.

"A few days ago," Seth said.

"Not the beginning of your story."

"No."

"Well?"

Lee stepped in. "There's not that much to tell."

"Oh?"

"Tarbh stampeded through our camp, Ike's and mine. Next thing I knew I was all alone, trapped in a rock shelter."

Seth picked it up. "When the stampede came through, their horses got loose. One of them was Jester. He and Clown showed up at my place a few days later. I was backtracking to return them when I found Ike dead, sitting against that boulder where I buried him."

Joe nodded. "We found him. Lonely spot for an old rider. But we didn't find anything else."

"Trrk didn't want anyone to find him, so he carried off all our equipment," Lee said. "And brought Seth to me."

"We finally got the communications sorted out," Seth said.

"It takes a while for the facilitators to work," Lee said. "Your brain has to learn to interpret the signals before you can understand. Like hearing with your skin."

Seth shook his head. "It took a lot longer to get to the point where we were wearing them. Things were pretty tense for a while. He was afraid to be found."

"He looks like he would be formidable in a fight."

"Yeah," Seth said. "But they, well, he says their fighting is controlled by strict rituals."

"Anyway," Lee stepped in. "He started to guide us

back, and he and Seth ran into the stink bear, and we decided we needed to bring him to Doc."

"And that's about it. We didn't want the word to get out that we were here, at least not until you knew."

"We still don't," Lee said. "I saw Adel Verlane headed to Jerdix's old place last night when I was coming to get Doc. And we hear she has been questioning our mental well-being."

"That she has."

Seth laid a hand on Lee's arm. "We think that the PAO needs to hear about Trrk directly, not by rumor. Doc promised to keep him under wraps."

"Good thought. But I think you should start by talking to Ro Vinz." Joe looked over at Trrk. "He's down at Tobin Canyon, and he'll need to know about this too."

"He doesn't," Lee said. "Not officially at least. Trrk does not want to be treated as a formal first contact for his species. He just wants to be able to stay at the place he's built up here and be one more settler."

"Still, Ro's the one to help you get the word to the PAO. Fact is she's meeting him here on Settlement Day. Her last stop."

"Okay. We'll ask Vinz for help seeing her. But nothing about Trrk unless we have to."

Seth leaned his shoulder into Lee's for support. He wasn't sure how she felt about dealing with the Ranger.

"I don't suppose your friend has any more of those translators," Joe said.

"'Fraid not." Seth quirked a smile at Lee, thinking of what it had taken to get the ones they had.

"He'll have an easier time of it if he can talk with

people." Joe turned toward the door. "Well, we'd better get to Vinz."

"No, let me go alone," Lee said. "While I ride to Tobin you two can run interference for Trrk and distract Adel if she discovers we've turned up. I can keep out of sight, be there in a couple of hours, and have a quiet talk with Vinz."

Seth took her hand. "No, you're worn out."

"She's got a point," Joe said. "But Ro won't be around the cabin at Tobin during the day anyway. He'll be out fishing. Lee can rest up and leave here in time to catch him when he comes in this evening."

Lee squeezed Seth's hand. "You need to be here when Trrk wakes up. He'll need a familiar face. And someone he can communicate with."

Someone male. But Seth didn't voice that. He had to let Lee take care of her part in this while he did his.

Chapter 22

Seth

Seth sat in a chair in Trrk's room at the hospital. Lee slept on the bench that folded down from the wall. Resting. Waiting for evening when she would leave for Tobin. Waiting for Trrk to show some sign of improvement. At least the smell had gone with the amputated end.

The Kelok hadn't regained consciousness, but Doc said all his vitals were stable. Good, but whether they were normal or not was something none of them could answer. Except Trrk, and he wasn't talking.

Seth got to his feet and moved the chair aside, giving himself a clear area between the bed and the door.

Enough for the opening sequence in the batayr martial arts form he hadn't practiced since they left the Village of Canes. The movement worked out the kinks from wrestling the drag with Trrk cross-country, and helped him focus.

What his pa had said about Trrk needing to be able to communicate made sense. As Seth understood it, the green stones woven into the hearing facilitator picked up the vibrations of someone talking and transmitted translated vibrations to the wearer's skin. The wearer's brain learned to read those like it would input through the ears. But what if those vibrations were amplified and broadcast? He wasn't technical enough to know how to do that, but it seemed like it ought to work.

Seth started as his choker tingled against his throat. "Brother," he heard. He looked around to see Trrk's eyes on him.

"You're awake," he said.

"Am I?" Trrk lifted a hand to gesture at the room. "This is not the *Long Flight*. I was dreaming."

"We're in Under Rim. At the medical facility."

"What have you done?" Trrk tried to push himself up. "Why have you brought me here?"

"Easy," Seth said. "Doc and my pa are the only ones who know you're here." Lee sat up. Seth held up a hand to keep her still. She nodded.

Trrk slumped back down. "You were to take me to the elder's abandoned home where no one would see me."

"Doc needed to bring you here to treat you. We told them you were a castaway, by yourself."

Trrk relaxed when he heard that. "Where is your spouse?"

"Right here." Seth held out his hand, and Lee came to take it.

"Just rest and get better," she said.

"I'm sorry about your tail." Seth hoped he was doing the right thing being upfront with Trrk, but the Kelok was a realist. "Doc had to amputate the end. The tissue was dead."

"My ... tail ..." Trrk lifted his head. "It is ..."

"Doc says the stump had already started to heal up."

Trrk clicked his beak once, weakly. "It does not matter. All that matters is that the message be delivered."

"Don't worry about that. The PAO is going to be here in Under Rim in a couple of days. We won't have to go to Portside to find her."

"The pouch is safe?"

"It is," Lee said and held up her saddlebags.

"Care for it until it is delivered."

"Of course. Now you rest."

"Don't worry," Seth added. "I'll be here."

Trrk relaxed.

"Trrk," Seth said, "is it possible to convert one of the hearing facilitators so it broadcasts rather than transmitting to only one person?"

"Convert? Yes." Trrk faded back to sleep before Seth could ask more.

Lee pulled him away as far as the door. "He seems okay."

"He woke up. And at least we know there's a way for

him to talk directly to people." It was possible. All he needed was someone with the necessary expertise.

The door opened. Doc came in and shut it behind him. "How's my patient? I saw some changes in his vitals."

Seth sighed with relief. "He woke up enough to talk to us."

"Coherently?"

"Yes. He was groggy, but he understood what I told him. He's asleep again now."

Doc smiled. "Best thing for him."

"We need to talk to Pa. Any way I can get in touch with him without word getting out?"

"He's in his office. I can have him stop by, just to fill me in on the search efforts. Or have a cup of tea before he gives up and goes home for the evening."

"Thanks, Doc."

Once he was gone, Seth grinned at Lee. "We can solve one problem. Get Trrk set up to speak for himself."

"So that's what you want to see Joe about?" Lee asked.

"Yeah, about getting Gwyn to help." Convenient that his twin sister was a communications specialist.

"Is that our biggest worry right now?"

"Well, no." When he thought about it. "But I can't stay with Trrk every minute." He laid his hand against her cheek. "Besides, it'll give me something to do while you're gone."

"Besides going to the house and facing the whole family?"

"That we need to do together. After all, you got me

into this in the first place."

"Now how did I do that?"

"Long story. You know how it goes."

"Are you saying I should never have let you loan me Jester?"

"And where would you be without him?" If Jester hadn't been along to come home without her, he'd still be waiting for her and Ike to show up at his place. And where would she be?

Chapter 23

Seth

A knock and the door opening stopped any further discussion of borrowed horses and other things. Seth stepped out of the way and let his pa into the room.

"Doc says you want to talk? I was coming anyway. To see what you want to do while Lee goes to Tobin," Joe said.

"We need Gwyn's help," Seth said. "Trrk says we can set up one of the devices to broadcast so he won't need me to translate."

"He doesn't look ready to help with that."

"That's why we need Gwyn." One of the reasons. They also needed equipment.

"Sorry," Joe said. "Gwyn made an emergency run to Portside for parts. She won't be back until tomorrow."

Seth shook his head. "I'll just have to stick with Trrk to translate."

"I sure wish you could come out to the house, even for a little while, and let the family know you're okay."

"Have you told anyone we're back yet?"

"Just Kiri, and she won't say anything until I tell her it's okay. Although she is righteously angry with both of you for all the worry."

Seth nodded. "And you don't like it when she's worried." Kiri was a friend to both him and Lee, once a fellow rider at Seven Wells, and now his stepmother.

Joe grinned. "It upsets your baby brother, and he's not even born yet."

Seth ran his hand through his hair. Even after spending the winter with them, he was still getting used to that idea. "It's not like we did this on purpose."

"I know. I know." Joe clasped his shoulder. "But she's not the only one who's worried."

"As soon as Lee fills Vinz in, and it doesn't matter if Adel knows we're here, you can tell the world."

"But not about your friend. You're right about letting the PAO know first. He may be just one castaway but, like it or not, he represents a whole lot more."

"Yeah," Seth said. A whole lot more a whole lot closer than anyone could imagine.

Doc stuck his head through the door from the waiting room. "Company. Adel Verlane's heading this way."

"You two stay here with your friend," Joe said.

"She'll be wanting to know if I've learned anything."

"What will you tell her?" Lee asked.

"The truth. That no one in the district has reported seeing you." He left, shutting the door behind him.

"I hate putting him in this position," Seth said.

"We'll have to answer to the rest of family for it."

Voices in the hall kept Seth from responding. Adel had gotten past Doc into the hospital wing.

"I'm sorry, Ranger, but Doc asked you to stay out of this area," Joe said.

"I just wanted to find out if you've heard anything." Adel sounded concerned.

"Let's go into the other room where we won't disturb Doc's patient."

"Marshal, I can't tell you how much it meant to me when I first arrived to discover I did know someone here on Carico. I was so disappointed when Lee wouldn't help with the survey."

"I'll bet she was," Lee whispered. "No handy scapegoat."

Seth put his finger to his lips. The voices were fainter. Joe and Adel must have moved into the waiting room but left the door open.

Adel was still talking. "... worried when I learned she was going into the wilds with that Willemsen person out there somewhere."

"It may sound strange to you," Joe said, "but all we can do now is wait. They must have had a good reason to so obviously disappear."

"You don't think something has happened to them?"

"If we'd found an abandoned camp, I would. But

they took everything with them and left no sign I could follow. I trust my son. I trust Lee. They will be in touch when they can."

"I wish I had your faith."

"Go back to Portside," Joe said. "Focus on getting ready for the survey. Take your mind off things."

"Not yet. If you are right, this is where they'll come. I'll give it a couple more days. After Settlement Day, I'll have to go back."

"Where are you staying?"

"At the ETB House. PAO Emmerling offered me a room there. Although it's eerie somehow. Maybe just because it's so empty with no one else there yet."

"I'm sure you can find plenty of things to do in town tomorrow. Lots to be done to set up for the festivities on Settlement Day."

"It'll be my first." She didn't sound enthused.

"The big celebration is always in Portside."

"I'll start small and save that for next year."

The voices faded and a door shut.

"Good," Lee said. "She's gone."

"She said she was staying where? ETB?" Seth asked.

"Emerging Territories Business Consortium."

"That was Jerdix's group?"

"Sounds like his demise didn't have too much effect on them. Doc says they own what we thought were his holdings here."

"Yeah, I remember Pa saying something about his stead being used as a guest house where people can get away from the city."

"The important thing is that Adel plans to stay there

through Settlement Day, right where we hoped to catch up to the PAO privately." Lee crossed her arms and paced.

The door opened, and Doc stepped in. "Verlane is gone for the moment. But she's got time on her hands. If my patient was in better shape, I would suggest you move him out of town. Someplace quiet and out of the way."

Seth looked at Trrk. He was watching them. "I am satisfactory," Trrk said.

"What?" Doc asked, moving to his patient.

"He says he is 'satisfactory'," Seth said.

"He is?" Doc turned to Trrk. "You are? I don't know what is considered normal, but you have had a serious injury. I expect you are dehydrated although I hesitated to address that without knowing more. And you have been unconscious, if not comatose."

"We ..." Trrk hesitated. "Torpor? A minimizing of functions to allow our bodies to heal. Now I should be up, eat, drink, stimulate blood flow and revitalize muscles."

Seth translated, wishing they had the speaker setup he'd been thinking about.

"Well, I do see a significant difference in your vital signs."

"Is there a place I can be taken where I can be active without fear of discovery?" Trrk looked from Seth to Lee. "Please."

"Fallen Pine?" Lee said.

"He wants to leave?" Doc nodded. "The cabin would be a good place for him to recuperate. Once he convinces me he really is ready."

"What do you wish to know?" Trrk asked.

Seth let Lee handle the translation as Doc questioned Trrk about Kelok biology. He checked to be sure the hall was clear before leaving Trrk's room. From the hallway door, he watched his pa and Adel outside. Joe pointed toward the cafe and inn. Adel played with the end of her braid and smiled before turning away and walking off. Joe waited until she was well away before coming back inside.

"She seems genuinely concerned about Lee," Joe said.

"Lee doesn't believe it," Seth said. "I don't know what went on between them, but Lee is sure Adel has some scheme she's playing out."

"I'll keep that in mind."

"Trrk's awake again. Doc's quizzing him about Kelok biology, but I think he's willing to let us move Trrk out of town."

"Home?"

Seth wished he could say yes and let his capable father take over, but he and Lee had promised to keep the Keloks' secret. "Fallen Pine, I think."

"Good enough. Not that I don't want you safe at the house where I can keep an eye on you, but you never know who might drop by." Joe paused with a quirk of his mouth. "Still, I can't help worrying that you'll disappear again."

With all the secrets, Seth wasn't surprised. "I'll try not to."

"I'll stay around the office a little longer, then go

home. Except I'll pick you and Trrk up and drop you at Fallen Pine on the way with no one the wiser."

"I want to stay here until Lee is ready to go to Tobin."

"Right. I'll swing by Ila's and the cafe. Check on progress for the Settlement Day picnic. Make myself visible." He grasped Seth's shoulder. "Do my best to act like I am distracting myself from my son being missing."

Chapter 24

Lee

It was evening when Lee slipped out and caught Clown from Doc's pasture. She only needed a couple hours to reach Tobin, and Joe said Vinz would probably stay out until almost dark. Fishing. But not like most people. His hobby was the natural history of the aquatic life within Carico's settled territory.

Seth tied her saddlebags on her saddle. "Are you sure you don't want to leave the pouch with me?"

"I'd better keep it close. Who knows? Maybe Emmerling will be having a secret tryst with Vinz at Tobin."

He grinned. "We could get so lucky." He ran a finger

over her choker. "Better leave this with me. We'll need it if we are going to cobble together a way of amplifying the vibrations."

"And hook that to a speaker. I didn't know you were that techie."

"I'm not, but Gwyn will be back tomorrow. Hopefully Pa can bring her to Fallen Pine to help."

"Do you really want to bring her into this?"

"If it'll let Trrk speak for himself."

"Can we even get the choker off?" The shackles Trrk had used on her and Seth when they'd been held captive had intricate closures that required his talons to release.

"I can cut it off if I need to. It's just rawhide." Seth turned her around. "Oh, this looks easy. Hold still."

It might have been simple, but he struggled with it while she tried to hold still and not interfere. When he worked it free, she rubbed her neck, feeling almost naked without it. "Good luck," she said.

"You too. Look out for Adel."

She put her arms around him, wanting to feel safe and secure for a little longer. He held her close. She rested her head on his shoulder, listening to his heart, feeling his breathing.

Clown's nose shoved at her. Seth laughed. "He's right. You'd better get going."

She stepped back. Hesitated.

"I'll look after Trrk," Seth said and offered her a leg up.

She took it and settled into the saddle. "And yourself."

"You're sure you can find Tobin?"

"Really? I found my way here, didn't I?"

"You want to come down the canyon to the pens, not up where the bunkhouse is." He took her hand. "That way you'll be out of sight of skimmer traffic."

"I know. I'll manage." She bent down to kiss him. And she went on her way.

She stayed in the trees off the trail, passing under tall palm-pines with their broad, segmented leaves spread wide. Grasses and wildflowers carpeted the openings with chartreuse dotted with vivid yellows and blues. The summer rains brought the land to life. Better to think about that than being separated from Seth again.

Thunderheads were building. She kept moving and hoped the storms would bypass her. She let Clown switch between a trot and a rolling lope, his preferred gait for distance on easy ground. Erratic breezes from surrounding thunderstorms gave some relief from the heat and humidity. None came close enough to threaten her.

She'd only been to Tobin a couple of times and then by skimmer. Once not long after she and Seth had met, when he still knew her as 'Anni Dulce', a waitress at Rajir's Cafe and a newcomer to Under Rim. A day of laughter, just the two of them, away from the rest of the world and everything that was to come. But even that had been tainted by the lie of who she was. At least now the secrets were shared between them, five villages of aliens worth.

About an hour south of Under Rim, she reached the

end of the palm-pines and came to the rocky tableland with its scattered copper trees. That was where she needed to find the head of the canyon she would follow down to the corrals at Tobin. The sun was noticeably lower. To the south, she could make out the point of a highland that dropped off sharply. She thought she remembered a point like that immediately south of Tobin.

She turned east and stayed within the palm-pines where the footing was better and she would be less visible to wandering Rangers. Still, storm-muggy air stifled her urge to push Clown into a lope. She only had a few miles to go.

She couldn't let Adel's maneuvering get in the way of delivering the pouch with its formal invitation to meet with Prime. Trrk had sacrificed too much to achieve Eta'ak's vision. A vision that fear kept Prime from embracing.

Lee wondered again why Adel was so concerned with discrediting her. Why was she a threat?

If only she'd done something about Adel sooner, back when they were at the Ranger academy. But initially Lee had admired the charismatic girl. If she'd turned Adel in the night she'd let the girl into the dorm long after hours? The night Adel had been tricked into helping upper-level students cheat on a survival test, only to discover she had been deceived and used. After that night, Adel had become increasingly competitive, driven to prove herself better at everything. She had developed a fine talent for polishing her own reputation so that people discounted any little misstep she might make. And Lee never trusted that Adel wouldn't use her part in that escapade against her somehow.

Which made Lee wonder why she should expect Vinz to believe her rather than Adel. Since the Jerdix thing three years before, she and Vinz met briefly four times a year to review her status. He had let her sidestep a final medical evaluation to end her medical suspension. Like he didn't want her back. And Adel had had weeks before he went on vacation to establish herself. Why wouldn't he take his assistant's word over Lee's? The only chance she had was to get to him and present her case without Adel's interference.

The thunderheads drifted off to the east. Far over there somewhere was Blue Canyon with its hidden villages of Keloks, and Eta'ak with her determination to present their case for recognition on their own terms before the humans stumbled on them. And Prime, who believed she could still protect her people by remaining hidden even in the face of evidence that that state of affairs couldn't last.

Lee let her cynic voice play it out. Trrk, one lone castaway with no known affiliation. Pack him off-world and hand him over to the Coalition to deal with. Oh, he's not alone? Well, Carico is designated a human world. Find somewhere else for the refugees. Refugees who had spent ten years building homes they were not going to willingly walk away from. She and Seth hadn't seen any evidence of defensive weapons, but they had been given only a limited view of one village. Why wouldn't the Keloks have sophisticated weapons? Their males were obviously fighters, and they had technology like the hearing facilitators, holographic conferencing, and a communications relay still functioning after ten years without maintenance. Things the humans on Carico had little, if any, access to.

Eta'ak was right. Lee had to deliver Prime's reluctant invitation to PAO Emmerling to meet and discuss a shared future. Trrk swore Prime would honor it once it was delivered. And both sides could work for a peaceful resolution, something that would help, not hinder, meeting the humans' settlement plan milestones.

So far Adel couldn't know anything about the Kelok. Adel, who was responsible for the satellite survey that inevitably would find the villages but would also heavily influence the outcome of the settlement plan review. If the settlers weren't meeting the milestones laid out in the plan, they risked having outside administration sent in by the Sol Terra Alliance to make it happen or even losing their settlement rights entirely. How could Adel benefit from any of that?

Lee admitted to herself that, ever since Jerdix, she had just reacted to what was thrown at her and avoided life-altering decisions. But now she couldn't step back and leave not only her future but the future of Carico to others. She was the envoy for Eta'ak and Trrk's people, one chance to avert a violent confrontation. She would deliver the message she had been entrusted with. Then she could turn her attention to Adel and whatever plan she was hatching.

Clown's hooves found a trace of trail that joined with another like streams flowing together. The trail led to a fence and through an open gate at the edge of the palm-pines, then across the cobbled tableland before it dropped into a ravine that cut through the rock. Lee rode down into Tobin Canyon. Not far now.

It might be late evening, but the rock walls held the day's heat like an oven. Dripping sweat, she dismounted and led Clown. A patch of bright chartreuse ahead fueled her hope for a spring where they could both drink. She found a trickle of water escaping from the rocks. It flowed into a pool someone had dug out in the fine soil of the ravine bottom. There were no tracks around it to suggest a human had been there in weeks.

She filled her water bottle while Clown drank eagerly. Desert horse. He never passed up water.

The water ran down in a burbling brook under vine trees and whipbrush that crowded the narrow canyon bottom. The trail wound through a semi-tunnel high enough for someone on horseback to pass, a sure sign that riders maintained it. Otherwise, it would close over about tarbh high.

The shadows filled the whole rift until the sun barely brushed the top of the rim. Sundown. She only had about half an hour of twilight, but little Damele would be full when it rose soon. The night wouldn't be completely dark.

A gate blocked her way, the gate into the pens at Tobin. She opened it, led Clown through, and closed it behind her. The huge set of corrals lay in the mouth of Tobin Canyon. Tarbh were trapped there and sorted on their spring and fall migrations. The camp itself perched up on the tableland overlooking the pens. 'Camp' was a misnomer. It was a permanent facility with a stone cookhouse and bunk rooms, solar power, and a communications antenna. When not in use for migration, the Under Rim Steaders' Co-op made it available for other uses, like Vinz's vacation.

The corrals were deserted. A ditch captured the creek water and took it around the edge of the pens to the larger stream flowing in from the west under the high point she had observed earlier. Where would Vinz be? He was here for aquatic life to study. So was he somewhere along the other stream? Down in the meadows below the pens? Or fixing himself a nice dinner in the cookhouse on the rim overlooking the corrals?

Chapter 25

Seth

Seth hunched low in the passenger seat of his pa's antiquated skimmer until they were out of Under Rim. Trrk was hidden in the back. Doc had equipped him with a monitoring device to keep track of his vital signs and lectured the Kelok on not over-exerting himself too soon. Now they were headed north while Lee rode south to find Rodahl Vinz and get his help to meet with the PAO.

Fallen Pine was a familiar haven, a place Seth had gone for privacy as a teenager, the place he had sought out in his mind-fog after he had been tortured by Jerdix. He wished Lee was with him so he knew she was safe.

"You're quiet," Joe said.

"Lots to think about."

"Lee expects Adel to go see Ro Vinz?"

"Yeah." Seth shrugged in the dark. Given Lee's feelings on Adel, he was almost looking forward to meeting the woman again. After they delivered the Keloks' message to the PAO.

"Makes sense. I'd be surprised if she hasn't filled him in on Lee going missing. Although Ro is pretty strict about not being disturbed on vacation for anything short of world annihilation."

"We should have just waited. Gotten to the PAO without going to him."

"No, Lee made a good call. And this way, she can give her side of the story before Adel gets a chance."

"I guess." He'd have his own explanations to make in a couple of days. To Kiri; to his sister, Gwyn, with a volatile nature and the expertise he needed to build a speech synthesizer for Trrk; to all the rest of his extended family. "Will you, will everybody, forgive us for not letting them know sooner that we're safe?"

"The sight of Trrk might help."

"Will they accept him?" Seth voiced his worry.

"That might take more time. Most people around here have never lived around non-human people. Knowing they exist and standing next to one are different experiences."

"I noticed."

"I expect you did. I'm looking forward to hearing the whole story."

"Soon. After we talk to the PAO."

"I'll hold you to that."

Joe talked about the routine happenings around Under Rim, leaving everything else unsaid for now. As they neared Fallen Pine, he stayed to the west. "I just want to go by the pasture and check on the horses," he said.

Seth nodded. That pasture was used for horses that weren't needed at the stead, usually retired horses and colts not old enough to start riding yet. They found the animals in an open meadow, grazing in the evening light. They lifted their heads at the sound of the skimmer and watched until Joe passed without stopping.

As they approached Fallen Pine, Seth pointed to a single horse in the smaller pasture near the cabin.

"Not ours," Joe said.

Seth looked again and recognized the raw-boned bay that loped away across the meadow. "Void! That's Whip Willemsen's horse."

"What?" Joe set the skimmer down before they reached the cabin. "Now how would you know that?"

Seth hesitated. Being tied to Willemsen wouldn't help with Adel's accusations. "We ran across him a few days ago," he said. "Other side of the Whitewater. I thought he was planning to hide out above the rim." He couldn't exactly tell everything he knew. He and Lee had diverted Willemsen from the secret villages before he saw any Keloks. Now he would be nursing injuries Lee had given him when he had made the mistake of grabbing hold of her. They had sent him into unsettled country away from Keloks and, conveniently for him, from human authorities who were looking for him.

Looked like he hadn't stayed there.

"More of the story you can't tell me yet?"

"Accidental meeting. He went his way; we went ours. We weren't in a position at the time to bring him back and turn him in."

"You realize Adel was hinting that you two had helped Whip escape a restitution work detail at the Ranger headquarters in Portside."

"We heard. Not likely after he turned me over to Jerdix." Ancient history but Seth had a more recent issue with Whip too, for laying hands on Lee, even if she had handled the situation herself.

"Didn't say I believed her," Joe said.

"Well, it looks like I have a chance to help you take him into custody. Now how do we do that without him seeing Trrk?"

"No problem. Tell Trrk to stay put while we get Willemsen corralled."

Seth went around the far end of the cabin on foot while Joe waited at the back door. As lightly as he could, Seth climbed onto the end of the waist-high porch and over the railing. From against the wall, he could see most of the one big room across the front, the seating area in front of the fireplace nearest him, a table on the far side, with the kitchen in back of that.

Whip stood at the stove with his back to the windows. Like he owned the place. Not that he'd had to break in. Like pretty much all outlying cabins, anyone's thumbprint opened the doors but left a record of who had entered. And Whip could easily know from the time he'd spent working around Under Rim that this place was rarely used.

Moving slowly, Seth eased to the front door. He tested the latch. Locked. He put his thumb on the scanner and shoved the door open as soon as the lock released.

Whip whirled around, raising the spatula like he was going to throw it, then let it fall. "Tarbhs' clackers! What are you doing here?" he said.

"Better question is what you're doing." Seth stepped clear of the door. "When we sent you on your way, you were supposed to hole up on top of the rim where you wouldn't be found."

"Yeah, well, Jerdix's old place was stripped bare, and I saw this place from up top."

"And just thought you'd make yourself at home." Seth shook his head. "Teach me to do favors for a frog-eel."

"Favors?"

"We should have let the beyonders have you."

"Not you and that sweet thing. You're both soft."

Seth stared. "You have a bad memory. I would think your knee and ribs would be reminding you how sweet and soft Lee is. Not to mention that purple and yellow mask around your nose." He grinned at the thought. "Well, you have run out of chances. Time the authorities dealt with you."

All Whip's bluster deflated. He backed into the corner. "No. No. You can't do that. She'll have me dead. Keep me away from that narky skreel."

"Who? Acting Principal Ranger Adel Verlane? You never said what you did to cross her."

"Five minutes. I'll be out of here in five minutes."

"We tried that, and here you are."

"How was I supposed to know you'd show up?"

"Pull that pan off the heat. You're going to sit down in that chair over there." Seth pointed at an armchair in the corner of the living room by the fireplace. "And you are going to stay there until the Marshal decides what to do with you."

"I'll be dead. I'm telling you."

"Sit down. You can explain that to him."

Whip hobbled across the room and flopped into the chair, pulling up a foot stool to prop up his leg. "That narky woman you run with almost killed me. Should be her the marshal takes in."

"Lee? Do you really want to tell him that? Get a few charges added to your restitution?" He moved to where he could see the hallway and called, "Pa, got him."

The back door opened and Joe came in. "Quick and easy."

"He's whining about being hurt. I told you he laid hold of Lee."

"Not the smartest move."

"And he's scared to death of Adel Verlane for some reason. Claims that's why he ran."

"Let's have a talk with him."

"Okay." The sooner they got Whip on the way, the sooner he could take care of Trrk. And get some rest himself.

Joe came into the front room. "Willemsen, I hoped you'd stay clear of Under Rim."

Whip pushed himself to his feet. "I'm hurt, Marshal.

I need the doc."

"So I hear."

"Don't you want my side of the story?"

"If you want to make a formal complaint."

"I ... uh ... maybe."

"You think about that."

Whip slumped back in the chair.

Joe went to the comm unit tucked away under the steep steps to the loft. "You wiped yourself from the comm memory," Joe said, turning assessing eyes on Whip.

"It's an old system," Whip said.

"But you know your way around tech."

"I used to, back before ... before I went to work riding. And that's what I was doing for my restitution. Gofer work on the system for the survey."

"Seems a little sensitive for restitution," Joe said.

"Just gofer work, like I said." Whip shifted in his chair.

"Seth says you have a problem going back to it."

"As long as she's there. That Ranger who was overseeing my work."

"So you didn't get along. Must have been pretty serious."

"Well, I didn't screw up my restitution six months before I was free and clear just for grins."

"Why don't you tell me about it?"

"Don't let her anywhere near me. That's all I'll say."

"That's not enough to keep me from sending you to Portside."

Whip pushed himself straighter in the chair. "It's like I said, I was assigned to the Rangers for part of my restitution service. You know, keeping equipment clean and working, doing maintenance around the office, grunt work. Then she found out I used to do tech work and put me to work on the computers that analyze the satellite data."

"Sounds like she put a fair amount of trust in you."

"That's what I thought. At first. I mean, she took an interest in me, made me feel ..." He hesitated, sucked in a breath.

"What happened?"

"Hey, I thought we really had something. You know, that might last once I was done with my service."

"So it was more than just giving you good work to do."

"I should have listened to her boss, Vinz. He said I should watch out for her." Whip rubbed at his bad knee, looked everywhere but at Joe. "When I got thinking about things, some of the programming didn't look right," he said so low Seth barely caught it.

"What do you mean? I need specifics, Willemsen." Joe crossed his arms over his chest. "You're not convincing me you need protection."

"The programming, it puts boundaries on what the computer flags as milestone changes. Like new ag land or reclaimed mining."

"Go on," Joe prodded.

Whip looked Joe in the eye and said in a rush, "It looked to me like it was going to exclude some things." He took a breath, slowed down. "Not give us credit, you know. But she told me to mind my own business and let her worry about that."

"And you did."

"Until one night when someone showed up after hours. Off-worlder. I just got a glimpse. It was a couple weeks after that big conference. She'd had me take her out to that big Seven Wells stead that day, and we got back late. Anyway, he wanted to know if everything was set. And she told him it was just the way he wanted it. And he walked to a map on the wall, and tapped it with a finger, and told her 'Good work'."

"They did this with you looking on?"

"Clackers, no." Whip hesitated. "She shoved me in the closet when she heard someone come into the building."

"Why not just send you down the hall to work somewhere?"

"No time." He swallowed and looked away. "I wasn't exactly dressed," he added.

"You weren't ..." Joe laughed.

"Yeah, well, she has big appetites. Anyway, she let me know I'd better keep anything I knew to myself. When I got back to my bunk, I started thinking about what I'd heard and what it could mean for Carico. But truth is it was pretty scary. So I grabbed a few things and got out of there before she decided she didn't trust me to keep quiet. Caught a ride to Wide Ford. Nobody knows me there."

"And you were just going to keep this to yourself?"

"No, no. I thought once I'd been gone a while and the whole evaluation thing was in progress, I could find a way of letting someone know."

"Know exactly what?"

Whip looked around the room, like he could somehow escape. He looked Joe in the eye again. "She's setting us up to fail the evaluation so her friends can take over Carico."

Chapter 26

Lee

Lee tied Clown at the tack shed. Was Vinz already at the cabin or still out and about? Either way, she wouldn't need to ride. She pulled the saddlebags from behind the saddle. They were her overnight bag. But they held something else, something she didn't want Vinz or Adel or anyone else seeing, the rawhide satchel with the messages for the PAO.

She looked around the shed for a safe place to leave it. When she lifted the lid on the critter-proof feed bin, she discovered it was full. She buried the satchel under the grain in one corner and hung the saddlebags on a rack. She unsaddled Clown and turned him loose in a small pasture below the corrals where he could graze.

Lee crossed the ditch on a narrow bridge and followed the footpath leading up the rim to the bunkhouse. She had had plenty of time to think about what she needed to say to Vinz. Trrk's presence could wait but getting to the PAO couldn't.

She could trust Vinz to listen to her. He had treated her fairly, and he was a friend of Kieron Dougherty and of Joe Reilly. But would he believe her? How much influence had Adel gained with him before he left on vacation?

She trudged up the steep path. The uneven rocks demanded her attention. She ducked the ribbon-worms dangling from the rock wall, the first place she'd ever encountered the odd creatures back when Seth had brought the person he knew then as Anni to Tobin for a day's outing. The long, thin growths hung from the wall like strips of yellow-green fabric, quiescent now in the evening shadows. Eta'ak had shown her how to collect them and marinate them for the Kelok version of ceviche.

Eta'ak. How was she doing without Trrk? Was she facing Prime's displeasure alone, trying to explain his absence? Or did she think he was dead?

Lee's foot caught the edge of a rock, reminding her to watch what she was doing. She almost hoped Vinz was out fishing so she could get something to eat and sit on something that didn't move under her before she had to deal with things. She needed a couple days of rest before facing him. Only a day ago, they hadn't even gotten Trrk to Doc's. The nap she had taken before leaving Under Rim hadn't been enough to recharge her.

She climbed a series of rock steps to where the trail cut through the last edge of rim. There the gap between rocks was barely wide enough for her to walk through. As she neared it, a shadow darkened the slot. She looked up from the rough footing to see Adel Verlane above her, filling the space. Scorch it!

"Who?" Adel peered down in the dying light. "Lee? Where have you been? What are you doing here?"

Lee sighed. She didn't have the energy to argue. "I thought I might find a shower and a bunk," she said.

"You're looking for ..." Adel stopped.

Looking for Vinz, Lee thought. She wasn't going to admit that. "Do you mind letting me by?" Lee stepped up on the rock ledge where Adel stood. "It's been a long day."

Adel didn't move. "Everyone's been looking for you for weeks."

"You want the story, come on up to the camp." If Adel was headed for the pens, Vinz probably wasn't at the camp. Lee saw no chance of getting Adel to leave without talking to him, but she could keep her from talking to him alone. "I'll tell you all about it."

"All right." Adel turned and climbed out of the slot into the open.

Too easy, Lee thought. What was Adel's game?

They walked side-by-side across the open ground to the long, low building of native rock that housed storage, a cookhouse big enough to feed a crew of half a dozen people, a shower room, and four small bunk rooms. Adel's skimmer sat in front of the cookhouse next to a rugged skybike. Vinz's, no doubt.

"Wonder who else is here," Lee said casually.

Adel ignored that. "I could give you a ride to Under Rim. That is where you're going, isn't it?"

Get rid of me so you can come back alone, Lee thought. "I'm not headed to Under Rim," she said. She climbed the steps and knocked at the cookhouse door.

"Nobody's here," Adel said. When Lee looked pointedly at the skybike, she added, "Not right now at least. I looked."

"No matter," Lee said and laid her thumb on the lock pad. The lock released, and she pushed the door open.

"Oh," Adel said. "You have access."

"Anybody does." Lee went inside and turned on the lights. "The lock pad just keeps track so the Steaders' Co-op will know who's been here."

Adel stopped in the doorway. "You really need to check in at the Marshal's Office in Under Rim."

"It's late. I can do that in the morning," Lee said. Where was Vinz? It was nearing full dark outside. Probably fished until the last light.

Lee walked around the long table in the middle of the room and the counter that separated the cook's realm from the diners. She went to the pantry and helped herself to a self-heating pouch of stew from the supplies the co-op left for anyone in need.

Adel stayed by the door, half her attention outside. "If you're not going to Under Rim, where are you headed?" she asked.

"The first bunk I can find." Lee found a bowl in the cabinets, set it on the counter, and dumped in the stew.

Her stomach rumbled in response to the aroma. She took a mouthful, chewed the tender chunk of meat, and swallowed. "Want some?" she asked. "There's plenty." She watched as Adel looked out the still-open door and shifted restlessly.

Adel came around the table and stopped at the end of the counter, blocking the way to the door. "What I want is for you to come with me," she said. "I don't know where you've been or what happened to you, but you obviously need help." Her attempt to sound sympathetic fell flat.

Lee continued eating, but her mind was racing. Bad move, letting Adel corner her. She tried to recall what she knew of the layout from her brief visits here years ago. She could go over the counter. Or there was a door in the corner behind her that led into the cook's quarters, which had a door to the porch. If she couldn't drag things out until Vinz showed up. She was too tired to want to play hide-and-seek in the dark.

She set the bowl down. "Nothing wrong with me that a good night's sleep won't fix." She tried to step past Adel. Sometimes she hated having to look up at people. It made it hard to be physically intimidating.

Adel didn't move.

Lee eased back, giving herself an arm's length between them. "Assistant Advisor Verlane. No, I hear it's Acting Principal Verlane, at least for a day or two more. Not bad." She reached out and straightened Adel's already perfectly straight collar. "You accomplish the survey work and staff work on the plan review, and you'll be off this rock to bigger things in no time." She looked into Adel's icy eyes.

"You think that's all I want? A Ranger promotion?"

What did Adel mean? What did she plan to get out of the project? Lee stepped away, took her bowl to the dish cleaner, and put it in. That put her closer to the door to the cook's quarters. It was cracked open. Vinz was probably using it. "Well, then, luck with that, whatever it is you want."

"What do you mean?"

"That I'm tired, and you're keeping me from a bed."

"You can sleep in the skimmer. I'll give you a ride to Portside."

Portside, now, not Under Rim. No way she was going to either one with Adel. And she knew she couldn't win a fight. She and Adel had trained together. They were evenly matched at the best of times, and Lee knew she was far from at her best.

Lee darted for the cook's door, slammed it behind her, and took time to turn on the lights so she could find her way across the unfamiliar room. She flung open the outside door, ducked along the wall, and around the corner of the building. Adel's footsteps thudded behind her. She crouched and ran for a line of copper trees growing along the rim.

Lee froze among the trunks and waited for her eyes to adjust to the moonless darkness. She couldn't hear any footsteps. Where was the woman?

A skimmer door snicked closed. Was Adel leaving? Or fetching a light?

Lee hunkered down and duck-walked from one concealing trunk to another. She froze as a bright light moved across the area. Scorch it!

The light moved away toward the trail down to the pens. As quietly as she could, Lee followed. A little voice urged her to take the Ranger's skimmer and leave, but what would that solve? Adel would get to Vinz and undermine anything Lee might say later. If Adel excelled at one thing, it was selling her version of things. And Lee needed Vinz to be willing to believe her.

The light disappeared through the rock gateway at the top of the path. Lee ran that far, trusting the rocks to block the sound of her steps. She slipped through the slot and crouched down. Even in the dark, her light-colored clothes would show up against the rocks.

Adel's light made a halo as she went around a boulder out of sight. The light bobbled like Adel nearly dropped it. The ribbon-worm colony hanging from the cliff must have taken the ranger by surprise. Lee felt her way as far as the boulder.

Was Adel looking for her or trying to get to Vinz? From her vantage on the slope, Lee couldn't see any other lights out in the meadows along the stream channel, but Vinz could be up in the other canyon, the one Lee hadn't come down.

Lee edged around the boulder. Once she rounded that, she'd be in plain sight of Adel the rest of the way to the bottom, if the Ranger looked back. Lee took a last step into the open.

Adel blocked her way. "You need help, Lee. Let me help you."

"You? How can you help me?" Keep her talking. Keep her away from Vinz. Lee backed up.

"Where have you been? What happened to you?"

"I got lost." Lee backed a little farther, drawing Adel to a wider spot.

"Let's go back to the cabin. You said you wanted to sleep." Adel turned her light on Lee, half-blinding her.

Lee dodged past Adel and around the boulder out of the light, stumbled on the rocks, slowed, felt her way along. Adel's boots thudded in pursuit, a patch of light guiding her footsteps, giving her speed.

Lee made it as far as the ribbon-worms before Adel caught up with her.

"Let's just go back to the cabin," Adel said. "We'll wait there for Vinz."

"Is that whose bike that is?"

"Yes. You know him. You can trust him."

Lee tore a long ribbon-worm from the wall, flung it at Adel, and ran. Adel caught her by the back of her shirt. Lee twisted away, lost her footing, and fell, a hard, clumsy fall into the scrumble of rocks below the trail.

Adel's light swept the rock field. Lee huddled down into the shadow and light. Kept her breathing deep and quiet. Became aware of pain-to-be in her ribs and her shoulder where she'd struck the rocks. She'd missed her chance. She couldn't win a direct confrontation. And she wouldn't reach Vinz before Adel got to him.

"Lee," Adel said, her voice soothing, like she spoke to a child or a crazy person. "Remember, when we were new at the academy? When you snuck me back into the dorm that night? I would have gotten in such trouble." Silence. The light probing. "Let me help you now."

Lee shrank deeper into the shadows. No kidding

about getting in trouble. They both could have been expelled. Lee remembered having that threat over her head for years.

The light turned away. Footsteps receded down the path. To where Vinz was.

Lee stood up, balancing precariously on a chunk of rock that had broken free from the cliff along with hundreds of others. She could see up over the edge onto the path. She reached up, secured her grip, and clambered up. Her shoulder ached where she'd landed on it and both forearms stung. Even in the dark, she could make out the bloody scrapes from the rocks.

Adel's light was almost to the bottom and the maze of pens. A lane ran along the foot of the slope, connecting the canyon Lee had come down to the one coming in from the right. The ditch ran along the lane, diverting the water around the corrals. Lee didn't see any light but Adel's. Where was Vinz?

Lee picked her way carefully along the narrow path to the bottom. As long as the light kept moving, she didn't have to worry about another ambush. She might not beat Adel to Vinz, but she could limit how much time Adel had to sell her story.

Adel's light moved off toward the right-hand canyon. She wasn't hesitating to think about direction. She must be confident she knew where to find Vinz. Any moment the light would go into the canyon, out of sight.

What time was it anyway? It seemed like hours since Lee had reached the camp. Lander wouldn't rise until after midnight, but Damele was just rising and full. About nine o'clock. And enough light to find her way.

Lee crossed the foot bridge and leaned against the tack room. She could wait there for Adel and Vinz to come back. Her tired body begged her to. But that would give Adel time with him. Besides, he might know another way up to the camp and bypass her. She pushed herself straight and stepped up onto the corral fence to see if she could see Vinz anywhere.

She could make out Clown's white splotches in the meadow. What was he watching? His head was high. Something had his attention. Something out into the meadows, not up the canyon where Adel had gone. Lee ran her eyes back and forth across the meadows slowly, trusting her peripheral vision to pick up movement. And she found it, dark against the pale grasses along the stream bank. Vinz. Who else could it be?

"Thank you, Clown," she murmured. She pushed her reluctant legs into a trot and headed for the gate she had let the horse through earlier. She could reach Vinz while Adel was looking for him up the canyon.

The tall grasses of the meadow seemed to reach out for her feet. She stumbled on, trying to judge her course to intercept the man. Get to Vinz; explain she needed to talk to Emmerling. He'd trust her. He had to trust her.

"Whoa there," a voice said. "Lee? Lee Vawn-Cory?"

Lee looked up. He was there, his pale face and hair floating in the dark a few feet in front of her. She'd almost walked into him.

Before she could say anything, a shout reached her. "Lee! There you are. Are you okay?" Adel jogged along the stream toward them, flashing her light on Lee.

"No," was all Lee could think of to say. She let her

legs fold under her and sat down. "I'm tired."

Vinz dropped to one knee next to her and held up a hand to stall Adel. "What happened to you?" he asked. "Are you hurt?"

Lee looked at her scraped arms. "Not much," she said.

"Sir," Adel said. "She's been missing for weeks. She refused my help and won't talk about where she's been or what happened." Adel moved around them so her light was in Lee's eyes. "She's not being rational."

"Douse it, Adel," Lee said. "Both the light and the attitude." She took a breath. This wasn't helping her case. She was just reinforcing Adel's claim. She pushed herself to her feet. Vinz took her arm to help her up. She looked him in the eye. "Sir, I apologize." She raised her hand to block Adel's light. "It's been a long few days, and I'm a little short on sleep."

"Adel," Vinz said. "Lower that light."

"But look at me, sir." Adel turned the light on herself.

Lee could barely keep from laughing. The usually impeccable Adel was soaked; her braid was coming loose; and she was covered with leaves, twigs, and algae from the creek. She must have fallen in. Lee couldn't imagine her purposefully looking like that. "Don't tell me," Lee said. "I did that to you?"

Adel pointed the light at the ground. "Sir, do you hear her? She isn't making any sense. She needs help."

"A good night's sleep would help," Lee said.

"Enough," Vinz said. "We'll sort this out up at the camp. Adel, lead the way."

Chapter 27

Seth

Seth stared across the room at Whip Willemsen. The man's accusation of Adel Verlane hung in the air.

"Repeat that," Joe Reilly said. Seth moved over beside him.

Willemsen shifted uneasily in the chair. "She's going to make it look like we're failing. The analysis will misread things. You know, development, rehabbed mine areas, lots of little things that add up until Carico hasn't met its milestones."

"Let me be sure I understand you. You're saying Adel Verlane is biasing the outcome of the survey so the evaluation won't give Carico credit for accomplishments." Joe spelled it out. "Why? The Sol Terra Alliance will just send in someone to take over administration to make sure we do meet all requirements by the 100-year deadline."

"Her friends, they're set up to be the new administration."

"And how do you know this?" Joe asked.

"About the survey? I was inputting the parameters. Guess she didn't think I'd know what it would do."

"And you don't have any idea who the man was that she talked to?" Joe asked.

"Well, truth is, I do. I've seen him before."

"Where? Who is he?"

"One of Jerdix's friends, name of Henry. That's all I ever heard."

"You're sure?" Joe prodded.

"He was around Jerdix's more than once. I've been calling the horse Henry so I wouldn't forget."

"You are hardly the most credible witness."

"That's why I got out of there."

Joe pinned him with his eyes until Whip cringed, then said, "Maybe I believe you; maybe I don't. But I'll keep you safe until we can sort it out."

Whip sagged with relief. "Thanks. Oh, wow. I won't be any problem. I swear I won't. Just keep me away from her."

"Pa." Seth stepped back and tipped his head toward the hallway. Joe followed him until they were out of Whip's sight. "We can't keep him here," Seth said. "Not with Trrk."

"Does make things interesting," Joe said. "We may

have to let him in on the secret."

"Are you crazy?"

"We have ourselves another tech. One here, now. Gwyn won't be back until at least midday tomorrow."

"He's a fugitive. He attacked Lee."

"I would say that Lee meted out quick, efficient punishment all on her own." Joe laid his hand on Seth's shoulder. "I'm not excusing him, just making use of what the Elements have given us. If what he says is true, we need him safe."

"And I promised Trrk he'd be safe."

"He is. But now we have two things to bring directly to the PAO's attention. Let's hope Lee has luck with Ro Vinz."

"You'll go to Emmerling about Adel? Not to Vinz?"

"Preferably both of them together."

"Okay. Look, can I get the gear from the skimmer?" The cabin was closing in around him. He needed to get outside, get some fresh air.

"You do that. Have Trrk wait out back. Meantime, I'd better send Kiri a blip that I'll be a little late."

"You're going home and leaving me alone with Whip and Trrk?"

"In case Verlane really is monitoring me." Joe grinned. "You can handle things here overnight, and my wife needs my loving attention."

Seth threw up his hands. "I did not need to hear that." He went down the hall and out the back door.

He stopped on the porch, taking time to come to grips with the situation. He remembered his first encounter with Whip. It had been at Tobin Canyon

Camp during migration three springs ago. Whip had been repping for Jerdix and got his fun prodding people, especially a green crew boss named Seth Reilly. But what Seth couldn't forget was the night he had left a community meeting in Under Rim and Whip and a partner had intercepted him, drugged him, and turned him over to Jerdix to be tortured. There had to be another way of making the synthesizer. Whip would be safe from Adel if he was locked up at the Marshal's Office.

In his mind, Seth replayed what Whip Willemsen had just said and tried to imagine how Lee would react. She should be getting close to Tobin Canyon Camp by this time. And Vinz, her key to reaching the PAO. And she didn't know that the stakes had now doubled — Keloks and the outcome of the evaluation.

But right now, he needed to get Trrk settled. He strode through the evening heat and opened the cargo compartment of the skimmer.

"May I come out now?" Trrk asked.

"Sorry about that. Someone's at the cabin."

"Will we go elsewhere?"

"No. We're staying here. Come on." Seth started for the cabin.

Trrk hesitated. "It is someone who can see me?"

"It is someone who can help build a synthesizer so you can talk to people without a translator."

"Oh."

"Remember the man we diverted from the villages?"

Trrk bobbed his head. "Beyond the river? The captive of your spouse."

"Yup. Well, it's him."

"You did not trust him."

"I still don't."

"I could build the synthesizer."

"On your own?"

"It is possible." Trrk's crest lifted then settled again. "But the chance of success is greater if I receive input on how the hearing facilitator may interact with your technologies."

"Are you willing to show yourself to him? We can control where he goes and who he talks to for a while."

Silently Trrk rubbed his tail above the amputation. Then he stepped out of the skimmer. "Let us go."

"Remember," Seth said, "you are a lone castaway. And you know nothing about what happened last time I saw him."

"Best if the past does not come up. I am burdened with enough untruths."

"Once Lee gets to the PAO, we can quit keeping secrets."

"I will have to answer for aiding you when I return to my people," Trrk said. His crest drooped.

"You are doing all of this for them. And by showing yourself, you aren't giving away the villages."

"Accurate. But someone will be held accountable for preventing Prime from rescinding her authorization. Better it be me than my spouse."

Seth knew that feeling. He wondered how far Lee had gotten on her way to Tobin Canyon and how Vinz would take what she had to say.

"If you're not well enough for this, say so. You can

rest in the bedroom without Whip seeing you."

Trrk stretched carefully. "I am satisfactory."

"You weren't a day ago."

"You do not understand my kind's way of recovering. Our bodies put everything into repairing damage, shutting down other functions. When we return to consciousness, we are ready for normal activity."

"True?"

Again Trrk's crest lifted and dropped. "I would not want to go on the hunt or into the arena yet. But it is better to move than be still."

"Okay. Stay outside for now and move around. I'll go check on things inside."

He left Trrk by the back porch and went in to be sure his pa still wanted to do this. Joe met him in the hallway.

"Trrk's just outside," Seth said. "We need to let Lee know what's going on."

"We need to do that face-to-face," Joe said. "This is not something for the comm system."

"Right." This was getting to be a tangled mess. "Did you know that Lee knew Adel at the academy?"

"I didn't."

"Ever since we first heard what spin Adel was putting on our disappearance, Lee's been asking how she would benefit from making us look unreliable."

"I wondered that myself," Joe said. "She was also pushing the idea that you had helped Willemsen. To discredit anything you might report if you did find out what he knows?"

"Makes sense," Seth said.

Joe led the way toward the front room, saying,

"We'll need more than suspicions to convince Ro Vinz."

"Couldn't help overhearing that," Whip said. "I saved a backup of the programming. Someplace most people wouldn't think to look. In case she decided to clean things up."

"You're just one surprise after another. Where is it?" Joe asked.

"Nope. That's my insurance. You keep me safe and let her plan out of the bag. I'll give you the evidence when it's needed."

"We can talk more about that later," Joe said. "For now, consider yourself in my custody."

"But," Seth said, "you are going to help us with a tech project."

"Hey, I'm no programmer. I was just inputting code."

"Well, this is more telecom than computers," Seth said.

"That I can do."

"We'll see." Joe eyed him.

"I can." Whip looked from one to the other. "I can."

"You'll get the chance to prove it," Joe said.

Whip dropped his eyes and shuffled his feet. "One more thing?"

"What's that?" Joe asked.

"Can I finish my dinner? I just got here this afternoon and it's my first good meal in weeks."

Joe chuckled. "Go ahead."

Seth went back outside. Trrk was working through the basics of the Kelok martial art form but with none of the flash and dash that characterized it. Not feeling as good as he wanted them to believe. Seth let it go.

"Don't stop," he told Trrk. "I'm just going to get some things from the skimmer."

He took advantage of the short walk to get himself together. The last few days had been hard, and his nap earlier had been far too short. Settlement Day was the day after tomorrow. Lee would deliver the Kelok invitation to the PAO, and they could pass the whole mess, except Trrk, off to the authorities. Trrk stayed with them until he could go home.

Seth hadn't brought much, only his saddlebags and some food Joe had gotten together for them. He and Lee had left the rest of their packs at Lickskillet with the horses. Was it just last night he had gotten Trrk to Ike's old cabin?

He slung his saddlebags over his shoulder and picked up the box of food. Might as well get on with this. Trrk waited near the back door. His crest and epaulet feathers sagged. The dun-colored down over his body looked dingy.

"Ready?" Seth asked. "We'll get some dinner."

"I do need food."

"Then let's go in and see what Whip thinks of you."

Trrk perked up. "I will enjoy startling this man. A small repayment for what he attempted to do to your spouse."

Seth agreed wholeheartedly.

Whip was sitting at the table eating when Seth returned to the front room. The man's eyes went past Seth and locked on Trrk. Whip scrambled up and backed to the wall, wide-eyed. "Wha... what... I said I'd help. Keep that thing off me."

Seth glanced over his shoulder and saw Trrk with his crest standing up and spread wide as he clacked his beak. That was more like him. "Don't scare him too bad," he said. "We need him to work with you."

Trrk let his crest slowly settle down on his neck. "First impressions are important."

Seth reminded himself that Whip couldn't understand Trrk. The rasping squawk was not reassuring. "Whip, meet my friend Trrk. You are going to help him build a speech synthesizer from a hearing facilitation device."

"Do what? A synthesizer? With that?"

"Yes," Seth said. "And this *person* can understand everything you say."

Whip moved, putting the table between himself and Trrk. "You're crazy."

Seth shrugged. "It feels that way some days. But if you want protection from Adel Verlane, you help Trrk cobble together a synthesizer."

"What in the Void is a hearing facilitation device?"

"This," Seth said, running a finger under the choker around his neck. "Trrk's people make them. We need one that transfers vibrations to a sound system instead of to skin."

"Okay," Whip said. "I've gotta wake up from this dream eventually. Until then, I'll go along. You're sure that thing won't hurt me?"

"I guess that depends on whether you behave. So sit down and finish your dinner. Trrk, make yourself comfortable. I'll fix us something to eat."

Seth waited until Trrk got settled on the rock hearth

before putting the supplies down on the kitchen counter. Whip perched on the edge of the bench behind the table and pulled his plate to him, his eyes never leaving Trrk.

"Looks like you three are all set," Joe said. "I'm off for home. Doc will be here first thing in the morning to check on Trrk. Whip, he'll look you over while he's here."

"I, uh, yeah. This knee's bad," Whip whined. "He won't tell anybody, will he?"

"Patient confidentiality. No one else will know you're here."

"You're sure you don't want to stay?" Seth asked.

"I've got better things to do." Joe grinned. "See you tomorrow sometime. After Lee gets back from Tobin."

"Okay." Seth watched his pa leave. Whip stayed on the backside of the table, nibbling at his food with his eyes on Trrk. Trrk squatted on the edge of the hearth with the bandaged end of his tail twitching from side to side. Seth turned his attention to food for him and the Kelok. This was going to be interesting.

Chapter 28

Lee

Lee made it all the way up to the camp, concentrating on putting one foot in front of the other. The last few days piled up on her. Her ribs and shoulder ached. The scrapes on her arms burned. She was afraid she would have to crawl up the ledges of the trail but managed to stay on her feet, pulling herself along the rock wall. She did her best to walk more or less normally across the level ground to the building and climb the steps with Vinz close behind her.

"Go sit down," he told her, pointing to the cookhouse. "And Adel, get yourself cleaned up. The shower room is two doors down."

"But sir —"

"Go on."

Lee chose one of the tall stools at the counter. She wasn't sure she could get back up if she sat on a chair.

"Let me see," Vinz said, taking her wrist and turning her arm over. He got a clean washcloth from a drawer and ran the hot water over it. "Not too bad."

She took the cloth and dabbed at the scratches. "I need to talk to you. Before she gets back."

"What's been going on?"

"A lot." Too much. "I need your help. I have a message for the PAO and her alone. Can you get her to see me?"

"Not without knowing more than I do now."

"It has to do with, uh, some beyonders out on the Whitewater."

"Beyonders. And you knew to come here looking for me. Which means you talked to Joe Reilly."

"Yes, sir. Please. If it was just you and me here ... but I can't say more where she might overhear. I didn't even share most of it with Joe."

"You're not giving me much to work with."

"Please. Time is short. I have to see the PAO before the satellites start collecting data."

"That shouldn't be for a few weeks."

"From what Adel broadcast recently, they are being deployed right after Settlement Day. The actual survey won't start until they're calibrated, but they will be gathering images."

"So they will reveal a few beyonders. I expect that."

"Not these beyonders. I can't explain, not until I talk

to the PAO. I promised, sir."

"I'll consider it. That's the best I can offer at the moment."

"Thank you." It didn't sound promising. Well, she could find a way to the PAO on her own if she needed to. Lee pushed herself to her feet. "There's one more thing. About Adel."

"It's apparent you two have some unresolved history."

Lee looked him in the eye. "Don't trust her. She's been spreading my personal —"

Adel thrust the door open. "What's she telling you?" She tossed her now-neat braid back and pulled her tunic straight. "Like I said, she's been listed as missing for at least two weeks. She and two others. It's been five days since we found the body of one of them in a shallow grave and not a sign of the others until now."

"Lee?"

"It was Ike Allred, from Seven Wells," she said. "We were caught in a narrow canyon by a stampede."

"He wasn't found in a canyon." Adel kept her voice quiet, calm.

"No, he must have made it out on the plateau before he died. That's where Seth found him and buried him."

"Seth? That would be Seth Reilly?" Vinz asked.

"The one she was involved with three years ago." Again, Adel conveyed information calmly.

"Sir," Lee said, trying to match Adel's control. "There's nothing more I can ... will ... say about it here."

"So you came here to find me. And found Adel."

"I just got here, looking for you, when she came in,"

Adel said. "She looked exhausted, and she wouldn't answer my questions."

Lee sat back on the stool. "I didn't come to talk to you."

"I was going to the comm," Adel said, pointing across the room into the kitchen area. "To let someone know I'd found her. And she ran out. I went after her. She seemed, I don't know, paranoid I guess."

"I've heard enough from her." Lee glared. "Acting Principal Adviser Verlane. She's been broadcasting warnings about me for days, about my mental health. 'Don't approach her. Just notify authorities.' Like I was some dangerous criminal. And when she found me here, she did her best to keep me from you."

"Me? Sir, down on the trail, she ran from me. She fell over the edge in the dark."

Lee held up her scraped forearms. "Clumsy me."

"Just listen to her. She's not rational."

Lee stood up. "Do you believe me?"

He shook his head. "I think, right now, you need to get some rest while I consider what you told me."

"While you listen to her side of the whole thing?"

"My turn to ask for trust," he said. "Take the second room. We'll talk in the morning."

Lee walked past Adel, keeping her back straight. Adel would have the last word. She'd lost. She wasn't going to let Adel see that. She entered the designated room.Tthe outer lock engaged behind her. When she thumbed the pad, the lock didn't release. Well, that worked both ways. The door also had a manual lock to give occupants privacy. She latched that. No surprise midnight visits to disrupt her sleep.

She heard Vinz and Adel outside. Sounded like he wasn't too happy with his assistant.

"So the satellite array is arriving sooner than expected?"

"Yes, sir. I probably should have gotten word to you, but there was nothing you needed to do. The ship should be in orbit tomorrow and can start deploying the satellites as soon as I coordinate with them on the pattern."

"Then don't you think you should be in Portside instead of worrying about one lost rider?"

"A lost Ranger, sir."

"Who has plenty of local resources capable of conducting a search."

"Yes, of course. I'll leave right now." Hesitation. An indrawn breath. "I can take Lee back with me and see she gets the help she obviously needs."

"No, wait until morning," he replied. "We'll discuss it then, after I've had time to think and Lee has had some sleep."

"Well, if that's what you want."

"Take the end room."

Sent to bed. Lee managed a grin. She had the night to figure out how she could avoid becoming Adel's passenger. She didn't know what Adel was up to, but Lee had no doubt that something would happen to her before they got to Portside. But what? How far would Adel go to protect her scheme, whatever that was?

Chapter 29

Seth

Seth stood on the porch of Fallen Pine cabin, looking out over the quiet dark of the meadow. Lander was high overhead, three-quarters full and waning. Damele was already down. The faintest hint of gray tinged the eastern sky. He wasn't sure what had wakened him; he was even less sure how he had managed to sleep at all. He was alone, for the moment. Trrk and Whip were presumably still sleeping, Trrk in the main bedroom by the back door and Whip in the loft.

Trrk and Whip had somehow managed to argue half the evening even when Whip couldn't understand what was being said. The project seemed to energize Trrk, but

Seth didn't miss the droop of his crest and the way he kept his tail stub tucked between his feet. From what Seth could figure out as he translated the technicalities, if not the colorful additions of Trrk's remarks, all they needed was a way to capture the output from the hearing facilitation device and feed it into a basic comm unit that could already transmit speech.

With the discussion about how to do that going nowhere but in circles, Seth had sent them both off to bed. Trrk laid claim to the downstairs bedroom, sending Whip up the steep steps to the sleeping loft in spite of his bad knee. Seth had settled for the couch where he would know if Whip tried to leave.

And he had slept soundly for the first time in two days. For a while. Now worry about Lee battled worry about Trrk, all under a swell of guilt about the lies and secrets that kept building up.

Soft sounds inside, stocking feet on the wood floor. Seth went back inside to see Whip slinking along the dark hallway toward the backdoor, boots in hand.

"Going somewhere?" Seth asked.

"To check on Henry," Whip said.

"Henry?"

"My horse."

"Before daylight?"

"I was awake."

"Yeah, well, he'll still be there after sunrise."

"Okay, truth is being shut in here with that beasty, I need some air."

"Take too much air, and we'll turn you over to the authorities. And watch how you talk about Trrk."

"I can't help it. Feathers and that beak. And then he's so tech smart. Just doesn't feel right."

"Get a working synthesizer together, and you won't have to stay around him."

Whip looked down at the boots in his hand. "I can check Henry later. I'll fix breakfast. What does that ... Trrk eat?"

"There's tarbh ham in the cooler."

Seth couldn't figure the man out. Maybe the cockiness was all bluff, at least when he didn't have backup. Whip was obviously scared of Adel and seemed willing to help if it kept him away from her. He wasn't comfortable with Trrk, but Seth's own initial reactions had been pretty negative too. Elements! He had more important things to do than watch over Whip Willemsen.

Or did he? If what Whip said about Adel's plans was true, the settlers' future on Carico depended on stopping her. And the Keloks' future too. Seth had a hunch that friends of Adel's with ties back to Jerdix wouldn't be sympathetic to sharing.

He let Trrk sleep. Time enough to wake him when Doc got there. Seth figured Doc would show up early so he could be back in town for his usual breakfast at Under Rim's inn and tavern with its proprietor Ila Jones. He always had breakfast at Ila's. People would notice if he wasn't there.

After he and Whip ate, Seth let Whip go out to the pasture. He went along to be safe. Whip fed a handful of dried roundfruit to his horse before running his hands over the animal, stopping to scratch favorite spots. Another surprise. Seth remembered Whip as one to treat a horse as a tool of his job, important, valuable even, but not an individual. Being alone and dependent on one horse seemed to have changed that.

The hum of a skimmer interrupted them. "I'd better get out of sight," Whip said, looking around for the nearest trees.

"Back to the cabin," Seth said. "It's just Doc."

"I'm okay." Whip looked away sheepishly. "No need for him to see me."

"Pa already told him you'd be here," Seth said, "so he'll want to look. You can explain to him how you got hurt." A satisfying thought.

"Your girl does know how to do damage."

"You're lucky she didn't do worse." Seth took that as a reminder not to worry. Lee could take care of herself.

"I just, well, all I really wanted to do was scare her, get her to go away, you know. She was such a meek little spinxi around Jerdix. I wouldn't really have ..."

"Save it for Doc. Not that he's likely to believe you either. Let's go." Seth pointed to the cabin.

Chapter 30

Seth

When Seth got back to the cabin with Whip in tow, Trrk was in the front room with Doc. His maimed tail was stretched across the table while Doc inspected the stub. At the sight of Whip, Trrk flipped the tail under the table.

"Willemsen, have a seat over there." Doc waved to the far chair by the fireplace. "I'll get to you next."

"I'm okay."

"The marshal said to check you over. I'll check you over. Now sit and let me finish with this patient."

"Whatever you say." Whip sat on the couch with his feet up and his back to Doc and Trrk.

Doc patted the table, and Trrk brought his tail back

up. "It's looking good," Doc said. "I'm interested in that lichen you used on it when you were first bitten. Interesting stuff."

Seth waited for Trrk to say something. When he didn't, Seth did it for him. Faster than translating anyway. "But it didn't seem to work that well. He still lost a big chunk of tail."

"That was from lack of blood flow, not an infection. This end is healthy and healing thanks to good care. You could make up more but now this will be more useful." He sprayed the stub with clear liquid temp skin that dried into a film. "There. It wasn't able to hold the edges of your wounds together, but this is just what it is meant to do." He ran a finger gently across it to adhere it.

The tail shivered at the touch. "It tickles," Trrk said.

Seth translated for Doc.

Doc smiled. "Good stuff, temp skin. It's meant to be sensitive. Keeps people careful with their injuries."

Trrk took his tail in hand and ran an extended claw lightly across the stub. "Could we have some of this?" he asked Seth.

"What for?" Seth asked.

Trrk bobbed his head. "The synthesizer. To amplify vibrations."

"Doc, can you let us have some temp skin?" Seth asked. "Trrk thinks he can use it in the speech synthesizer, but I don't know if the aid kit here is up to date or not." Temp skin was a standard component for both humans and animals. But it did lose effectiveness over time.

"Help yourself." Doc handed Seth the container. "I

hope it helps make this speech contraption. I have a feeling Trrk should be able to speak for himself. You can't hide him forever."

"Just a day or two," Seth said. At least Doc had a professional obligation to protect his patients' privacy.

"Trrk, don't let these two keep you from resting, understand me?" Doc waited for Trrk to bob his head. "Good. Now, let me take a look at Willemsen. Shall we go back to the bedroom?"

Whip looked at Seth and Trrk. "Yeah, fine," he said and got to his feet.

"After you," Doc said and watched him hobble toward the hall. "Fight?" he asked.

"Something like that," Whip said without looking at him.

"How long ago?"

"Seven days," Seth answered for him. "Lee objected when Whip tried to assault her."

Doc's eyebrows raised. "Joe said you found him here."

"We did. We parted company after Lee's encounter with him. We weren't somewhere we could report him, and we weren't going to drag him around back of beyond with us. We didn't think he'd be stupid enough to show up here."

"Quite a mess."

"Yes, it is."

While Doc was in with Whip, Seth got Trrk something to eat. "You really think the temp skin will do the trick for the synthesizer?" he asked.

"Like a drumhead," Trrk answered.

"Doc is happy with the way your tail looks."

"It heals." Trrk tucked it away under the table out of sight.

"Does it hurt a lot?"

"Do not concern yourself."

Seth let it go. He couldn't begin to know what Trrk was feeling or what the injury might mean within the Kelok culture. They had made jokes about Seth's tailless status. And now Trrk would have to face humans injured and incomplete.

Doc reappeared. "No permanent damage. Was Lee injured?"

"No, no, she wasn't."

"Should I be worried about her, given her history?"

"More like it freed her somehow. By defending herself, I think." Seth wasn't sure how to describe it.

"Good to know." Doc gathered up his kit and headed for the door. "Ro Vinz called me from Tobin Canyon. He's bringing Lee in for evaluation."

"He's what?" So she'd gotten to Vinz, but it didn't sound like that was going well.

Doc stopped at the door. "I got the impression she insisted on coming to me instead of to Portside."

"She never cleared that medical suspension, did she?"

"Not to my knowledge."

Seth forced a grin. "At least we can trust you to sort it out."

"You can trust me to do a thorough and honest evaluation of her condition to the best of my ability."

"Sure, Doc. I just meant, well, I know she's okay,

better than she's been in a while, and I know you'll see that."

"Don't worry about Lee. I gather she's working on a meeting with the PAO? To introduce Trrk before rumors start flying?"

"That's right."

"Okay. Now listen to me. You stay here with these two until you hear from your father. Won't help if you appear to be assisting a fugitive."

"I do know that."

"I'd best be on my way. Vinz and Lee will probably beat me to town as it is."

"Tell her ..."

"I'll tell her you are fine and to focus on her job. I'm glad you two are back together. You're good for each other."

Doc got in his skimmer and was gone, leaving Seth alone with Trrk and Whip who were already arguing over how to best utilize the temp skin. Seth didn't understand how they did that when Whip couldn't understand a word Trrk said. Lots of gesturing and sketching diagrams.

Anyway, Lee had made contact with Vinz. And Doc would be able to counter any claims Adel made about Lee's competence. And they had Trrk if they needed to introduce him to Vinz to convince him of the need for a meeting with the PAO. But where had Adel gone when she had left town? The guest house? Or was she with Vinz and Lee?

Chapter 31

Lee

Lee sat cross-legged on the bottom bunk in the little room. She'd been awake since the narrow window had shown a hint of gray. She'd heard Vinz's door just before sunrise, but nothing from the other side yet. They were going to have to break in the door to get her to go with Adel.

A sharp rap on her door. "Breakfast," Vinz said.

"I think I'll just leave the door closed," she called back. She heard Adel's door open. "Until after she's gone," she added.

"I thought you wanted to go to Portside."

"I didn't say anything about Portside. I said I need to

see the PAO. I don't think I'll do either if Adel has her way."

"You aren't helping your case," he said.

"No, she sounds completely paranoid." Adel's voice. "What does she want to talk to the PAO about? And why would I care?"

"You think I need medical attention? Have Doc Legat in Under Rim come get me. He's the closest."

"See, she admits she needs care." Adel sounded triumphant. "There are specialists in Portside better able to deal with this."

"Doc, or I'm not leaving this room." How much did that sound like a child's tantrum? Even with her voice as steady as she could make it. "Doc's the only one I trust right now."

Silence, except for shifting feet. "Okay. I'll see if he's available," Vinz said. "Now open the door, and I'll give you this tray."

"I don't think so."

"You're going to let her dictate terms?" Adel said.

"My call. Come on."

Two pairs of feet walked away. Lee leaned back against the wall and whispered, "Doc, you'd better not be out on a call."

Vinz was back in a matter of minutes. "The doctor says to bring you to him. He has a house call he needs to make first thing."

"I can wait."

"I promise I will see you safely to him. Now come to the kitchen before you convince me Adel is right about your state of mind." The outer lock clicked open.

Scorch it. What could she do? She eased to her feet and straightened slowly, favoring her bruised ribs. She did not want Adel to realize she was hurt. She released the inner lock and followed Vinz to the kitchen.

Adel sat on a stool at the counter, toying with the end of her braid. The slight smile on her face reinforced Lee's distrust of her. Lee pulled out a bench and sat down with the long table between them. Vinz pushed the tray of food across the table to her.

"I sent blips to Kieron Dougherty and Joe Reilly to let them know you are here." Vinz brought her a mug of tea. "Also the central marshal's office in Portside to cancel the bulletins about you."

Adel flipped her braid behind her back. "Whip Willemsen hasn't been found yet either."

Whip? Lee shook her head. "Doesn't have anything to do with me."

"What about Willemsen?" Vinz asked. "He's missing too?"

"They both disappeared about the same time, in the same area," Adel said.

"Weren't Ike and I at Seth's on our way to explore the plateau for Seven Wells when you were spreading the word of Willemsen's escape?" Lee asked.

"Enough. Adel, we'll discuss Willemsen later." Vinz turned to look at Lee. "Did you leave anything with your gear that you need?"

Lee thought about one diplomatic pouch concealed in the feed bin and shook her head. "No, nothing that can't wait."

"Okay. You clean up the dishes. Adel, strip the

bedding from the rooms you two used and put them in the cleaner. Leave this place ready for someone else."

Lee placed the half-hour skimmer ride to Under Rim with Adel at the controls right up with her first days as Eta'ak's captive for uncomfortable experiences. Adel spoke to her like she was a child, or incompetent, trying to get her to talk about where she'd been and what had happened to her. It might all sound very solicitous if anyone was listening, say if Adel was recording it. Lee sat square in her seat, eyes ahead, with a mental wall between them, and answered with uninformative single syllables when pushed to answer at all. At least with Vinz following them on his skybike, she felt more or less safe.

As they approached Under Rim, Adel slowed. "You're sure you want to go to this village medic?"

"The med center's on the left. Park in back." At least Trrk was safely at Fallen Pine where Adel wouldn't find out about him.

Adel parked the skimmer at the hospital door. Lee hopped out as the vehicle came to a stop. Her bruised ribs reminded her to move carefully.

Vinz landed next to her. "You look a little stiff."

"Too many miles," she said. "It doesn't look like Doc is back yet. I'll just go in and wait."

"We couldn't leave you alone," Adel said. "Sir, I can stay with her if you want to get back to Tobin. "

"No rush," Vinz said. "I need to talk to Doc. Lee, inside." He went with her through the door.

Lee led the way along the corridor past the first room where Trrk had been and the tiny seating area across from it, past another room on each side, and through the door into the lobby facing the esplanade. At the reception counter inside the street door a sign announced that Doc was out on a call and gave options for scheduling an appointment, having Doc call when he got back, or calling him if it was an emergency.

"No staff?" Adel asked.

"Typical in these small districts," Vinz said.

"We should take her to Portside, where she can get appropriate care."

Lee sat down in a chair. "Doc can always have me locked up at the marshal's office if he thinks it's necessary. Or put me in a quarantine stall at the vet's. Those are pretty secure."

The look Vinz gave her said she was trying his patience. But he turned to Adel. "Go to the inn and see if there's room on the jumper run today. That'll get you back to Portside tonight so you'll be ready for the satellite delivery."

"I can take the skimmer," Adel said. "Set it on autopilot and sleep on the way. I can still be in Portside late tonight sometime."

"Leave it for me. I may need it."

"Are you sure there is a run today? I heard they were pretty erratic."

"It's the day before Settlement Day. People want to get to Portside."

Adel hesitated, then said, "All right."

A bell tinkled back in the clinic hallway. Lee pushed herself to her feet. "Sounds like Doc's back."

Chapter 32

Lee

Doc came into the lobby. "Lee, I'm glad to see you alive and well." He ran critical eyes over her. "Or mostly well."

"Good to see you too, Doc." Like she hadn't seen him a day before. Trust him to keep secrets when a patient was concerned.

"Ranger Vinz." Doc turned to her escorts. "You asked for my services?"

"More accurately, Lee did. I'm concerned about her, and she insisted on seeing you rather than going to Portside."

"They're worried about my state of mind," Lee said.

"She's under a medical suspension," Adel said with

a look of concern.

"I am well aware of my patient's history," Doc said. "For the record, this is a voluntary evaluation, I take it."

Vinz shook his head. "Under the circumstances, it is not. I need to know that her recent disappearance isn't connected to her past trauma."

"It's not," Lee said.

"And that it hasn't reactivated any stress-induced reactions."

"Understood," Doc said. "So involuntary evaluation —"

"I voluntarily submit to evaluation," Lee said. "Let's get this cleared up so I can get on with things."

"Involuntary," Vinz reiterated. "Subject to confinement until I receive the official report."

"Confinement!" Lee stepped back, away from Vinz and from Adel. So much for getting Vinz to help her see the PAO. But the look on Adel's face made her think. Confinement would put her safely out of reach for a while. She bowed her head to Doc. "Okay, where would you like to confine me?"

"First door on the right in the hospital," Doc said. "Ranger, you are welcome to escort her. Then you'll have to wait outside the patient's room."

"Fine." Vinz pointed Lee toward the door.

"Does the door lock?" Adel asked. She hesitated, then added, "For her safety."

"I agreed to submit to evaluation," Lee protested.

Doc raised his hand to silence her. "There's an alarm so I know if patients are following directives."

"Let's go," Vinz said. "Adel, move the vehicles over

behind the store, away from the emergency entrance, and get yourself a seat on the jumper to Portside. Then wait here. I'll be at the cafe having a mug of tea."

"There's a sitting area inside the back door where she can see the hallway and the door to the room," Doc said.

Adel flipped her braid behind her back and stalked into the hospital corridor, heading for the vehicles in back. Lee followed, turning into the room Doc had designated. "The sooner we can get this over, the better," she said. "I still need to talk to the PAO."

"Let me know when you're ready to explain why," Vinz said.

"I can't," she said firmly. "The whole point is for her to be the first to hear what I have to tell her."

"You'll have to give me more than that before I bother her."

Lee sat on the edge of the bed. "Maybe when Doc has done his thing, you'll accept my word that it is important and that she would rather have a heads-up now than be taken by surprise later."

"We'll see."

Doc waited in the doorway, watching Vinz leave the building. "Will you stay put?" he asked. "Your medical suspension gives him the authority to have you confined long enough for an evaluation."

"I said I agreed. Just get it over with." She pushed aside her frustration with Vinz. "Was your house call this morning to see Trrk? Is he okay?"

"It was, and he is doing all right. Working on the synthesizer contraption they are trying to build has given him something to focus on."

"Gwyn got back early?"

Doc hesitated, then shook his head. "I couldn't say. Now settle in, and I'll start the diagnostics."

"I thought this was a mental evaluation."

"You know that begins with your physical condition, especially those ribs you are favoring. We'll see how much of your story I can read."

"Hey, the ribs are new. Last night. Like the scrapes on my arms. I was trying to avoid Adel."

He laid a finger on his lips. "Monitor Room Two," he said to the air. "Involuntary confinement, monitor audio and run general diagnostics. Activate." He pointed at the bed and left.

Monitor audio? Well, he had protocols to follow. She pulled off her boots and kicked them into a corner. She lay down on the bed and practiced mindful breathing, careful not to overstretch bruised ribs.

At least Seth and Trrk were making progress. It would be nice if Trrk could speak for himself. Trrk. She might have to introduce him to Vinz. That should be a good enough reason for him to quietly set up a meeting. And give Emmerling cause to believe the invitation was legitimate.

Which brought other concerns to mind. Would Prime show up if Emmerling accepted? Trrk thought she would as long as Lee, as envoy, never received official word not to deliver the message. As long as Eta'ak had any influence left.

The diplomatic pouch, with its written invitation in both Sol Standard and Kelok color writing, the woven story cloth, and the formal stole-of-office, was hidden in the feed bin at Tobin Canyon. No way Adel could know it existed. No one did except for Lee and Seth and Trrk. It should be safe where it was, but she needed to retrieve it before she could go to Emmerling.

Her brain buzzed on. Who was helping with the synthesizer? Joe had said Gwyn wouldn't be back until later today. But Doc had said he 'couldn't say', not that he didn't know who was helping. Lee felt like she was holding a tangled ball of string. Pull the right one, and it would all straighten out neatly. Pull the wrong one, and it would knot up beyond hope.

The door opened, and Lee got to her feet. Doc stuck his head in. "Back on the bed," he said. "Your guard is here. Very solicitous."

"Not you too." Lee shook her head. "I got these bruises trying to get away from her."

"She did say something about you running from her."

"And you believed her?"

"Take it easy," he said. "That's for Vinz to sort out. I'm more concerned about the level of stress you are showing."

Lee shut up and lay back on the bed. Keeping secrets was stressful, and she couldn't explain that to him without giving away secrets. Keep it simple. "I'm worried about Trrk. And I'm being confined against my will. Is that stress enough for you?"

"I thought you were doing this voluntarily."

"I volunteer for the evaluation. I object to the confinement. And to Adel Verlane."

"So noted."

Lee shifted on the diagnostic bed and adjusted it so that she was sitting and could see the door. "There, Doc. I'm cooperating."

"Thank you. Now, can I go get breakfast while the scanners do their work?"

"Just as long as you lock the door so no one disturbs me."

"Try to relax a little." He laid a hand on her shoulder. "You've been through these evaluations before."

"Go eat," she said. She had been through both the physical and mental evaluations before and after her undercover assignment with Jerdix. No way she could speed those up except by not erecting barriers.

She didn't have time for this. She needed to be finding a way of reaching the PAO in case Vinz decided not to help. She settled her hands in her lap and focused on her breath rising and falling. Calm, patient, in balance.

Doc hadn't darkened the big windows into the hallway, so Lee saw Adel meet him outside her door. Apparently, he hadn't activated the sound dampening either. Lee could plainly hear their conversation.

"How is she, Doctor? She's had us pretty worried with this paranoia about me wanting to hurt her."

"Paranoia?"

"I ... I don't like to tell tales."

"It might help."

"I knew her at the academy and, well, she always had a little trouble fitting in, switching between pushing to join in and isolating herself, but always very competitive."

Look who was talking. Lee reached for the alert to

call Doc back in, then hesitated. If she objected, argued, would she be falling into the picture Adel was setting up? No, trust Doc. He knew her. He'd see through Adel's act, see the ice in those gray eyes. He would.

"Thank you for that perspective," Doc said. "Let's leave her alone for now. Let the scanners do their thing."

"Of course," Adel said, but, as Doc walked away, she lingered, staring through the glass at Lee. She gave a little wave and strolled away with a confident set to her shoulders.

Lee refocused on her breath, on waiting, being calm, not letting Adel drive up her heart rate, her adrenaline. Trrk and Seth could take care of themselves. Joe would take care of them. She just had to prove to Doc that she was nothing more than stressed by a crazy situation.

Lee had nearly reached a steady meditative state when a tapping noise disturbed her. She looked up to see Adel outside the door. The Ranger waved before turning away.

Harassment. Lee struggled to recapture her calm. An image flashed in her mind of herself at sixteen, slinking away in embarrassment after Adel and her gang had set her up to think she was meeting a popular boy. Adel had been correct when she told Doc that Lee hadn't fit in. Academically she had been Adel's equal or better. It had never meant anything when constantly faced with the social isolation that Adel manipulated her into.

"We're not sixteen anymore," Lee whispered to herself. "And I'm not alone now."

The scanners couldn't read her mind, but they could

read infinitesimal changes in everything from her brain activity to a myriad of chemical changes in her body. And Doc knew she had reason to be stressed. He knew about Trrk. As long as her reactions were within norms for her situation, she'd be okay.

Vinz came in from the plaza. Adel met him in the hall outside Lee's door. She kept her back to Lee and spoke too quietly to be heard. The set of her shoulders, her gestures, her glances at Lee all spoke of some plea of concern. Lee did her best to look at ease, patiently waiting out the scans.

Adel turned to face Lee through the windows and raised her voice. "She knows the fugitive Willemsen who ran away from his work detail with us. Can it be coincidence that she disappeared at the same time? What can she have gotten herself mixed up in?"

"About Willemsen. You said earlier that he ran?" Vinz said.

"It was after you left on vacation. He failed to report the morning after he drove me out to Seven Wells to meet with Kieron Dougherty."

"Now why would he do that? He was close to finishing his restitution."

"I don't know, but Lee was at Seven Wells that day. And two weeks later when I was spreading the word to outlying steads to watch for him, she was at Seth Reilly's place, up north of Wide Ford."

"The edge of beyond," Vinz said. "And then she and Reilly disappeared?"

"We found the body of the old man who went with her; he was buried in a makeshift grave. And when she finally turns up, it's way over here near Under Rim. She's got me very concerned."

If she didn't know better, Lee thought she might almost buy into the picture of concern Adel was painting. She started to get up, but Vinz was watching and held up a hand, shaking his head. "I'll keep that in mind," he said to Adel. "What time do you leave for Portside?"

"Half past one," Adel said. "But I really don't feel right leaving Lee like this. Whatever happened to her, she needs friends around her."

"That's kind of you. It can't be easy for you, having her accuse you of wishing her harm. But you do seem to upset her."

"Still, I don't want to abandon her."

"She has family here," Vinz said. "Don't worry."

"Well, if you say so."

"Now go get yourself a cup of tea. I'll stay and watch her."

"Yes, sir." Adel took a last long look at Lee, then turned away.

Lee lay back, uncomfortably aware of Vinz's eyes on her. She wanted to speak up for herself but arguing now would only sound defensive. Better to just prove herself.

Chapter 33

Lee

Lee shifted restlessly. An hour since Doc had left her to the scans. Boredom. Was that part of the diagnostics? Lie on the bed and wait. Guaranteed to make a person fidget. He might have provided something to read at least.

Lee found Vinz was less intrusive about his observations than Adel had been. But Adel wanted to upset her. Vinz just pulled a chair into the hall across from her door and focused his attention on a tablet. The results of his natural history studies at Tobin, maybe. But even his quiet presence made her uneasy.

The door from the lobby slid open. Good. Doc was

back to rescue her.

But it wasn't Doc. It was Joe Reilly. Vinz got to his feet.

"Morning, Joe."

"Ro. Doc said you were here. What happened at Tobin?" Joe asked.

"Lee showed up."

"Is she okay?"

"Not really. But I finally got her pinned down for a full evaluation." Vinz nodded in Lee's direction.

Lee gave Joe a thumbs up to reassure him. He looked from her back to Vinz.

"Getting her cleared to go back to the Rangers?"

Vinz shook his head. "We'll see what Doc says. She showed up at Tobin looking for me, wanting me to set up a meeting with PAO Emmerling. But she wouldn't say why. And apparently she and my assistant had a run-in."

"That doesn't sound like Lee."

"No. But you've met Adel. I wouldn't say it's her style either."

"Can I talk with Lee?" Joe asked.

"She's in the middle of some scans."

Lee shook her head. Not Adel's style? Vinz didn't know her very well then. But she'd always managed to convince people she was the victim, not the aggressor. Lee wished Doc had darkened the windows and muffled the sound. Being unable to speak up for herself wasn't helping her maintain her composure. Then Adel walked in from the back door. The last thing Lee needed.

"Marshal, I didn't expect you here," Adel said. "It's always good to see you."

"Adel."

"Is your son back? Was he with Lee?" She turned to face Lee through the window. "It's hard for me to see her like this, so different from the girl I knew at the academy."

"In what way?" Vinz asked.

"She's being so secretive, so distrusting even of Doc. Her wild story of needing to see the PAO without any explanation. Her paranoia about me. I guess that hurts the most. How can she think I would hurt her?"

Maybe because you cornered me at Tobin, Lee thought. She felt like she was watching a broadcast rather than seeing something played out on the other side of the windows.

"Then it's good she's here," Joe said.

"Once Doc finishes his evaluation, maybe we can get the full story from her," Vinz said.

"I hope so," Adel said. "But can we believe her?" She laid her hand on the window and shook her head.

Lee rolled her eyes. What a show.

"Don't worry about her," Joe said. "She's in the best of hands."

"I hated to commit her," Vinz said, "but it seemed the only way."

"You'll be staying in Under Rim?" Joe asked.

"I had planned to be here through Settlement Day anyway," Vinz answered. "But we'll see what Doc says about moving her to Portside."

Adel turned to Vinz, twisting her braid between her fingers. "Sir, please, let me stay, at least until we know what the doctor finds. And I could take her to Portside if that's what he recommends."

Vinz laid a hand on her shoulder. "Okay."

"Thank you. It means a lot."

"Are you already staying at the guest house?"

"Yes, sir."

"Go take your name off the transport list. You can wait here."

"I'll watch over her."

Adel left and came back. Vinz left. Doc came back, darkened the windows, and left Lee alone with the lights dimmed and a quiet, bland voice asking her seemingly mundane questions requiring yes or no answers, allowing no clarification. Before she was done with this part of Doc's evaluation, she almost wished for her fishbowl. At least then she had the view of her watchers to distract her. On the other hand, now she could get up and move around.

Was the glass one-way? Was Doc sitting outside watching her? Was Adel watching?

The computer voice repeated a question. She hadn't answered within the allotted seconds. Only enough time to react, not to think. And no time to let your mind wander. Exhausting. How many questions could they come up with to decide if she was within the behavioral norms?

"Are you happy?" the voice asked.

Lee hesitated. The countdown began beeping. "No," she said. Of course she wasn't happy being locked in this room answering silly questions.

"Are you sad?"

"I'm frustrated."

"Please respond yes or no only. Are you sad?"

"No." Angry, scared. More scared, the longer this took. "Well, yes, I'm sad." Sad that people didn't trust her; that they paid attention to Adel's hints and suggestions; that she couldn't simply deliver a message and get on with her life.

"Only your initial response will count. That is the final question. Please wait for further instructions."

And wait. And wait. And wait a while longer. Not very restful, being isolated and probably observed. If Adel or Vinz stood guard, she couldn't tell with the windows to the hallway darkened and the sound dampeners on. Perfect for an invalid; frustrating when she was bored. Anything to take her mind off the thoughts piling up in her head. Maybe that was the purpose.

Seth would be practicing batayr somehow even in the limited space. She envied him that, but she'd never been able to master the meditative side of the art. She needed to work on that.

What were he and Trrk doing now? Catching up on rest? Fretting over how she was progressing on their goal?

What argument would convince Vinz to use his personal connection with Emmerling to arrange a meeting? Trrk? Seeing the Kelok should override Vinz's uncertainty about Lee's credibility. And Trrk's presence would sell the PAO on the reality of the invitation to meet with Prime. Like she hadn't gone through all this in her head a zillion times already.

She stood in front of the door, the largest clear

space in the room, and took the opening stance of the batayr form. And discovered she couldn't remember more than about three moves. She really was falling apart. No wonder people worried about her.

Just momentary. Just the stress. Get that diplomatic pouch and the message with it delivered so she could relax, and she'd be fine.

Someone tapped at the door, and it opened. Doc came in. "There," he said. "Enough of that." He cleared the windows.

Back to the fishbowl, Lee thought. Better than sensory deprivation. "What next?" she asked, trying to sound calm and accepting. Not succeeding, not to her own ears at least.

"You can relax. Get some sleep if you can."

"When can I leave?"

"Don't get in a rush. I have to evaluate the results thoroughly. And you know you've been under a lot of stress, and you're physically exhausted."

"Not exhausted."

"My point is I am not releasing you to Vinz until I'm satisfied."

"So I stay here?"

"You stay here. For a while."

Doc left the lights dim but the windows clear. Lee's stomach suggested it was time for food. She drank some water. Lay down. Stared at the ceiling. Wondered what Seth was doing, and Trrk with his injured tail. And Eta'ak waiting in the Village of Canes for any word of them. Poor Eta'ak.

So many lies and secrets. Did that make Adel right,

in a way? That Lee couldn't be trusted? Lee wondered if she was seeing things clearly or if the stretch of days under Kelok influence had skewed her perceptions. Was it right to keep secrets from Joe or Vinz? People she wanted help from. She paced.

Boots on the hallway floor. Deliberate. Too heavy for Adel. Then lighter scuffs like the shoes Doc wore.

Vinz's voice. "Well, Doc, what do you think?"

"It's too soon to give you a conclusive answer."

"I'm not asking for a definitive diagnosis. But time is short with the survey work about to begin. Am I going to be tied up dealing with this?"

"You've let her status drag on this long."

"Obviously I made a mistake."

"Well, if you're asking if you can reinstate her right now, I would say no." Silence. Then Doc said, "Come to my office, and we'll talk."

Lee felt like she'd been punched in the gut. Not that she wanted to go back to the Rangers. She wanted to deliver the message to the PAO, pass off the Kelok contact to experts, and go back to work at Seven Wells. Or to Seth's stead and raise horses and maybe even kids someday. No, it was just hearing Doc say it, hearing that he doubted her. Because if he did, if he would admit it without even seeing all the data ... "Yes, I'm stressed," she said to the monitoring equipment, or to the air. "I'm frustrated. I need to finish what I started, not be shut up here. Just let me go do what I need to do." She sank down on the bed. "Just let me go."

She heard the lobby door open again. Doc coming back? But it was Joe Reilly who came into her room and brought up the lights. "Are you bouncing off walls yet?" he asked.

Lee nodded, aware the room was monitored. "How are things at the house?"

"Fine. Doc suggested I bring you some lunch and see for myself that you are surviving."

"Thanks. I'm afraid he's not going to let me out of here anytime soon."

Joe set the box of food down. "Tam wants to know when you're coming back to work for him."

Lee recognized the pungent aroma of the special curry from Rajir's Cafe. "He always asks." She had waited tables there when she'd been undercover, investigating Jerdix. She had met Seth there. "I may have to," she said.

"You have a job," Joe said. "I talked to Kieron Dougherty. He'll be here tomorrow evening to take you back to Seven Wells."

"The boss is coming? You know I can't do that yet. There's ..." She stopped herself. Doc might know about Trrk, but she didn't need to get it on the record. "I have something I need to finish."

"You could let us take care of it. Looks to me like you deserve a break."

If Joe didn't trust her, she had no credibility left. No way she could deliver the message and convince the PAO it was legitimate. "Thanks for the food," she said. "But I'm not hungry."

Chapter 34

Lee

Adel intruded on Lee's depression. Not that Lee cared when the only ones who trusted her were clear up at Fallen Pine.

Adel set down a water bottle. "Doc thought you might want this." She roamed the room, looking at the dark, silent monitors, pretty much anything except Lee. "Where is Seth anyway? I thought he'd be here at your side."

"Busy," Lee said.

"Not as committed to you as you'd like?" Adel leaned on the *committed*.

"Leave him out of it."

"It?"

"Whatever this is between you and me. In fact, leave me out of it too. Go do your job."

"My job. Is that what you want?"

"I wouldn't touch it." Go back to the Rangers? Never.

"You like this life, riding around on a horse in the middle of wilderness? You can have it. I can see to that."

"Is that a promise?" Letting Adel rattle her wasn't going to help anything.

"Might be. If that's what you want." Adel went out and shut the door behind her, leaving Lee wondering what that had been about.

She heard the outer door close and waited to be sure Adel was gone. Then she peeked out. No alarm sounded. Were the monitors in her room off? The hospital wing was empty. Lee went out and looked into the lobby. Empty too. But she heard voices in Doc's office. Doc and Joe. Deciding her fate, no doubt. She went back and closed herself in the room.

A minute later Doc came from the lobby. Maybe there had been an alarm after all.

"When can I get out of here?" she asked. "I do have something I need to do." As he knew.

"You may have to leave that to Seth to handle."

Joe had been talking to him. "Come on, Doc," she said.

"I know you. You will put off taking care of yourself until you think everything else is settled. Not this time."

"I promise you, I will get all rested up, as soon as —" As soon as what, she wondered. As she delivered the message to the PAO? Orchestrated the meeting between the PAO and Prime? Would she be able to leave the negotiations after that to others? Or was she up to her neck in human-Kelok relations for the rest of her life?

She didn't know what Doc read in her face, but he shook his head. "See what I mean?" he said.

"It's important."

"I understand that. But you are not the only one who can handle things."

Wanna bet? Lee thought. If he knew the whole story. But they had promised to keep the villages secret until the PAO was briefed. Too many people already knew about Trrk. And Eta'ak had entrusted the message to her to deliver; to a female as was proper in Kelok culture. "I promised," she said. "Let me keep my promise if you want to relieve my stress."

He lightened the windows. "What exactly is that promise?"

"It includes keeping a secret. Just trust me."

"I have to trust what the diagnostics tell me, which is that you are exhausted and stressed to the point of compromising your judgment."

"Fine, after I talk to the PAO I'll take a vacation or something."

"Vinz says you've proven to him these last three years that you don't take your well-being seriously, and he feels responsible for you. When I can lift your suspension and let you go back to the Rangers, he'll give you the choice to do so or to resign. Until then, he wants you under medical care, preferably in Portside or even off world."

"Ah, Doc. It's a little stress. Understandable, don't you think?"

"I told him I don't have cause to lock you up. But I would like you to rest here tonight where you won't be disturbed by anyone, well-meaning family included. In the morning I'll have to release you to his custody." He took her by the shoulders. "It'll be okay. The good news is that PAO Emmerling will be here late tomorrow evening."

"I know, I know."

"Let young Seth and his friend take care of things. You rest. I mean that."

"Am I going to be under guard all night?"

"I did tell Vinz that one or both of them could sleep here." He pointed her toward the bed. "You have full access to the library files. Relax. Doctor's orders."

He went out, closing the door behind him. Adel must have come back. Lee heard him in the hallway, talking with her, her saccharine voice expressing concern. "Vinz said I could stay here tonight and watch over her," Adel told him. "He's going back to that camp where he's been staying."

"Make yourself at home," Doc replied. "Just do not disturb my patient."

"Of course," Adel said.

"For now, I'll be at the inn if you need me."

Lee listened as Doc's footsteps retreated and the lobby door closed. Her room door opened and Adel stood in the opening. "I'll make sure you aren't bothered," she said. "You need your rest."

"Thanks so much," Lee replied. "Shut the door on

your way out."

Adel smiled. "Poor Lee. Carico hasn't treated you well, has it?"

"Let's see how well it treats you by the time you finish the survey work."

"I hope it's going to be very good to me." Adel stepped back into the hall and closed the door.

What did she mean by that? She sounded so smug. Lee wondered again what she was up to. More than just a successful assignment that could garner her a promotion.

Lee had her own assignment, and Emmerling would be in Under Rim the next day. She just had to convince Vinz to let her stay through Settlement Day.

Scorch it. The pouch she was charged with delivering was sitting in the feed bin at Tobin Canyon. She had to retrieve it. Sneak out, maybe borrow Adel's skimmer. She could get in and out of the corral area unnoticed if she was careful, even with Vinz at the camp. And, in the morning, she'd be right back here with no one the wiser and could have Doc get a message to Seth. Chances were good that he would go to check on Trrk anyway. She might not get the rest Doc prescribed, but she felt less stressed already. No problem, once she got past Adel. She'd wait until the middle of the night. Until then a little sleep wouldn't hurt.

Lee heard Doc come through and peek into her room around eleven before going out the back door, presumably to his cottage at the edge of the forest behind the parking area. She waited until after midnight, growing more impatient by the minute but determined to let the village and Adel settle in for the night. Finally, she slipped out into the hallway and cat-footed her way into the lobby, then out through the clinic side to avoid passing the room where Adel was sleeping, the one where they had brought Trrk.

The parking area was dark. She stayed tight against the building to avoid the motion detectors designed to pick up approaching vehicles or people. Adel's skimmer was parked behind the community hall. Vinz's skybike was gone.

Holding her breath, she laid her thumb on the scan pad of the skimmer door. If Vinz had deactivated her identification when he placed her on medical suspension ... But the door opened to her thumb and, when she started the motor, it hummed to life. Free and clear. She eased the skimmer into motion.

The passenger door flew open, and Adel jumped in. "Not without me, you don't," she said.

Lee let the skimmer slow. So much for her grand exit.

"Don't stop now," Adel said. "This is the best move you've made yet."

Chapter 35

Seth

With Doc gone back to town, Whip was cocky again, blustering about hammering out the synthesizer in no time. Seth escorted him to the cellar to see what kind of spare parts might be there. In a back corner they found two small comm units that Whip pounced on. "Just what we need," he crowed. "Old but they look intact. Meant for skimmers. Find a way to feed the information from that contraption into one of these and we're there."

Seth decided the synthesizer idea wasn't that complicated if he ignored all the jargon. The hearing facilitation device picked up Trrk's vocalizations, translated them to Sol Standard, and generated "speech" in the form of faint vibrations that the wearer "heard" through their skin rather than their ears. How all that was done might as well be magic for all Trrk explained about it. But it did work. All the synthesizer needed to do, in theory, was to pick up the device's output and amplify that "speech" so it could be heard instead of felt.

But either it was magic, or the wearer's skin and brain did some translating of their own to make it understandable, because the first few attempts produced nothing that sounded to Seth like speech. Especially since with his own device he heard the translation and Trrk's vocalization and the garble all at the same time. He had to go outside to get away from it.

Lee was in Under Rim. She needed to know about Whip's claim. And he was stuck here with an injured alien and an escapee who needed to stay hidden for now. All he could do was trust his pa to handle things in town.

He found a place under the palm-pines at the edge of the meadow and began the batayr form. He had hardly practiced it since they had left the Kelok villages. Time to get back to some kind of routine. When he couldn't do anything else, he could let the flow and focus ground him. And not give in to the temptation to ride into town to be with Lee.

He repeated the form once and then again as the day grew warmer. The stretching and movement felt deeply good. Satisfied, he returned to the cabin and stuck his head in the door. "Progress?" he asked.

"Almost got it," Whip said.

"The solution lies in the correct arrangement of the hearing facilitator," Trrk said. "In the spacing of the beads and the pattern of the webbing."

"But that's just rawhide, isn't it?" Seth asked.

"It is infested with mycelium of a fungus we grow. Critical to the function of the device."

"Now you tell me," Seth said, running a finger between his neck and the choker.

"What's he saying?" Whip asked.

"It's about spacing and pattern," Seth replied. Whip didn't need the details.

"I had that figured out from what he's been doing."

"Good," Seth said. "Anything I can help with?"

"No," Trrk said and shook his head. "We are close."

"I'll be right out front then." Seth closed the door and stretched out on the bench that doubled as a bunk on the porch. Mycelium, huh? How much did they really know about the Keloks? Easy to think of them as primitives from what little he and Lee had seen of them living as they did in rock shelters, relying on hunting and gathering to survive. Whose real habitat, Trrk and Eta'ak had explained, was aboard starships, calling no planet home. Who apparently incorporated fungi into their technology.

And who were highly social beings, which might explain why working on the synthesizer with Whip energized Trrk. Seth thought he would give them a little longer before insisting Trrk rest. He was supposed to be recuperating.

And once they finished the synthesizer, what did he

do with Whip? He'd like to lock him up, but how? Too bad they didn't have a set of Trrk's rawhide shackles, the ones he and Lee had worn when they had been held captive. Someday he'd get a chance to have Trrk show him the trick to the closure on those.

A shrill neigh brought him half off the bunk. He had fallen asleep. Now what had the horse stirred up? He got to his feet.

He couldn't see either Trrk or Whip inside. What the ... He opened the door.

Trrk stretched on his belly on the couch, his injured tail draped over the end. Asleep. Well, that was good. He needed it. But where was Whip?

Trrk blinked and raised his head. "Brother? What is it?"

"Where's Whip?"

"We got the synthesizer to work adequately. Then he went up to the loft. I do not believe he truly trusts that I will not eat him." Trrk's crest flared in what Seth knew to be laughter. "He did prove a useful assistant."

"I'm glad you got the thing working," Seth said. "I'll check on Whip. You take it easy."

"Yes. I should allow my ... my injury to heal."

"I'm sorry about your tail," Seth said. "Doc says there was no way to save it."

"I trust he was correct."

"It'll heal though, almost good as new."

"Almost."

But Seth sensed that wasn't good enough somehow. "I'll fix lunch in a while," he said, unable to think of anything reassuring.

"That would be good."

Seth climbed up to the loft. "Hey, Whip, you getting hungry?"

But the loft was empty. No Whip; no gear; nothing to show the man had ever been there.

Oh, Void! There went their only evidence of Adel's plot. Seth nearly broke his neck getting down from the loft. "He took off," he told Trrk. "He's gone."

Trrk got to his feet. "We will hunt him."

"I will," Seth replied. "He can't have gotten far. You stay here."

"I am responsible. I failed to guard him. Was that not your name for me? Guard?"

"The only thing you are responsible for right now is getting better." Seth thought for a moment. "He left in a hurry. He may hope he can swing back and get supplies while we hunt for him."

"You believe he might do so?"

"He needs food if he's going to keep hiding out. You watch over things here. I'll go after him."

"Go with care," Trrk said reluctantly. "A hunted animal will defend itself."

"That's why I'm worried about him coming back here."

Seth grabbed his saddlebags, shoved biscuits and trail bars in on top of the usual survival gear, and headed for the back door before Trrk could say more.

The tack shed door stood wide open. Whip's saddle was missing as Seth had expected. Along with Henry, the horse.

The pasture gate was also open, but the most recent

tracks went in, not out. Whip had left through the pasture. There was a back gate out of the field on a trail that led toward the rim that loomed a thousand feet high on the northern skyline. On top the country was unsettled and virtually unexplored. That was where Seth and Lee had sent Whip to hide when they had diverted him away from the Kelok villages.

Seth slung a nosebag with some grain over his shoulder with the saddlebags, grabbed a halter off a hook — no handy bridle or spare saddle in sight — and ran for the other pasture and his pa's horses. Once he spotted the animals, he forced himself to walk, to study them. He recognized a little bay, Ratchet, an older gelding he knew he could ride bareback. He whistled, started across the meadow at a walk, and hoped. He whistled again and repeated it as he went. "Come on, horses," he said under his breath. "Come to me."

Chapter 36

Seth

Seth caught the little bay gelding. "I'm going to regret this," he muttered as he swung up on Ratchet's bare back and headed for the trail Whip had taken. His own fault the man had been able to take off. Too trusting. And Trrk should be resting, not watching over a slimy frog-eel like Whip. He ought to let Whip go, report him to the authorities, and let him take his chances.

But he pushed Ratchet into a lope. He hated to admit it, but they needed Whip. If he was telling the truth, he could help stop a plot to sabotage the review of the planet's settlement plan.

And he knew about Trrk.

The tracks of Whip's horse stayed on the faint trail. Looked like he was going for speed rather than evasion. Did he really think he could get away? Or was he gaining time to set up an ambush? Seth slowed his pursuit and thought about the terrain. The best sites for that would be as the trail twisted its way up between the rocks of the rim, not down in the open forest. Why couldn't the fool just stay put?

The day was hot. Beneath him, Ratchet's back turned sweaty. The horse he followed was trotting now as the slope steepened. The rim loomed above. Betting Whip wouldn't lie in wait until he reached the narrow upper trail, if at all, Seth pushed his horse faster. Once Whip reached the top, he could go anywhere, and Seth didn't know that country at all.

Ratchet's ears pricked forward, and his head came up. Seth slowed the horse and left the trail to swing around a thicket of young trees, letting the animal's attention guide him. Something, probably Whip's horse, was up ahead near an opening in the trees just below where Seth knew the trail started switching back and forth across the slope. He hadn't been there in three years, not since Jerdix had died. But he couldn't let those memories distract him. Where was Whip?

He slid to the ground and led the bay into the thicket where he tied the horse. "Be patient." He patted the horse's neck and slipped around the thicket. From the edge of the trees, he studied the ground up ahead where Ratchet had been focused.

Movement. The flip of a horse's tail. Carico's equivalent of insects might not like human or horse blood but were still attracted by moisture. Like a sweaty horse. The animal stamped a foot. There, in another thicket.

Seth worked around on the side away from the trail. Definitely Whip's horse, tied to a tree. But no Whip. Seth crept through the trees to the trail.

Boot tracks going up, plain to see. Not the way Seth would go about setting up an ambush. Too obvious.

Staying off to the side, Seth climbed up the slope. With a horse, the trail was the best way up here. On foot, he could scramble through the rocks, downed timber, and towering old trees. Above the treetops he could see the crag Jerdix had fallen from more than three years before.

He heard a clatter and crash of falling rocks and someone cursing. He moved back toward the trail, where Whip was trying to clear a jumble of stones to make a path around a fallen tree blocking the way.

"Need help?" he asked.

"Tarbh's clackers." Whip dropped the pot-sized rock he held. It narrowly missed his foot. "What are you doing here?"

"What do you think?" Seth asked. "That we'd just let you go?"

"Man can hope, can't he?"

"I thought you wanted protection?"

"I got thinking." Whip sat down on the tree trunk. "You were right back when you told me to stay up top until the snow flies. I don't figure you or your marshal daddy can protect me. Not from that bitch lizard."

"I guess you're going to find out. Let's go." Seth

waved a hand down the trail toward the horses.

"Make me."

Seth ran his fingers through his hair. "You haven't healed up from your last fight. You really want another?"

"She didn't fight fair."

"Fair? That's priceless coming from you." He shook his head. He didn't want to get physical. "Fine. Stay here. Go camp out up top." He started down the trail. "I'll just take your horse back with me."

Footfalls behind him. Seth spun and stepped toward Whip, ready to fight if he had to. "Besides," he said. "What are you going to do for supplies?"

Whip deflated. "You just can't give a guy a break."

"We did, back the other side of the Whitewater a few days ago. And again last night when Pa didn't haul you off and lock you up. More than you deserve."

"What does that mean?"

"Lee collected from you already for trying to assault her. But you turned me over to Jerdix."

"And when you took him down, I lost a good job and a future doing something besides chasing tarbh for a living."

"You see that high point on the rim up there?" Seth pointed at the crag.

"What about it?"

"Your old boss, who was going to give you that good future, he died at the bottom of that cliff."

"That was here?"

"You remember that little black rod Jerdix carried?"

"Yeah, some kind of recorder or something."

"A pain-pleasure rod." Seth's skin crawled at the

thought. "Illegal anywhere in the Coalition, not that that probably matters to you. By the end he was addicted to the pleasure setting. He dove off that cliff trying to catch his precious rod when it fell. No one but himself to blame."

Whip looked at the two-hundred foot cliff. "That's what that was?"

"Be glad you never learned firsthand."

"The Ranger." Whip turned away from the rim. "I think she has one. At least I saw something like it in her office one time."

Seth's throat tightened. Adel with a rod? Adel in town with Lee. "I'd be afraid of her, too, if I was you. Now come on. You're safer with us than on your own. Let's go."

Chapter 37

Seth

Something woke Seth. He lay still and listened. Nothing. The front room at Fallen Pine was dark. He was surprised he had actually slept after learning Adel had a rod. Overhead, he heard the squeak of the bunk in the loft. So Whip was where he belonged, where Seth had confined him when they got back to the cabin.

Outside, the meadow was silver. Lander was up and a little less than half. The sky showed the faintest hint of the coming dawn. Settlement Day.

His mind jumped. Adel had a rod like the one Jerdix had used on him three years ago. Seth shuddered and hoped his pa had understood the blip he had sent —

isolate Lee. He hadn't wanted to say too much, but if they kept Lee away from everyone, Adel couldn't hurt her.

The lights of a skimmer came into view. Seth pulled on his clothes and went out on the porch. A vehicle with marshal's markings came to a stop. Seth tried to swallow down the lump in his throat. At this hour something had to be wrong.

Joe got out and stopped at the bottom of the steps. "They're gone," he said. "Lee and Verlane are gone."

Seth sank down on the top step. "When? How?"

"Adel stayed in one of the hospital rooms last night. When Doc checked in on Lee about an hour ago both of them were gone. And the Ranger skimmer."

"You didn't get my message."

"I did. And passed it to Doc. She was isolated in her room."

"But not locked in."

"No." Joe laid a hand on his shoulder. "Look, Adel probably just went back to Portside early."

Seth stood up. "Whip says she has a rod."

"She what?"

"Adel has a rod. And I don't believe she went back to Portside alone."

"Okay. If — admittedly a big if — if Lee did leave by herself, why and where would she have gone?"

"I don't know." Seth left the steps and paced across the ground. "Unless she saw an opportunity to get to the PAO."

"Emmerling will be in Under Rim tonight," Joe said. "Lee knows that."

"When Vinz brought her to the hospital, did she have a satchel made of rawhide about so big?" Seth measured out a hand-span wide and half again that long.

"Not that I know of."

"Check with Doc. If she didn't, she must have left it at Tobin Canyon. And she'll need it for her meeting with the PAO."

"So you think she headed to Tobin to get it?"

"Maybe got Adel to take her somehow." Not likely but possible.

"Vinz didn't answer when Doc called Tobin."

Seth thought about the layout. "He might not have heard the comm, either asleep or already out after his fish."

"We'll start at Tobin then."

"Let me talk to Trrk. I'll have to leave him here with Whip. And Whip took off for the rim yesterday. I had to go run him down."

"Fool."

"That's when he told me about the rod. I guess I can't blame him for being scared of Adel." Seth knew he was. He was terrified for Lee's sake.

"Is Trrk well enough to leave with him?"

"More or less. You have a set of restraints with you?"

"I do."

"Would you get Whip out of the loft and shackle him? I'll go fill Trrk in." Seth didn't wait for an answer. He went inside to wake Trrk.

"The envoy is at risk?" Trrk was off the bed instantly. "We must find her." Seth didn't miss the wobble in his step.

"I will do that," Seth said. "My father will help. And there are others as well. I need you to stay here and guard our prisoner."

Trrk's crest drooped, and he lowered his head. "I have failed at that once."

"I trust you. You'll keep him safe," Seth said. "We need him. The things he knows can change the whole future of this planet."

"I am ... I am not what I was." Trrk tucked his tail behind him.

The tail. Seth looked him in the eye. "You got a tailless one initiated into your clan."

"Somehow." Trrk's crest flared a little, a tiny chuckle.

"Even injured, you are more than a match for Whip."

"I thank you for that confidence."

"Just the truth." Seth bobbed his head. "Gotta go."

"Find her."

In the front room Whip was whining about the shackles. "Lost your privileges when you took off," Seth told him. "Go back to sleep."

"You can't leave me here with that beaky coblynau."

Seth suppressed a laugh at the reference to a mythical haunter of mines. "Can. Will. Behave and you'll be fine."

"But ..." Whip dropped his hands and quit pulling at the restraints. "Just, well, be careful of that woman. Okay?"

"Okay."

Shaking his head in surprise at Whip's concern, Seth filled a water bottle and stuffed some food into his saddlebags. Just in case. He hoped he'd be back in a few hours but couldn't know for sure. Where had Lee gotten to?

How far to Tobin from Fallen Pine? He ran the figures in his head: Fallen Pine to home to Under Rim to Tobin. About an hour normally. Less than that in the marshal's skimmer. By how much?

For a long time they didn't talk. Seth got the feeling his pa was waiting for him to fill in some blanks in the story. Or was that his guilt over secrets nagging at him? Finally he said, "Lee probably left her gear in the tack shed by the corrals. She wouldn't have told Vinz about the satchel."

"What's in this satchel?" Joe asked.

Reasonable question. How to answer? "Proof," Seth said. "Trrk didn't plan to come with us until he got hurt. He gave us some things to show the PAO to convince her of what he is."

"With him here, is it necessary?"

"It's important to him. Cultural."

"You and Lee really fell into a situation, didn't you?"

"Never know what you'll find back of beyond," Seth said.

"A castaway alien of an unknown species. That tops anything I could dream up."

Seth forced a laugh. "From the stories you told when we were kids, I find that hard to believe." He hoped he would get to see Joe's face when he learned the full story.

"I have to wonder what your Trrk is like when he's healthy. Not a pacifist, I would guess."

Seth chose his words carefully. "From what he has

told me, his people channel their aggression into ritual. They fight for status, to settle disputes, but within strict guidelines. He says you lose if you seriously injure an opponent. It shows you have not learned proper control."

"Pretty high-tech gadget, that translator. I'm guessing back of beyond is not his usual habitat. I'm amazed he was able to survive off the land."

"So is he."

It was light enough to see the country around them. Joe approached Tobin Canyon Camp from the north. "We'll start with Vinz," he said. "See if he's seen either of them."

"No skimmer," Seth said.

"But looks like Ro is just coming in from somewhere."

Vinz's skybike was setting down in front of the cabin. Vinz got off and waited for them. "What's up?" he asked as they got out.

"It's Lee and your assistant," Joe said. "Both left Doc's sometime during the night."

"They did?"

"Then you haven't seen them. Seth thought Lee might have come looking for something in her gear."

"I've been down on the flats searching for a specimen in the pools. Interesting little thing that only comes out at night. You ought to —"

"Ro," Joe said. "Lee?"

"She said she left her stuff in the tack shed. She didn't seem very worried about it when we went to town. What makes you think they're together?"

"You think Adel would have left on her own? Wasn't

she supposed to be guarding your prisoner?"

"Now that's harsh, Joe. You know I only committed Lee because she has been avoiding closing out her medical suspension."

"Well, she's gone and the one you left with her is gone too, along with the Ranger skimmer."

"Verlane was very concerned about Lee. If Lee insisted on leaving, maybe Adel went with her."

"I've heard some pretty strong allegations against your assistant the last couple of days," Joe said.

Vinz nodded. "It's apparent that the two of them don't get along."

"Lee's not my source."

Vinz tensed. "Who then?"

"I won't say more until I check some things out."

"Well, let's just see if we can find them. There's a tracker on the bike. It should pick up the one on the skimmer."

"Fine. While we do that, Seth, go on down to the tack room and see if Lee's gear is still there."

Seth hurried across the yard. Vinz didn't seem very concerned, not like Dougherty would be. But Joe would get him on track.

He stopped in the slot where the trail cut through the rimrock and studied the corrals spread out below him. No sign of a skimmer. He could see Clown's white splotches out in the meadow. She wasn't there. Well, he hadn't expected her to be. But she might have come and gone.

He trotted down the steep, rocky trail as quickly as he could. The tack room door was secure. He went inside. Her saddle was on a rack with the saddle blanket draped over it and the bridle hanging on the hook. The saddlebags hung over the rack next to it.

He unbuckled the bags. No sign of the diplomatic pouch. But why would she have left the saddlebags if she'd come back? She kept too many basics in them from comb to clean socks. Did she hide the pouch when she first got there to keep it safe until she talked to Vinz? He looked around. The room was nearly empty. A couple spare ropes and saddle blankets, tools and supplies to repair the fences, and a metal bin used for storing horse feed.

He lifted the lid. It was almost full. No pouch. He dug his hands into the grain. There, in one corner. He lifted out the rawhide satchel, shook it free of grain, and started to slide it into Lee's saddlebags. When he saw a length of fabric Lee carried as everything from extra blanket to towel to dress, he changed his mind. He twisted the cloth into a sack around the satchel, tucked it under his arm, and left the saddlebags propped up on the lid of the feed bin. If she did show up, her gear would be waiting for her, and she might, maybe, piece the missing wrap together with him and the satchel. It was her dressiest, one he had given her and that she would want to wear to meet with the PAO.

"Where are you?" he asked. The morning chorus of frog-eels didn't give him a good answer.

Chapter 38

Eta'ak

All through the day Eta'ak squatted before the viewscreen, an unwelcome presence in the Village of Lichens. People went silent as they neared her or chose a path wide around her. She did her best not to look, not to see that they averted their eyes. It was easy to tell herself that what was on the screen was of greater importance, but hard to believe it.

She waited until the depths of night to go to the galley for food and visit the bathing area. The village was silent then, empty except for two of Second's hunters. Standing watch over her or the broadcasts or both. They ignored her. She curled against the pillar of stone next to the monitoring station and slept restlessly.

All through the second day she sat with her back to the cavern, to the people, still surrounded by an invisible barrier. She spun thread from her drop spindle, a soothing repetition of movement requiring even tension. As much a distraction from her surroundings as the scanning of broadcasts was.

Still no mention of Trrk or the envoys. The Ranger female who had been so frequently seen reporting on the search for the two humans also made no appearance. Which suggested what? Only that attention had turned to the First-Comers' celebration day on the morrow? Or that there was a silencing of information that officials wanted kept secret?

The cavern reeked of fear and anger. And all day, preparations went on around her. Villagers cleared space, packing away looms and nets and baskets and all the paraphernalia of daily living, so that those from the other villages could come together. This had been their first refuge on this world and now, possibly, their last.

Village of Lichens occupied the largest cavern of any of the villages. There they had first established themselves before they had gained skills and courage enough to spread out. The last pinnace they had used to shuttle to the surface remained intact, hidden at the back behind woven-mat walls, still functional perhaps, if they had fuel for it. Its communications center served the village.

In it were stores the hunters had left hidden away since they had grounded. Now they brought out both handheld and tripod-mounted energy weapons to place around the front of the cavern. Eta'ak had last seen those deployed during a trade dispute some time before they had come to this world. Now they would defend against the First-Comers. If it came to that. Eta'ak cast a prayer to the Infinite One — something she had not done in years — that her plan for peaceful negotiations might still succeed.

It was a tiny thing, a quick blip amongst the day's announcements confirming the pending arrival of a ship carrying the satellite array to be deployed to re-survey the planet. Eta'ak froze the screen and turned.

But no one would look her way. Her voice would be unheard. She turned up the volume on the translated broadcast and replayed it in a loop.

It took only moments before Second was at her side, lowering the volume, tailing her aside to establish one of his hunters before the screen.

Eta'ak stood, eyes lowered but watching the explosion of activity. The male who replaced her scanned through the log and incoming broadcasts for the flag words but found only the arrival schedule she had spotted. Second dispatched another hunter to the village communications station to send the message that would call all the Keloks to Village of Lichens. Around the plaza, females huddled together, trying to calm the girl-children. Gunners checked their weapons as if the First-Comers were already in their sights.

"Oh, Trrk," Eta'ak whispered. "Our time runs short." Then she caught a snippet of information she had missed. Planetary Administrative Officer Emmerling would visit communities during the morrow's celebrations. Her last stop would be the district of Under Rim. Home of the envoys' clan. Is that where they had gone? To wait for the administrator? She kept her hope to herself. Nothing short of the PAO's public acceptance of the invitation could reach through Prime's protectionism now.

Nan C Ballard

Chapter 39

Lee

Lee eased the skimmer across the dark parking area while her mind raced. "Where to?" she asked. Her voice was steadier than she expected.

"Go east." Adel pointed. "Stay away from the road."

Where in the Void were they headed? There wasn't much out that way unless you went far enough to reach the Whitewater and the secret villages. No trails. That terrain would challenge a skimmer. It had been hard enough with horses and the drag. "How far?" she asked.

"Until I tell you otherwise." Adel watched her steadily.

"Okay." Lee put her attention on the vehicle. She

didn't have the near-instinctive reactions to easily handle rough terrain. In the dark. Not like someone who used a skimmer routinely. She had only driven half a dozen times a year since she'd gone to work at Seven Wells.

"You want to go to the PAO." Adel said. "To tell her what? What did you find out?"

"Nothing that concerns you." What did Adel think she knew? This couldn't be about Trrk. No way she could know about him.

"It's not about the survey? I thought ... Never mind. Just keep going."

Lee complied, trying to think how to gain the advantage. Once they were clear of town and observers, would Adel want to turn south toward Jerdix's old stead or, if her goal was Portside, to follow the main trail from Under Rim to Wide Ford? She could hope for the latter. It went through pretty empty country for a couple hundred miles. And that was her element, not Adel's.

Definitely past Jerdix's old place now. Did Adel have some connection to the dead man? Or was her staying there now simply what was available with Settlement Day coming up?

Lee kept going, most of her attention on the craft. She needed to constantly correct its path. Its lift worked better over ground than treetops. How long had they been traveling? Only twenty minutes or so, maybe ten miles at the speed she was going. She began edging their route a little south, a little toward the main trail. And west of that lay Tobin Canyon.

"Turn back east, due east," Adel said. "You want to

stay away from Vinz."

"So just where are we going?" she asked.

"Someplace quiet where we can talk."

"Just talk?"

"Without being interrupted."

Lee could think of one place, a place where she had everything she needed to escape into the hills. "Okay. There's an abandoned stead out this way," Lee said. "It hasn't been used in years."

Adel hesitated. "Someplace where Vinz won't find us?"

"No reason I know of that he'd look for me there." Why was Adel so interested in avoiding Vinz?

"Okay. Go there. It's your chance to get out from under his control."

"If you say so."

Lee drove slowly. She couldn't see the ground beneath the trees, couldn't anticipate slopes or gullies. The skimmer could compensate for a lot but needed guidance without some kind of trail to scan in on. Adel didn't comment. She didn't seem to be in a hurry.

"Shouldn't you be worrying about getting the survey going?" Lee asked. "Why waste your time on me?"

"Would you believe I took this job partly because I heard you were on this hunk of rock. It's a big job and I thought we could help each other out."

"You could have saved yourself some trouble if you'd talked to me first." Lee kept her eyes on the terrain ahead. They were getting out of the forest into the tableland. It was after midnight. Lander was coming up, joining Damele, both waning gibbous. In their light she could make out the vast rocky stretch. Better for the skimmer than the timber. She turned east. Now if she could find Lickskillet on her own in the dark.

"I was just figuring things out when you disappeared." Adel shifted in her seat. "Safely out of Vinz's reach without me doing a thing."

"Wouldn't want me to tarnish you with your boss." And now Adel had everyone Lee knew looking sideways at her, waiting for her to break down.

"You don't get it. You have more to worry about than I do."

"What? That I lose my Ranger career? I walked away from that three years ago."

"What's so important that you have to see the PAO? Who happens to be friends with Vinz."

"Like I said. Nothing to do with you. Or with Vinz or the Rangers." Except that Vinz could help her get together with Emmerling. Except he was an obstacle at this point, using her medical suspension to control her. But why would that matter to Adel? "You wanted to talk, well, talk. What's going on?"

"I watched them with you," Adel said. "Marshal Reilly, Doc — so solicitous, so supportive. But I can't trust even them; only you. You finally gave me the opening I needed when you ran."

"So we can have a private chat, right?" Because Adel trusted her? Lee didn't believe it.

"You'll understand soon. There." Adel pointed. "Is that it?"

Lee recognized the low rock building at the foot of a little rise. Ike's old place. Whipbrush and a lone water-finder tree gave away the spring. Somewhere down in the meadow along the trickle of water there should be three horses that she and Seth had left here a day ago. Could she force the skimmer down hard enough to give her a brief advantage, let her get away?

"Gently," Adel cautioned.

Was the woman psychic? Lee brought the skimmer to rest in front of the cabin where Doc had parked two nights before.

Lee reached to open her door, to burst out and run before Adel could reach her.

"Doors lock." The Ranger skimmer obeyed Adel. Lee eased back into her seat.

Adel studied her silently, then held out her hand. "Give me your boots."

"My ..."

"Come on. The boots. I don't want you running before we have a chance to talk."

Lee pulled off her boots and handed them over. What was Adel up to?

"Socks too."

Lee pulled off her socks and made a show of shoving one into a boot top while she dropped the other and pushed it under the seat with her foot, hoping Adel hadn't noticed. Evidence she had been in the skimmer in case she vanished. Did Adel really want to talk? Or to dump her here? Why not out in the middle of the tableland somewhere? Adel's motives eluded her.

"Unlock," Adel said. The doors complied. "You can get out now. Walk toward the building." Adel waited until Lee stepped out to open her own door. "Inside," she repeated. "Out of sight."

Lee thought about sprinting past the cabin and disappearing into the whipbrush along the creek. But she couldn't outrun Adel barefoot. She walked to the breezeway in the center of the cabin. Why was it always barefoot? Jerdix had left her barefoot too. In an inch of fresh hail.

Adel flashed a light around the space. "Sit down."

"Just tell me what you want."

"A talk. Without interruptions. Now sit, please. Over there." She pointed at a chair. In the one place where she could corner Lee between the wall and the old wood-fired cook stove. Next to where Trrk had been lying when Lee had gotten there with Doc. Lee picked her barefoot way across the detritus on the packed-clay floor.

Rock walls enclosed rooms on both sides of the breezeway. Overhead Lee could glimpse flecks of moonlight through the roof, a continuous layer of slender poles once covered by an insulating layer of dirt that was long gone to wind and rain. Nice place, once upon a time.

"How does anyone live like this?" Adel said, sweeping a hand around.

Lee couldn't help a chuckle at that disconnect between them. "Comfortably, once it's cleaned up." She meant that. Once it had been a pleasant home. The doors into the enclosed rooms on each side were shut now, hiding their contents. But the breezeway would have been the main living area, at least in good weather.

Adel shined the light around again, more slowly this

time. Someone had just walked away, leaving dishes on the table and wood stacked by the stove. Dust coated it all. Seth had fixed a bed for Trrk on the floor against that wall there. And Lee had stowed their packs in one of the rooms. But they hadn't touched what had been left so long ago.

"Sit," Adel repeated.

Lee pushed the chair around and straddled it, putting the straight back between her and Adel. A slender beam of moonlight caught the chair, revealing a carved 'A'. For Allred, Ike, her old partner who must have left everything after his wife died in the pandemic forty years earlier. A tea kettle sat on the cold stove, a cutting board on the table, and next to it a bowl big enough to mix bread. Ike always kept his tools neat and near at hand. *Look over me now, Uncle*. She sent the thought silently into the night.

She sat still and quiet. She didn't want to have a private talk. She wanted to retrieve the satchel from Tobin and deliver it with Prime's invitation. She should have run sooner, run faster. Barefoot? She still should have run.

Could she distract Adel somehow, get her away from the cabin for even a couple of minutes, back to the skimmer maybe? Long enough to hide. Adel didn't know she had horses nearby and the packs she and Seth had left behind. Lee could afford to wait.

Adel found another chair. She pulled it over in front of Lee and sank down on it. "Is this what it takes to have a private conversation with you?" she asked.

"You had a chance at Tobin," Lee said. "Or at Doc's."

"I said private. This has to be between you and me. I've been trying to get you safely away from Vinz ever since I ran into you at Tobin." Adel turned off the light.

Lee listened to the scratchings and scufflings in the dark corners and across the roof overhead. The residents of the ruin. "Well, there's nobody here but us and the rock rats."

"This isn't funny. There's too much at stake. Can't you let go of whatever you've got against me for five minutes and listen?"

Lee knew she should keep quiet. She wasn't a teenager now. She had a diplomatic mission to carry out. But she was in no mood to listen to Adel. "You're the one that came to Carico."

"And ever since I got here, I've been worried about you."

"Worried? You expect me to believe that?"

"You gave up everything you worked for all those years at the academy. Hiding out, playing settler. And then I learned Vinz had you under a medical suspension." Adel leaned forward in her chair. "What happened to you?"

"Nothing I want to talk to you about."

"When did we become unfriends? What did I ever do to you?"

"When were we ever friends?" Lee shifted, feeling trapped against the wall. "When did we do anything except try to out-compete each other?"

"How else was I supposed to get your attention?"

"My attention?" Lee stared at Adel, trying to piece that together with her memories.

"It's ancient history, I know." Adel stood up, stepped away, half-hidden in the darkness. "But I had the worst crush on you back then. You with legends for parents, who was so good at everything."

"Crush?" Lee was glad it was dark in the breezeway. Her expression must have been comical.

"All those years I spent trying to impress you, to get you to see me."

"I did see you," Lee said. "Trying to beat me at everything. Trying to take every boy who liked me."

"Trying to keep them from liking you."

"Why?"

"It sounds stupid now, but so you would like me."

Lee sat in the dark, trying to rethink their history. "That's not how I saw it."

"I guess not. Hey, we were teenagers. I got over it at some point but by then I guess competing with you was just what I did." She came over, stood close enough that Lee could see her face even in the dark. "But when I got here and found you in such trouble with the suspension and everything, I had to try and help somehow."

"Crush?" Lee said again, still in the past.

Adel sat down. "Will you listen to me, please? Really listen. Because now I desperately need help with something, and I can't trust anyone else."

"Help?" Were they living in different realities?

"It's about the survey and the evaluation and Carico's future. I think Vinz might be interfering somehow."

That pulled Lee away from grappling with a new view of Adel. Vinz? Then she heard the hum of a vehicle.

Seth coming to her rescue? But it sounded wrong, more like Vinz's skybike.

Adel heard too. "Go. Vinz can't find you. Do not let him find you."

Chapter 40

Lee

Adel stood up. "Hurry. Get out of sight. He'll keep you under that medical hold until he can stash you out of the way somewhere for good."

"What are you talking about?" Lee struggled to switch gears.

"No time." Adel hid in the shadows, looking out. "Hide. I'll get rid of him."

Not the time to debate. Lee didn't want to get dragged back to Doc's without getting to the satchel. And Adel had her curious. She ducked out of the breezeway, hugged the wall until she heard the skybike land on the other side of the cabin, then sprinted for the cover of the whipbrush along the little stream. From there she could see through the breezeway to the bike next to the skimmer. And Adel going out to meet him.

Vinz stepped off the bike. "Verlane. What are you doing here?"

"It's Lee, sir. Something she said. I thought I might find Seth Reilly here."

"In the middle of the night? I couldn't believe it when the alarm activated."

"Alarm, sir?" Adel was out in the moonlight now.

"I set the location alarm on the skimmer. A precaution in case Lee decided to run."

"I didn't know. I'm sorry to disturb you." Adel moved toward the skimmer, drawing him away from the cabin.

"No matter. Maybe this is for the best." Lee saw his shoulders shrug in the moonlight. He stepped closer to Adel. "The programming is installed for the survey?"

"Yes, sir." Adel sounded puzzled by the change the conversation was taking. "It'll need some calibration, but the algorithms are in place." She flipped her braid behind her back and faced him squarely.

"Very good," Vinz said. "But then such a promising career should end on a success."

End? Lee didn't like the sound of that.

Vinz continued. "Yes, you were an up-and-coming ranger. Too bad you got caught with this." He held something up.

Adel stepped back, staring at Vinz. "What's that thing?"

Lee's eyes locked on the silhouette of a black rod, a hand-span long and as big around as a finger. She swallowed down her panic at the sight.

"A pain-pleasure rod, you know." Vinz held it higher and turned it in his hand so it caught the moonlight. "Prohibited throughout the Coalition. And I just found it in your skimmer."

"By the Rings, I've never seen that thing before."

"But you have. And your playmate Willemsen will swear to it."

"Will's part of this?" Adel paused. "Or is that why he ran? To get away from you."

"He served his purpose. You both have."

Adel spread her hands. "I can be reasonable. Tell me what you want. We can ... we can just climb in the skimmer and ..."

"Where's Lee? Give her to me, and we'll talk."

"Lee? She's in Under Rim."

"No, she's not."

She backed away, away from the cabin, from Lee. "You set me up. And now you're using Lee." She stabbed at Vinz with a finger. "We trusted you. Everybody trusted you."

"Yes, and now — you two taking off together in the middle of the night. This rod. All I need to explain your demise."

Adel darted for the skimmer. Vinz lunged at her, rod extended like a fencer. She shrieked, stumbled.

Run, Lee yelled silently in her mind. The sight of the rod froze her. She couldn't make herself draw Vinz's attention.

Vinz stepped back. "Forgive me. Wrong setting. My trusty assistant. Who would imagine she was addicted?

The pleasure setting will do that. Like that fool Jerdix."

"Who?" Adel asked, circling away from him.

"Before your time. Ask your friend Lee about him, if you ever get a chance," he said. "But we've managed to pull the plan together without him."

"You and who else?" Adel asked. She backed into the skimmer. He lunged at her again.

She moaned, a deep, dreadful sound. The memory of the rod's pleasure setting tingled on Lee's nerves. She forced herself to her feet, to go help Adel.

Vinz had hold of Adel. He jabbed the rod into her. She collapsed. He leaned over her, extended the rod. She grabbed his arm, thrust a foot up into him, and threw him over her. Then she was on her feet, running, out of Lee's sight behind the cabin.

Lee watched Vinz roll to his feet and pick up the rod he had dropped. "You, come back here. We're not done." He disappeared after Adel.

Lee held tight, a rock rat hiding from a spinxi. Adel rounded the corner on her side of the cabin, and Lee hissed at her. Adel dove into the brush before Vinz came around the building flashing a light. Lee pushed Adel's face down and buried her own in the crook of her arm. She could feel Adel shaking. Reaction to the rod.

The light panned over them again, then dropped. "You won't get far," Vinz shouted. Lee peeked up. The light moved around toward the other side of the building.

"This way," Lee whispered and crawled upstream. To the spring. Sure enough, a box about two feet by four feet square was set into the wet area, collecting water to flow into a pipe to the cabin.

"In here." She slid the lid partly to one side. Hoping the box was deep but not too deep, she swung her feet inside, dropped down, and found herself waist deep in water. "Hurry."

Adel slipped in next to her. Lee pulled her down and settled the lid into place. Shoulder to shoulder they hunched chin-deep in the cold, fresh water and listened for any sign of Vinz looking for them.

Over the gentle chuckling of the water Lee heard the cabin doors slamming, undecipherable bumps and drags, and the skimmer door closing. Then Vinz's voice again. "It's a long walk. You can make it. But by then it won't matter."

He stopped. Waiting for a response? They didn't give it to him. He went on. "Everyone will know the story. How you orchestrated the escape of Willemsen and now Lee. And the rod. Don't forget your possession of that. Prohibited anywhere in the Coalition."

Lee forced herself to stay still and quiet.

"A rod addict and an unstable ex-ranger. That's enough to make even Joe Reilly doubt you."

The skimmer door shut. Lee listened to the faint hum as it circled and circled. Looking for them. Did it have a thermal scanner? Probably — they were used to count animals during survey work. So he did want to find them. Lee sank deeper into the cold water, crammed tight against Adel. "I owe you an apology," Lee said. "Someone's scheming, but it isn't you."

"He's sabotaging the survey," Adel said. "That's why I couldn't trust anybody."

"Except me." Lee closed her eyes and tried to readjust years of perspective.

"Except you."

"And you've really been trying to protect me from him?"

Adel shivered. "Really. So, what do we do now?"

"We're going to Under Rim."

"That's what he expects. It has to be," Adel said. "He knows we won't let this go. Besides, I doubt he left us his bike."

"So he plants his story and then comes back to deal with us when he has time." Easy enough to drop them somewhere so far out that they never made it back alive. Except Lee had already come back from a place like that. "But he has to find us first," Lee said. "And we have something he doesn't know we have."

"What's that?"

"Three horses," Lee said. "Our ride out of here."

Chapter 41

Seth

When Seth got back from the Tobin Canyon tack room, Vinz and his pa were intent on the skybike's readout. Seth stowed the pouch, still covered in Lee's wrap, in a storage compartment in Joe's skimmer before joining them.

"Snowstorm Peak?" Joe questioned.

"That general direction," Vinz said.

"Makes no sense to me. How about you, Seth?" Joe moved aside to let Seth see the screen.

Seth shook his head. "West? I can't think of any reason Lee would head that way." Except that it was away from Lickskillet and the distant Kelok villages.

"Well, let's go see. Right now, they seem to be staying put." Vinz straddled the bike.

"We'll follow you." Joe headed to the skimmer. Seth hurried after him.

"Any thoughts?" Joe asked as they followed Vinz away from Tobin. "Is Lee in charge? Or Verlane?"

"I'd say Adel just because I don't think Lee's ever been west of here before."

"That country gets rough around the mountain."

"Maybe they headed for West End." The only community out that way, on the far side of Snowstorm Mountain. "But Lee needs to be in Under Rim tonight. She'll do everything she can to get there."

"Ro doesn't seem to be too concerned," Joe said. "I take it Lee hadn't been back."

"Her horse, even her saddlebags were there. I retrieved the pouch. Trrk and I will have to go to the PAO ourselves if Lee can't." If Lee was still missing.

The day was starting to heat up by the time Vinz's skybike slowed and began circling. Joe set the skimmer down on the rocky tableland to wait.

"Looks like a canyon," he said. "Tough ground for a skimmer."

Seth couldn't sit still. He got out and walked toward the rim of the canyon, the kind of rim you could hop a skimmer down if there was a wide enough bottom to follow. There wasn't, not quite. A dark brown shape sat down there among the blue-green boulders and yellowish whipweed, a skimmer on its side with the roof tight against the rocks. He waved to his pa before scrambling down the first place he could find.

Seth climbed a boulder and pulled the door, now facing the sky, open. There was no one in the vehicle. It didn't look badly damaged, not like it had crashed from above. More like someone had misjudged the boulder and tipped it over into the wall.

Seth backed off and began looking for tracks. Whoever had exited the craft had rock-hopped away, never setting foot on soft ground that would leave a sign. Every fiber screamed at him to do something to find Lee. He breathed the anxiety down. No one badly injured could have exited the skimmer without leaving some sign. She was okay. And, if she had a chance, she would be heading to Tobin for the pouch.

"Void," Vinz said when he reached the skimmer.

"They're gone," Seth said.

"It looks almost drivable."

"Maybe," Joe said. "Once you get it upright."

Vinz climbed up and peered inside. "I'm going in," he said. "See what they might have left."

"Wait," Joe said. "Better let me do that. This is a possible kidnapping."

"You're the marshal." Vinz dropped to the ground.

Joe took his place on the boulder and let himself down into the skimmer. Seth made himself stay put and wait at a distance. Vinz paced up and down the sandy bottom. Maybe he was more concerned than he had seemed earlier.

Joe's head appeared out of the door with a bleak expression. He held up a black rod, a hand-span long and the diameter of a finger.

Seth's guts twisted and his breathing stopped.

"Whip was right," he forced out.

"What is it?" Vinz came closer. "Elements and All, a P-and-P rod. That had to be your girl's."

"Never, no way." Seth stared at Vinz. "You know her history. How can you even think that?"

"But that would mean ..."

"I told you I had allegations against Verlane," Joe said. "Seth, go get me a bag for this from the side compartment of my skimmer."

Seth tore his eyes from that innocuous little rod. "Sure."

He focused on climbing the rock rim of the canyon. Jerdix had used a rod on him repeatedly on a random setting so he never knew what to expect. It had taken him months afterward to get to where he could stand to be touched by another person. With intensive treatment for the physical changes it made in his brain as well as the psychological effects, he had learned to overcome his aversion to the rod to a point. It didn't mean he wanted to be anywhere near one. It did mean that he knew without a doubt that Lee would never willingly hold one.

Which left Adel. Who was somewhere nearby with Lee. And, if Jerdix was any example, would come back for the rod.

He got the evidence bag and climbed back down to the wreck. Vinz was out of sight. Inside the craft, Seth guessed. Joe bagged the rod, started to hand it to Seth, and pulled it back. "Sorry."

"You know that isn't Lee's," Seth said, keeping his voice low.

"I know. And Doc will be able to confirm that."

Vinz put his head out of the wreck. "The emergency pack is missing. So they are well supplied for a couple of days. And I pulled this." He held up a little cube. "The tracker. For counting wildlife. It detects heat."

"That'll help," Joe said. "It should work in my skimmer."

"It should." Vinz passed the cube to Joe. "You scan around here. I'll circle back towards town and see if the one on my bike picks up anything along their most likely route."

Joe looked over the area again, then nodded. "Anything is possible."

"Okay. But Joe ..."

"What?"

"If you find them, be careful."

"We'll be cautious." Joe started up the slope. "Come on, son."

Seth hurried after him but, once they reached the vehicles, he slowed. Something didn't feel right about the whole thing.

"Don't worry," Joe said. "This heat scanner will find every rock rat in the canyon."

Seth turned around, surveying the country. "I couldn't find any sign that they'd been there. And Lee wouldn't have tackled that canyon with a skimmer. She's barely driven one in years."

"So Adel must have been at the controls."

"I guess. But it just doesn't make any sense."

"Now you know how we felt, searching that plateau for you. At least we have good reason to believe one of them wants to hide."

"And I'm telling you, Lee will do everything she can to get her message to the PAO tonight."

"I sure wish you'd trust me with the real reason that is so important."

Seth shook his head. "Sorry. It's not my secret to share. But you'll find out tonight. If Lee can't make it, Trrk and I will have to do it ourselves."

"Fair enough." Joe plugged the tracker into the dash of his skimmer. "Let's see what we can find here."

"They'd have to be in the canyon. We'd see them on this tableland."

"We'll find out. If the tracker doesn't pick up anything within a reasonable distance from here, I'll drop you back at Fallen Pine and get together a search team," Joe said. "We'll find her."

Chapter 42

Lee

Lee listened to the hum of Vinz's skimmer fading into the distance. She could feel Adel shivering next to her. Reaction to Vinz and the rod, not to mention the cold water up to their chins. "He's gone," she said.

"Are you sure?" Adel asked.

"Yes." As sure as she could be. Lee pushed the spring box lid aside and climbed out. She turned back and extended her hand to Adel. Adel looked her in the eye before taking it and pulling herself out.

Lee slid the lid back into place. "You'll be okay," she said.

"You don't know what he did."

"Yes, I do. I really do." She shivered herself and not just from the cool pre-dawn air. "Let's get dried off."

She picked her way through the dark in her bare feet. She had spare socks in the packs, but she wondered where her boots were. Probably in the skimmer Vinz had taken, along with the sock she had shoved under the seat. How would he explain that, if anybody found it?

Lee opened the door to one of the enclosed rooms and felt around in the dark. "Scorch that man!"

"What?" Adel asked.

"Seth and I left our packs here. Dry clothes, food, saddles. All gone."

"You were here?"

"A couple days ago. Before I went to Tobin Canyon."

"So your partner took your equipment."

"No, we left everything here. It had to be Vinz."

"And he was waiting for you to run so he could track the skimmer and leave you stranded somewhere?"

"Better for him if I do disappear," Lee said. "But we've got horses, if I can find them. He didn't take those." She looked down at her bare feet. If there were dishes left in the kitchen, what else was there? "Any chance you still have a flashlight?"

"I do." Adel pulled one from a pocket. "He didn't bother searching me."

Lee took the light and looked around the room where they had left the packs. It must have been the main living space, part sitting area, part workshop, part kitchen prep area. No useful moccasins lying around.

She crossed to the other room. The bedroom. The

bed was made. A woman's clothes hung in the closet. Ike's wife's things, her great-aunt's. Dead some forty years. In a cabinet, she found folded clothes and towels. And on the wall by the door a pair of boots hung tops down on a boot rack. More her size than Ike's. She took down the boots and discovered socks stuffed inside them. A little bit of luck.

She grabbed two towels to go with the boots and went out into the gray pre-dawn. She passed Adel a towel. After drying off the best she could, she sat down, pulled on the socks, and put on the boots, soft, well-worn, and only half a size too big. Better than too small. She went back into the bedroom for a second pair of socks to help the fit. Blessed socks.

Adel finished toweling off her long, thick hair and began rebraiding it. "Whose place was this?"

"Family. Ike Allred."

"The man who died?"

"Yes. Once, a long time ago, he lived here with his wife. Looks like he just walked away and left everything when she died."

"But family?"

"His wife was my great aunt."

Adel stopped braiding her hair. "But you're from Kasba-on-Oasis."

"I grew up there. But my mother is from here and her sister still lives here. My cousin is married to Seth's sister. This is home now. Under Rim, Seven Wells, Carico. And I am not going to let a rogue ranger spoil it."

"You heard what Vinz said to me. He's setting me up to take the blame for what he has done."

"Yup. But I am going to talk to the PAO tonight anyway, and she's going to listen to me, not to Vinz."

Adel shook her head. "You know they're friends. Very good friends."

"I have such a surprise for her that she'll have to listen. Time to hunt up the horses. I need to get to Tobin Canyon."

"Where Vinz is staying." Adel shook her head.

"I'm betting Vinz'll head to town for the celebrations where he can plant seeds of doubt about both of us. Anyway, I don't need to go up to the cabin. Just the tack room."

"If this doesn't have anything to do with the survey, why are we wasting time on it?"

"I promise you it is important. And that we'll deal with Vinz and his plans too."

"I said you were the only one I could trust. I guess I've got to stand by that."

"Get comfortable," Lee said with a grin. "I'll be back with our rides."

Vinz had missed the halters hanging on the outside wall. Lee slung them over her shoulder and hoped the horses hadn't wandered too far. "Great Aunt Lori, you had good boots," she said as she strode along the little creek.

Lander was still in the sky. And she saw Creamy, his pale hide almost glowing in the moonlight. Tinker was a dark shadow near him. The roan's coat was better camouflage, but she soon spotted him a little away from the others.

Predictably Creamy lifted his head and stood while

she walked up to him. "Sorry, no treats," she said as she put the lead rope around his neck and slipped the halter on. She scratched his favorite spot on his chest.

Leading Creamy, she walked in Tinker's general direction. He wasn't always cooperative but with Creamy involved, he stood still as she approached. "Such a good horse," she said as she haltered him. She looked at the roan who was watching from a few steps away. "You just tag along this time," she told him.

Horses in tow, she returned to Adel. "Take Creamy."

"No saddles?"

"Thanks to Vinz." She tied the lead rope into a loop for reins. "Come on. I'll give you a leg up."

"I haven't ridden in years."

"Creamy will take care of you."

"Why is it I always end up in an adventure around you?" Adel stepped into Lee's cupped hands and settled on the horse's round back.

"At least Creamy is well padded," Lee said. Tinker was not only leaner, he was tall. Lee looked around for a convenient mounting block. No luck. She took a good hold on a hunk of mane and swung up, catching her heel on Tinker's far hip, and dragging herself on. By some miracle, the horse stood still through all of that. "All set?" she asked Adel.

"Lead on."

Lee followed the little creek down across the tableland rather than heading straight toward Tobin as she expected Vinz would have done if he had gone there when he left them. A low rim ran east-west across the country, the one Tobin Canyon Camp sat on top of. She wanted to come into the pens from the meadows below, get to the tack room, and then go up Tobin Canyon toward Under Rim without being seen. Surely Vinz wouldn't be indulging in his fish finding hobby after his encounter with Adel. Not on Settlement Day.

Riding bareback was great for learning balance or when you were playing around. It quickly lost its appeal as Lee tried to find a comfortable way to straddle Tinker's prominent backbone. Her shifting just made the sensitive horse tense. It was still faster than walking.

Discomfort aside, they made good progress. The roan followed along, stopping to nibble on something, then galloping to catch up. The other two mostly ignored him. Lee pushed aside the feeling that they were headed the wrong direction. Sometimes direct wasn't best.

Dawn found them at the top of a barely visible trail off the rim. "Down that?" Adel asked.

"Might want to walk." Lee slid to the ground, hanging on to Tinker's mane until her legs wanted to work properly.

Adel followed suit and pulled her sweaty pants away from her skin. But she hadn't complained once. She rubbed Creamy's neck and followed Lee.

The trail wasn't as steep as Lee expected. It cut through the rimrock and switched back and forth across the slope to come out a little above the mouth of a draw that opened into the valley below.

"Should be easy going from here," she said. "Ready to ride?"

"I'll walk a ways," Adel said.

"Good idea."

Adel came up to walk next to Lee. "You said you experienced that rod thing?" she asked.

Lee nodded, not wanting to talk about it.

"A lot of your file is blocked as confidential."

"Good." Leave it that way.

"Vinz said something about addiction. How can anybody become addicted to that?"

"I thought he used both settings on you." The memory of the pleasure setting still shook Lee.

"He did. It was horrible."

"Yeah." Lee stopped and faced her. "It still releases all those pleasure chemicals into your system. And no, I was never addicted."

"That isn't what I was thinking."

"What then?"

"He said something about Jerdix and a plan. Jerdix is the one who died three years ago, isn't he?"

"He did. Sounds like his plan didn't." Lee started walking again. Jerdix again. Wouldn't he stay in his grave?

"What was that?" Adel asked. "His plan."

"If anyone ever figured that out, they never told me."

"And why would Vinz have been associated with him?"

"I didn't know he was," Lee said.

"He's been on Carico a long time. He's friends with Joe Reilly and Kieron Dougherty at Seven Wells. I know he's close to the PAO. Has he been hiding in plain sight all this time?"

Lee thought about Jerdix diving off a cliff trying to retrieve his rod. "Back then he was pretty critical of

Jerdix's addiction. Maybe because that tangled up whatever plan was in the works?"

"I liked Vinz at first. Even though I was new, he seemed to trust me. He didn't watch over everything I did. But the more I saw, the more I began to wonder about him and why he had picked someone as inexperienced as I am for the job. By the conference, I knew he had something he was hiding."

"I think he has set both of us up."

"You?"

"I think he planned to bring me back for the survey; you know, give me a fresh chance. While using my history to cast suspicion on me. Like you've been doing."

"Me? Elements. Is that what it looked like? I was just so worried about you."

Somehow, Lee actually believed her. "Okay. So he has the two of us —"

"Three. I think Will ... Willemsen is part of it too."

"Whip? Helping Vinz?" Lee shook her head in disgust.

"No, another dupe. He wouldn't help, not to set me up."

Lee raised an eyebrow. "If you say so. The real question is what Vinz has planned." Lee felt the strands of this new problem pulling her. Not now. "Do you trust me?" she asked. "Or do you believe I should be committed for treatment?"

"I never did. I did everything I could to get you away before he got you to Doc's."

Lee ran their encounter at Tobin through her head. "True enough. Anyway, I have something I have to finish before I worry about Vinz."

"Will you tell me what this big surprise is that you have for the PAO?"

"It's a secret I promised to take directly to Emmerling. What happens with it after that will be up to her."

"After that, will you help me clear my name — our names — and find out what Vinz has planned?"

Lee nodded. "That I can promise."

Adel flipped her braid behind her back and straightened her tunic. "Then let's go."

Chapter 43

Seth

Seth fidgeted in his seat. Nothing. They had searched the canyon from the wrecked skimmer down to Snow Creek, the main stream coming off Snowstorm Mountain. After looping over the tableland on both sides, they followed Snow Creek downstream to where it met Tobin Canyon at the corrals. Clown watched them from the pasture. Joe hopped the skimmer up to land by the cabin.

"I don't see how they could have walked this far yet," Seth said.

"Unlikely," Joe said, "but best to make sure."

Vinz's gear was scattered around. Seth thought he

would be going to Under Rim, probably to the guest house where the PAO was staying that night. He must not have had time to pack up before they had shown up. Privately Seth hoped he and Lee could catch Emmerling in town. He didn't remember much of the night he'd spent in Jerdix's barn and didn't want to, but he knew he wanted to stay a long ways away.

"Guess that's it." Seth stood on the porch, looking around the quiet camp.

"We'll find her," Joe said.

"Or she'll find us." That's what would happen, he told himself. Wherever the PAO was that evening was where Lee would be. "Time to get me back to Fallen Pine. See how Trrk and Whip are getting on."

"Whip. Now there's a puzzle," Joe said. "Struts and whines but any mention of Adel Verlane has him terrified."

"They've got that speech synthesizer figured out, so you can lock him up." He got in the skimmer, not willing to admit the pleasure he got from seeing the marks Lee had left on the man. But he held onto that reminder that Lee could take care of herself.

They headed toward Under Rim. Seth stared out the window, trying to make sense of what they had seen. "You know, if that had been Dougherty this morning, he would have had a few choice words for whoever wrecked that skimmer. Vinz didn't seem..." Seth sought the right word. "He didn't seem very surprised."

"Ro's a practical man. No point wasting breath on things you can't help."

"He never even asked who was making allegations

against his employee and what those were."

"No, he didn't, did he?"

"Pa, I know he's your friend."

"I've known him a long time."

"Honestly, I've never liked the way he handled Lee. I mean the way he let things drag out. He didn't try to get her to carry through with any ongoing treatment, just let her retreat to Seven Wells."

"I wouldn't be second-guessing him on that. He does have access to her confidential records."

"And I was with her every day until the only thing I could see to do for her was walk away and quit propping her up." Seth shook his head. "But my point is that Vinz didn't react like I expected. Guess I shouldn't measure him against Dougherty or you."

"No, but I'm curious myself. Hate to say it, but let's keep both Trrk and Whip to ourselves for now."

Joe bypassed Under Rim and the festivities that would be underway already. Settlement Day was a time for big community picnics and fairs from the eastern mining districts to West End. PAO Emmerling would make whistlestops from town to town and, this year, end up in Under Rim.

"Better if you three stay at Fallen Pine," Joe said as he approached the cabin.

"Trrk and I have to be where we can talk to the PAO," Seth said. "In case Lee doesn't make it." Where was she now? What was she doing?

"Then I'll be back for you this evening. Might be best to wait for Emmerling at the guest house."

"The... Can't we catch her in town?"

"How public do you want the meeting to be?"

"Okay. The guest house." He didn't have to go near the barn, the stall where Jerdix had hung him by his wrists. Seth had never been in the house. But Lee had.

Whip met them on the porch. "Did you find them? Where is she?"

"No idea," Seth said. "No sign of either one of them."

"Clackers! What happened to her?" He froze for a moment and his expression changed. "I'm out of here."

"Whoa," Joe said. "You're not going anywhere. You don't think we'd let anything happen to our prime witness, do you?"

"Witness? Oh, yeah. You promise you'll keep me safe?"

"I'll do my best. So don't cram it up."

"Okay, okay."

"Good. Seth said you got the synthesizer working."

"Yesterday." Whip grinned. "Come see. I think I liked that Trrk better when I couldn't understand him." He opened the door and let them into the cool interior.

Trrk perched on the edge of the couch with his tail curled around his feet. A handheld comm unit and what looked like a small hand drum sat on the low table next to him. "My brother, have you found the female?"

What Trrk said echoed weirdly as Seth got the translation from his choker and the comm both. He slipped a finger under the choker and held it away from his skin.

"Not yet," he answered. "Looks like she and Adel left town together. We found the Ranger skimmer wrecked and no sign of them." He thought about the last time

Lee had disappeared without a trace. "You wouldn't know anything about it, would you?"

Trrk stood up, stretched tall, and lowered his beak. "I have no knowledge."

Seth couldn't ask what he wanted. Whether other Keloks might be involved. Not with his pa and Whip standing there. "I'm sorry I said that." Seth bowed his head to Trrk. "You were with me last night."

Trrk relaxed a little. "My brother, take me to the wreck, and I will find her."

"Are you sure you are well enough?"

"I am sure."

Seth turned to Joe. "He's a better tracker than I'll ever be, Pa."

"Vinz'll be expecting me in town," Joe said.

"I can't just sit here all day," Seth said.

"We must find the female," Trrk said. "She must deliver the message."

"Can we use your old Steadhand?" Seth asked. "Does Kiri need it?"

Joe's mouth quirked. "I got her a new one. She told me what would happen the first time the old one stranded her once the baby comes. Okay. I'll drop you off at the stead, and you can come back with the skimmer to get Trrk."

"What about me?" Whip asked.

"Better keep him with us," Seth said. "Unless you want to lock him up in town."

"Not today."

"Marshal," Whip said. "Any chance you'd take these off me now?" He held up his shackled hands.

Joe looked at Seth. Seth shook his head. "Not yet. I don't want to have to be worrying about what you're up to."

"I'll stay put. Promise." Whip looked at Trrk who snapped his beak. "He says he'll run me down and have my gizzards for lunch if I don't."

Trrk bobbed his head. "I did threaten harm. I believe you can unbind him without worry."

Seth studied Whip like he would an unpredictable horse. "Okay, take them off."

"Your call." Joe took the restraints off.

"Thanks, Marshal."

"Thank Trrk. He's vouching for you. You can answer to him."

"I'll be right here." Whip plopped into a chair. Trrk's crest riffled up in what Seth knew was a laugh.

"I'll be back soon," Seth said.

Chapter 44

Lee

Lee slid off Tinker to open the gate that barred their way. The cool had dissipated under the morning sun, and her seat and legs were wet with sweat from the horse's bare back. "This should be the big holding field below Tobin Canyon Camp," she told Adel. "We'll keep in the clumps of whipbrush out of sight as much as we can, just in case Vinz is here."

"If he is?"

"Don't beg trouble." Lee handed Tinker's rope to Adel. "Go on a little ways until that roan horse decides to follow through the gate." They could leave Seth's favorite at Tobin with Tinker. Lee looked forward to switching to Clown. If she had to get on a horse again for a while. Tinker's backbone threatened lasting damage.

After a minute of snorty, wild horse behavior, the roan raced through the gate with his head and tail high, gave a couple spectacular bucks, and came to a halt. "Yes, we see you, you wild thing," Lee told him as she shut the gate.

She looked ahead to the pens at the mouth of the canyon. Not much farther. Walking in Lori's boots would be better than getting back on Tinker. The boots didn't fit that badly.

As she took Tinker's lead back, she caught a flash of movement on the tableland above the pens. A skimmer left the cabin, heading toward Under Rim.

"Who was that?" Adel got off of Creamy.

"Not sure," Lee said. "It didn't look right for yours. Could have been a marshal's office rig." That could have been their ride home.

"Nice to know somebody's looking for us." Adel tucked loose hairs behind her ears. Not her usual impeccable self after the morning they had had.

"Just hope Vinz isn't there." Lee led the way into the maze of whipbrush and meadows.

They made it halfway across the meadow complex when Lee heard Clown neighing in the distance. Lonely horse. He must have sensed his buddies.

"So much for secrecy," Lee said. At least the others didn't answer him, but the roan trotted stiff-legged ahead of them, ears swiveling to locate the sound. Clown neighed again, and the roan broke into a lope.

Tinker tugged at his lead, wanting to follow. Creamy plodded faster.

Lee found an opening in the brush where she could see the rim and the trail down from the cabin. No sign of movement. Maybe Vinz really had gone to town. She took that chance and strode across the open meadow, eager to reach the pens. The horses had given them away, anyway.

The roan didn't hesitate to go through the gate into the smaller field where Clown waited anxiously for his friends. Lee shut the gate behind them. Still no sign of Vinz coming to check on things. She crossed the meadow, brought all four horses into a corral, and shut them in.

"I'll be right back," she told Adel and jogged to the tack room. The pouch would be there, safely hidden away, even if Vinz had taken everything else like he had at Lickskillet.

He hadn't, but someone had been there. Someone had moved her saddlebags from the rack next to her saddle. They sat on top of the feed bin with one side unbuckled. She looked inside. The only thing missing was the bronze and gold wrap Seth had given her, the one she planned to wear when she delivered the message to the PAO.

It had to be Seth. Who else would take that one thing and why? Had he found the pouch? She felt around in the grain, but it was gone. Trust Seth to get set to go to the PAO himself if she didn't show up. And it was safely out of reach of Vinz. What would the rogue ranger have thought if he had found the pouch with its invitations, story cloth, and stole-of-office? Quite a puzzle.

She took Clown's halter and went back to the corral.

"Did you find what you need?" Adel asked.

"It's gone," Lee answered. "I think Seth took it. It's proof of what I have to tell Emmerling."

"What makes you think you can trust her? Do you know how tight she and Vinz are?"

"I don't have a choice," Lee said. "The message is for the planetary administrative officer, no one else. We'll just have to see what comes next."

"We? I'm not even in on the secret."

"We. Vinz is going to be mixed up with it all."

"You are still going to help sort out what he's up to?"

"I won't let that get lost in the rest of this. I promise we are going to put that blame squarely where it belongs. On Rodahl Vinz."

Lee had Adel lead Creamy and Clown to the hitching rail by the tack shed while she turned Tinker and the roan loose in the field. Would Vinz notice the switch if he came back? Would it matter if he did?

Lee wasn't looking forward to another couple of hours horseback. Tinker's spine had left its impression on her. From the way Adel moved, she must be almost as sore. Lee put her saddle on Creamy and left Adel to cinch it up. The saddle would make it easier for the novice rider.

Her mind jumped back to Lickskillet. So Adel had had a crush on her back when. All the competition to attract her attention, not show her up. Lee shook her head at that. She'd never had a clue. It shed a different light on a lot of things Adel had done, back then and in recent weeks, like trying to get her away from Vinz. Allies? Now that was a strange concept for her to grasp.

The tack room didn't hold a convenient spare saddle, but there were a couple old saddle blankets. Lee tied one on Clown. He was rounder-backed than Tinker. With the padding, she might be able to ride.

"Where are we going?" Adel asked as they led the horses up the lane past the pens to the gate into Tobin Canyon.

"Away from here before Vinz shows up."

"But then?"

"Toward Under Rim and figure the rest out as we go." It was mid-morning at the latest. They needed to be in Under Rim as festivities wound down that evening. What to do in the meantime? "I'd go back to Doc's if I thought we could get there without being seen." Lee had trusted Doc this far.

"How about the guest house?" Adel asked. "Where I'm staying."

Lee locked down memories of what had been Jerdix's house. "Won't Vinz show up there?"

"Maybe, but my room is out in the bunkhouse. It should be safe enough if we can leave the horses out of sight somewhere."

It was audacious. Lee gave her that. "Someone might search your room, Vinz or the marshal, looking for clues to find us."

"I don't think Vinz wants to. Better if we aren't around. He'll spend his time establishing our evil doings."

"Good for us that I know the truth. And that some

key people will believe me." Joe would. Dougherty would. Even if they thought Vinz was their friend. "If Vinz isn't looking, we're safe enough. Seth knows I will do everything in my power to be there tonight. If they don't have a trail to follow, he will wait for me."

"Must be some secret."

"How about if we find a place between here and there to hole up and get some rest. Then we'll get to Jerdix's — I mean the guest house — this afternoon and wait for Emmerling."

Lee led the way up Tobin Canyon. She had come down that trail two days earlier hoping Vinz would help her meet with the PAO. That certainly hadn't worked out as planned.

Once up out of the canyon, she angled east. They had time to take a roundabout way. She wanted to arrive in Under Rim late enough for the PAO to be there so she could deliver her message before Vinz or anyone else interfered. She trusted that Seth would be on the same mission and would have the pouch. He probably had the same idea she'd had, to introduce Trrk as confirmation of the legitimacy of the invitation. But he didn't know about Vinz and Adel's suspicions. Not that it mattered to their primary purpose.

They got up into the forest before the day got much hotter. Heat was good. Heat led to thunderstorms. Thunderstorms would push people indoors for their celebrations, and she wouldn't have to deal with people scattered all over town.

Before midday they reached the main trail coming up from Wide Ford.

"Are you sure you don't want to go wait at the guest house?" Adel asked. "It can't be that far away."

Lee was tempted. "No," she said. "Let's find someplace we can get out of sight and wait. I don't want to risk Vinz finding us."

"Lead the way then."

Chapter 45

Seth

"You're sure?" Whip pointed out of the skimmer. "There's not a narky thing out here."

"Except a wrecked Ranger skimmer." Seth drove slower. "Somewhere along this little canyon."

"What were they doing out here?"

"Ask them when we find them."

"Now wait. You promised to protect me from that narky bitch."

Seth began to wish his pa had locked Whip up in town. "When we do find them, how about if we let Trrk referee?"

Whip shut up and stared out the window.

"Relax," Seth said. "They weren't here this morning.

We're just giving Trrk a chance to scout the wreck site and see what he can find that we didn't."

"You don't get it," Whip said. "I thought she really liked me. Her. You've seen her. Central raised and taught. She's traveled. And she treated me fine, like I was worth her time. When I found out she was just jinking me for kicks while she planned to undermine my home, it made me sick. What do you think she'd do to the one who blasted her plans?"

He'd really fallen for the Ranger. Seth pushed aside a twinge of sympathy. "Pa promised we'd keep you safe from Verlane. We didn't say anything about Lee."

"Lee?"

"You think she's forgotten what you tried to do over the other side of the Whitewater?"

"I just tried to scare her."

"Explain that to her. As long as you keep your hands to yourself, she'll probably leave you alone."

Whip rubbed his sore knee and kept quiet.

"There," Seth said. "That's where we were parked this morning. The wreck's down below." He parked the old Steadhand and got out. When he opened the cargo space, Trrk bounced out with a little of his old energy. Whip was slower to join them.

"I don't know if my leg'll get me down that," he said, looking off the edge.

"Stay here then," Seth said and locked the skimmer.

"I'll give it a try," Whip said.

"Both wait here," Trrk said. "To not confuse the scents."

"Okay." Seth found a rock to sit on where he could

see the wreck.

Trrk approached the wreck slowly, beak up and open, like he tasted as much as smelled the air. He circled, worked his way closer, and finally climbed up and opened the door. He leaned in, wrapping his tail around the door for support, careful of the injured end. When he stood up, he held something in his hand. He trotted a little ways up the canyon and then down before climbing up to rejoin them.

He opened his hand. "Your female's," he said. "They left nothing else."

One of Lee's socks. "Nothing?" Seth asked. It made no sense. Why would she have left one sock behind?

"It was concealed under the pilot's seat," Trrk said. "But they did not leave the craft here."

"What do you mean?"

"Your female and another have been in the craft recently. And two more, your sire and another male."

"Pa searched it."

"But did not pilot it. The other did, after your female did, and was here with your sire."

"Vinz," Seth said. "What about Lee?"

"There is no sign that either female was outside the craft at this location. I also believe that your packs were in the storage compartment at some time."

"We left those at Ike's old place when Doc came for you." Seth was glad he was sitting. "So Vinz somehow got the skimmer and brought it here without Lee and Adel. But they had been in it first."

"Correct."

"This is just a guess," Seth said. "Lee drove the

Ranger skimmer out of Under Rim with Adel as a passenger and went to Ike's place on Lickskillet. You're sure it was Lee, not Adel, who drove?"

"The ranger female did not sit in the pilot's seat after your female."

"So either on her own or because Adel forced her, but Lee was at the controls. Maybe they loaded up our gear from Lickskillet and went to Tobin Canyon to pick up what Lee left there. Where they ran into Vinz? Which leaves the question of why Vinz drove out here and wrecked the skimmer in a canyon he had to know he couldn't negotiate."

"Then brought you and your sire to it, saying he knew nothing about it."

Seth studied Whip. "Any chance Vinz and Adel are in on the sabotage together?"

"Could be," Whip said. "He was the one that set it up for me to do my restitution with the Rangers. Said he remembered me from when everybody was hunting Jerdix and thought I deserved a chance."

"They planned for you to get the blame for the programming."

"How could she?" Whip turned away.

Trrk came closer to Seth, leaving Whip to himself. "I do not understand human behavior, but it appears possible that your female is being held by the two rangers near the place you call Tobin, which they use as a base."

Had Lee been at Tobin earlier, when he and his pa had been there? Tied up in one of the bunkrooms where they hadn't looked. Or had they disposed of her body somewhere? "Come on, we're going to Tobin Canyon."

Seth took the most direct route possible across the tableland to Tobin Canyon Camp. At that point he didn't care if Vinz was there or not.

"You crash in there like a cram of tarbh, you'll get her killed," Whip said.

Seth eased up. "Ideas?"

"Leave the skimmer out of sight of the camp and walk in?"

"No. Vinz is expecting people to be searching for them. I'll drop off you and Trrk before we get there, and I'll go up and check the situation out."

"So we're supposed to just hang around?" Whip asked.

"Yeah. No. You two can sneak down Snow Creek and check out the pens." He could trust Whip that far. Trrk would be with him. But something was niggling at him, the more Whip talked. "Are you really that scared of Adel? Scared that she'll hurt you?"

"Void, no," Whip said. "She's hurt me as bad as she ever could already."

"Then why all the 'don't let her near me' stuff?"

"I just know I don't want to lay eyes on her. It'd rip the guts right out of me to have her admit to my face what she's done to me, what she plans to do to my world."

"Is she a threat to Lee?"

"I don't know."

Seth dropped down into Snow Creek and let Trrk and Whip out. "Take it slow," he told Trrk. "No need to push yourself."

"I am capable."

"I know." But Seth could also see the Kelok was tired. "If no one is at the bunkhouse, I'll hop the skimmer down to the pens to meet you."

"And if you don't come?" Whip asked.

"Come looking for me and expect trouble."

Seth hopped the skimmer back onto the tableland, circled, and came into Tobin Canyon Camp as if he was coming from town. No sign of Vinz's sky bike. But that didn't mean Adel wasn't there, holding Lee prisoner.

He parked boldly by the steps and climbed out. The back of his neck crawled, like he was being watched. "Anybody home?" he called out. No answer. He went into the cookhouse. Nothing had changed since he and his pa had been there earlier. He checked the storage room and the cook's quarters where Vinz's gear lay scattered around. He looked into each of the bunk rooms and the shower room before crossing the yard to the comm vault. It was empty too. From there he could see down over the pens and the fields. No Clown. Was he hidden in the whipbrush? Then he saw two horses dozing in the shade, Tinker and his roan.

How? It had to be Lee. Coming from Lickskillet with the horses and leaving them here when she reclaimed Clown. Why leave with two horses? Was Adel with her, riding Creamy?

He ran to the skimmer, hopped it off the rim, and parked by the tack shed. Trrk and Whip hadn't gotten there yet. Sure enough, Lee's saddle and saddlebags were gone. He studied the tracks. Two people, probably women from the size of the boots, had been there and had led two horses up the lane toward the gate into Tobin Canyon. But neither matched Lee's for size or wear. Her boots, like his own, had holes in the soles.

When he saw Trrk and Whip coming, he waved at them to hurry. "Check this out, Trrk. What do you make of the trail?"

Trrk took a maddening amount of time going over the ground around the tack shed, the hitching rail, and up the lane. "These belong to your female and to the other female who was in the wrecked skimmer," he said. "They seem to be cooperating. There is no scent of force or dispute."

"Working together?" Seth shook his head. "Why?"

"The sign is not sufficient to answer that," Trrk said, with a flip of his crest, a touch of his old humor.

"Lee came for..." Seth broke off, remembering Whip. "... for what she left, that I already took. And now she's headed to Under Rim." She was okay.

"With Adel." Whip sagged back against the hitching rail. "Just leave me here. I'll walk. Somewhere."

"'Fraid not," Seth said. "It's tough but we still need you to tell what you know."

"I can't do that to her."

"Yes, you can. You will. For Carico."

"Yeah, for Carico."

Seth laid his hand on Whip's shoulder. "Load up. Let's go."

Chapter 46

Lee

"Enough!" Lee shouted into the thunder. To think she'd been hoping for storms to cool things off. It was early afternoon, long before they wanted to slip unnoticed into town. Or maybe the guest house where Emmerling would spend the night. She and Adel were still debating that. Now she just wanted to get dry, get something to eat, and get some rest. The downpour continued, drenching them and making their horses duck their heads and flatten their ears even under the shelter of the trees.

"I'm tired of being wet," Adel said. She stood against the trunk of a tree where the canopy provided the most protection. "Isn't this supposed to be a desert?"

"High desert transitioning to palm-pine forest," Lee answered. "During the summer rainy season."

"My boots were finally drying out from the spring box."

"Well, the spring hid us from Vinz and his tracker device." Lee moved closer to the tree trunk, squishing in her borrowed boots. She'd been walking. The saddle blanket wasn't enough protection for her to stay on a horse any longer.

"Why are we staying here again?" Adel asked, shaking water from the end of her braid.

"It's way too early. Emmerling won't even be to Under Rim until near dark."

"The guest house should be quiet," Adel said. "Everyone will be at the festivities. We could get dry and rest. You don't plan to corner the PAO looking like that, do you?"

Lee had to admit she needed a shower and a change of clothes. The latter would be hard to pull off unless she could hook up with Seth before he took the message to the PAO himself. He had her dress. "Okay, okay. We'll risk sneaking into your room."

The rain eased up. They led their horses out from under the tree, and Lee waited for Adel to mount.

"What's that?" Adel stepped away from her horse, listening.

"Scorch it. It's a skimmer." Now what? They were in fairly thick forest and well off the trail.

The skimmer's hum grew louder. The two horses faced back the way they had come, ears on high alert.

"What under the Seven Rings of Gimokodan is that?" Eyes wide, Adel froze.

"Trrk!" Lee thrust Clown's reins at Adel and ran to greet the Kelok. She stopped short of throwing her arms around him. Not a respectful way to treat a male. "I am so glad to see you."

"And I you." He bowed his head politely. "Please stay here. I will guide your spouse to you."

"Seth's here too?" Of course he was. "Wait, you got a synthesizer working." She put her hand to her neck where she no longer wore the hearing facilitator.

"Yes. Please wait. He is not far."

Lee watched Trrk disappear among the tree trunks.

"What was that?" Adel said.

"Who," Lee corrected. "That is my friend Trrk. I plan to introduce him to the PAO tonight."

"But that is not one of the known species. And I heard it speaking to you in Standard."

"He has a translator," Lee said. "He's a castaway. I'll tell you the whole story later. After the PAO hears it."

"No wonder you've been so secretive. A first contact."

"Not technically. He's not requesting contact with the Coalition. Just a place to live here on Carico." She took the horses from Adel who was still staring after Trrk. By the time she got them tied, the skimmer twisted its way into view between the trees. Joe's battered Steadhand. Trrk followed on foot.

The vehicle stopped, and Seth burst from the driver's door. "Come here. Away from her," he said. "Do you know what she's been planning?"

Lee crossed the space to him in a few steps and shut him up with a kiss. "It's all right. I'm all right."

He held her tight, his breath warm on her neck. "We were afraid she had taken you. And then when we found the wrecked skimmer —"

Lee pushed him back. "The what?"

"The ranger skimmer, out toward Snowstorm Peak. But Trrk said you hadn't been there."

"Whoa. Vinz took the skimmer when we, or Adel I should say, got away from him at Lickskillet. He never saw me."

"Vinz?"

Trrk bobbed his head to Lee. "Perhaps if she tells her story chronologically?"

"First," Lee said, "I want to know what you think Adel has been planning."

"She's setting up the survey so Carico will fail the evaluation," Seth said. "We have a witness."

"Not Adel." Lee turned to her companion.

"Vinz," Adel said. "He's the one. I swear on the Rings, it was him. He set us all up, me, Lee, and Will Willemsen."

"Tell that to him." Seth pointed to the passenger's seat. A man crawled out, eyes on the ground.

"Will?" Adel took a step forward.

"Whip?" Lee glared.

"Go on," Seth said. "Tell Lee what you told me."

"She..." Whip squared himself and pointed at Adel. "She had me install programming that would interpret the survey wrong," he said. But when he looked at Adel, his attempt at his old cockiness collapsed. "How could you do that?"

"It wasn't me. I just passed on the programming that Vinz gave me. I hadn't even looked at it yet."

"You had one of those rod things. I saw it in your room."

"No, never." Adel's eyes widened. "He used it on me, Lee. You saw him. It wasn't mine."

"Then what did Whip see?" Seth asked.

"This, only this." Adel reached into a pocket in the back of her shirt and pulled out a black rod.

Lee couldn't help backing up and took Seth's hand when he stiffened.

"It's a kubotan," Adel said. "For self-defense. Vinz gave it ..." Her voice trailed off. "He's been setting me up ever since I got here. Oh, Will. Is that why you left?"

"I thought you were sabotaging the survey. And I couldn't turn you in, even for that. I couldn't."

Adel put the kubotan away and went to him. "Willem Willemsen, you should have trusted me."

"I never had anybody I could trust," Whip said. "Jerdix. He treated me good until that all fell apart. But I didn't think, how could I think someone like you..."

Adel didn't say anything, just stood eye to eye with him, took his face in her hands, and kissed him. He buried his face against her neck and held on tight.

"We were beginning to wonder about Vinz," Seth said. "He said he used the locator on the skimmer to find it wrecked in the bottom of a draw. And Pa found a rod when he searched it. But when I took Trrk back, he said you and Adel had been in it but hadn't gotten out at the wreck site."

"I left Doc's to go get the pouch ..."

"We have it."

"I thought you did. Anyway, Vinz showed up at Ike's old place while Adel was trying to convince me to trust her. I got away before he saw me, but I heard him telling Adel how he was going to ruin her name. He used the rod on her to emphasize his point. But she got away from him, and we hid."

She looked at Adel before continuing. "He didn't even look very hard. Just threatened what would happen if we showed up in town. He suspected I was there too. He found the packs and hauled everything away with him. He must have tethered his bike behind the skimmer."

"But the skimmer had a tracker," Seth said.

"We were in the spring box. Cold water. Our heat signatures wouldn't have looked any bigger than a couple rock rats."

"Smart."

"We caught the horses. He'd missed the halters you hung on the wall. And we went to Tobin, figuring he'd be in town making sure Adel was thoroughly framed. I checked for the pouch, switched horses, and here we are. And if I don't sit on another horse for a week, I'll be happy. Tinker is a horrible ride bareback."

"Ow." He ran a thumb along her cheekbone. "How to ruin my plans for our reunion."

"You!" She dropped her forehead against his chest with a laugh. They were almost to their goal. Almost. "Hey. Where'd Whip come from?"

"He was making himself at home at Fallen Pine. He told us about Adel's plan, at least what he thought was her plan. And he helped Trrk cobble together the synthesizer."

"So he's one of the good guys now?"

Seth shrugged. "So so. But he is a witness to the programming. And Adel seems happy to see him."

Adel had Whip by the hand, coming their way. Whip hung on with a death grip, looking like a scared puppy. Adel gave him a little shove forward.

"Anni, I mean Lee. About the other day, across the river. I'm sorry. I was angry and scared, but I shouldn't have done what I did."

Lee looked at him without answering.

"I shouldn't have grabbed on to you. I guess you thought I meant worse, but I didn't. I just wanted to scare you away." He looked to Adel, and she nodded. He took a deep breath. "Not your fault Jerdix turned out to be a crook. And if you want to turn me in for what I did, I'll own it."

Days ago, the feel of his hands on her had brought back memories of Jerdix before him. Her knee slamming into Whip's nose had given her back the power Jerdix had stolen. But he was still a waste of space, and she hated that they relied on him for anything, much less stopping Vinz's plans. "I'll think about it," Lee said.

"One more thing?"

"What's that?"

"Next fight we're in, I want you on my side. You're narky."

Lee shook her head. "You want to take responsibility for him?" she asked Adel.

"He's redeemable."

Whip took Adel's hand again. "And I can help. I know my way around Jerdix's place, that's this guest house now. I know a place we can wait, if they haven't changed things too much."

"Not the barn," Seth said.

"No, no. There's an outbuilding hidden in the trees where riders used to hang out waiting for him to tell what he wanted. Nice place. Unless it's been gutted like the one on the rim."

"Far enough from the main house not to be noticed?" Seth asked.

"Yeah. And there's a place for the horses and where you can put the skimmer under cover."

Seth put his hands on Lee's shoulders. "Are you okay taking the skimmer there with these two?"

"If Trrk'll be with me," she said. "You're going to bring the horses?"

"I'll meet you there. We've almost got this in the trap."

"If nobody bolts at the gate." She stepped back from him. "Let's go."

Chapter 47

Seth

Good thing Whip had given detailed directions to the hideout. Even so, Seth had trouble finding it, especially since he didn't want to be seen by anyone around Jerdix's old stead. On the outside, the log building looked weathered into its surroundings and half-overrun by brush. The skimmer was parked under a shed off one side.

Seth led the horses into the shed at the other end of the building and unsaddled. He'd had time on the ride to wrestle with the idea of their mismatched crew. The world had flipped. Whip and Adel were on their side; Vinz was the bad guy. Did they unload that to

Emmerling before or after Lee presented Prime's invitation?

Lee joined him as he tied Clown and Creamy, with their very visible coats, inside. In the private shelter of the shed, he greeted her with an eagerly returned kiss. The feel of her against him nearly distracted him completely.

"I missed you too," she said.

"You had me worried."

"I know. Sorry. I just wanted to sneak down and retrieve the pouch."

"Do we have to go inside right now?"

She shook her head. "Trrk's resting next to the door. Adel and Whip retreated to the loft to clear up things between them."

"Want to do the same?"

"Ah, for the luxury," she said. "But I'm still wondering how we pull off things tonight."

Focused on the job, as usual. He opened his arms and stepped back. "Just keep watch until Emmerling shows up? Now that we're here, I don't like the idea of facing her in town with everyone around."

"I wish we knew what her plans were."

"And what about Vinz? From what I've heard, he'll be with her."

"Ready to undercut anything we say." Lee frowned.

"We have Trrk to support the invitation. Maybe the whole survey question can wait until tomorrow."

"Can we get to Joe this afternoon and make sure he knows what we've learned? And get him to encourage Emmerling to come back here at some point before it gets too late?"

"You're not going anywhere near town." Vinz would have her locked up at Doc's in a blink. "But I can go. Vinz already knows I'm not missing, and he has no control over me."

"You'll be mobbed by family."

"With luck, I can get to Pa without them seeing me." He hated to think about the people still worrying about him and Lee. Just get through tonight, and they could have a grand reunion.

"I plan to sneak into the main house," she said. "I'll find a place we can wait."

He read the tension around her eyes. "What?"

"Hard not to remember the last time I was in that house."

"Jerdix. I've been so busy blocking out the barn in my head, I didn't think."

"I'll be okay."

He held her close. "I love you, you know."

"Love you too."

He savored that moment, soaking up the feeling to get him through the chaos of the rest of the day.

She topped off the pause with a kiss full of promise before easing away. "You should talk to Trrk before you leave. Fill him in on our plan, brother to brother."

"Make sure he rests. He's not as well as he'd like us to believe. But I sure was glad to have him with us today."

"Go tell him that," she said. "Remind him we need him tonight to pull this off."

"We do. Guess we should go in. Then I'll walk into town, find Pa. Stay out of the way of everybody else.

And be here to escort the Keloks' official envoy tonight."

Seth timed it to get to Under Rim late in the afternoon when everyone would be gathering to eat. The summer rains cooperated. A thunder cell moved over and drenched the whole area, sure to drive the festivities into the community hall. He came out of the forest behind the Marshal's Office anyway, the one place he expected to be deserted. His pa's official vehicle sat there next to a shiny little Surrey that he guessed was Kiri's new skimmer. He came in the back door of the office as he had done since childhood.

From the tiny front lobby, he could see across the plaza. People were gathered on the porch of the community hall and undoubtedly inside. Most of them he recognized. No way he could slip through unnoticed to find his pa.

A chair scuffed on the floor just outside, and Joe appeared in the door. He came in and moved back away from the front. "My office," he said. Seth followed him out of the public space into the depths of the building.

"Close the door," Joe said.

"Somebody here?" Seth asked.

"Not in the building, but town's too busy. Did you find them?"

Seth nodded. "Both of them."

"Trrk tracked them down?"

"Sort of. Interesting thing is neither of them had been anywhere around the wreck."

"What?"

"Trrk said they had been in the skimmer, with Lee driving, but he couldn't detect any sign of them outside.

Just Vinz, in the driver's seat and around inside and out."

"He's sure?"

"Positive. And he found one of Lee's socks under the driver's seat. But when we got to Tobin, they had been there, at least the tack shed and pens. Two of the horses we left at Ike's old place were there and Lee's horse was missing. We caught up to them out of town."

"Where are they now?"

"An outlying shed at Jerdix's old place. Whip knew about it."

"Wait. What about Whip and Adel?"

"Cozy as a spinxi pair."

Joe sank into his chair and leaned his elbows on his desk. "Is there a beginning you can start at?"

"You're not going to like it."

"Stick to what you know is true; not what you think. Let me put the pieces together myself."

"Okay." Seth sat down. "Lee took the Ranger skimmer last night to retrieve something from the tack shed at Tobin. Adel saw her leaving and tagged along. They ended up at Ike Allred's old place."

"Down on Lickskillet?"

"Yup. While they were talking things out, Vinz showed up. Lee got out of sight when they heard the sky bike, but Adel didn't. Lee overheard what went on between them. It got pretty intense."

"Save that. I want to hear it straight from Adel."

Seth nodded. "Okay. Adel got away from Vinz. She and Lee hid in the spring box. When they finally came out, Vinz was gone. The skimmer and his sky bike were gone. And the packs and saddles we had left in the cabin were gone."

"Wait. You had been there?"

"I waited there with Trrk while Lee came and got Doc. When we brought Trrk to town, we left our stuff there."

"Okay. So Lee and Adel were stranded at Ike's."

"They caught the horses and rode to Tobin. Lee figured they could sneak into the tack shed for what she wanted and leave without Vinz seeing them. From what he said, they thought he was going to Under Rim anyway."

"They were right. He's been here since I got back from dropping you off."

"From what Lee said, they got to Tobin right after you and I had been there. She saw us leave from out in the meadows. She figured out that I had what she was looking for, and they headed this way. We tracked them down in the palm-pines."

"So Lee, Adel, and Whip are co-existing? And Adel knows about Trrk?"

"And I was the only one we thought could come to town and figure out the best way to talk to the PAO."

"What about the rod Vinz found in the skimmer? Whip said he saw one in Adel's room."

"Adel carries a kubaton that Vinz gave her for self-defense. She says Vinz used the rod on her at Lickskillet as a threat."

"You're suggesting that Ro Vinz set up the wreck, and the rod is his."

"I gave you the pieces I know. Adel and Whip can fill in more blanks."

Joe ran a hand over his face. "I've known Ro since before you were born. He came to Carico to run the last survey twenty-five years ago."

"I know. Look, can we introduce Trrk first before we open that mess?"

"Probably a good idea." Joe leaned back. "Go back to the guest house and get ready. I'll suggest to Emmerling and Ro that we go there after she has dinner with the district arbiters. I'll tell her you have something to share about what you found back of beyond. I'll probably bring Doc and Kieron Dougherty too."

"Dougherty is here?"

"I'm expecting him anytime. That's why I was over here instead of at the hall."

"Don't let Vinz know Lee and Adel are here."

"I won't."

"All right. We'll wait at the guest house for you."

"Good." Joe stood up. "I'd better get back out front before somebody comes looking for me."

"Pa, thanks. And the secret, all of it, will come out tonight."

"That part I am looking forward to."

Chapter 48

Lee

Lee had a little time to herself with Adel and Whip doing their own thing and Trrk taking his rest guarding the cabin door. She took advantage of it to shower. It appeared that one of the ways Jerdix rewarded his less-than-legal help had been with comfort. However ignored this hideaway might be under the current management, its basic infrastructure functioned.

She'd had the chance at Doc's to get cleaned up, and there was that soak in the spring box this morning, but the last real shower she'd had must have been in the Village of Canes where the Keloks had piped solar-heated water through hollowed out canes. And before that had been days earlier when she and Ike had been at Seth's place, their last stop before they headed out on their exploration of new grazing land for Kieron Dougherty and the Seven Wells Stead.

She let the hot water run over her and inspected her collection of minor injuries – the scraped arms and sore ribs from her fall at Tobin trying to beat Adel to Vinz; the tender rawness from riding Tinker bareback; the sundry scratches and bruises from the days of travel. All in all, nothing serious.

The only thing she had to wear that was clean was the silky wrap she was saving for the presentation; the one Seth had brought from her saddlebags. Looking around, she found spare clothes in a closet, brand new as far as she could tell. Supplies for Jerdix's crew maybe. Not much selection and only one pair of pants close enough to her size that she could keep them up with a belt. She didn't worry about the fit of a shirt. Baggy was fine in the summer heat.

She stretched out on a bunk that doubled as seating in the main room of the hideaway and tried to get some sleep. She'd had nothing but snatches of naps since the night locked in at Tobin Canyon Camp. Okay, that had been night before last. Not as bad as it seemed. And, it turned out, she wasn't tired enough to sleep with her chance to complete her mission finally within sight. Her mind raced on.

They had gone through so much to get to this point. She wanted to get it right, to get Emmerling to accept the invitation. Eta'ak had given her instructions for her role as the Kelok envoy. The rawhide satchel Seth had retrieved from Tobin held two copies of the invitation, one written in Sol Standard and one in the color-writing of the Kelok. And a cloth that Eta'ak had woven to tell the Keloks' story, again in their color-writing. And lastly a long, narrow, multi-colored stole-of-office Lee was to wear around her neck as a symbol of her authority. That she was to pass to the PAO to wear at the meeting with Prime to indicate they were meeting in peace.

She wanted to have the invitation committed to memory.

Prime, leader of Kelok Gra'a Tral — the Exiles of Blue Canyon — invites Charlyn Emmerling, Planetary Administrative Officer of Carico, to meet together so that we may discuss our peaceful coexistence on this world.

She and Eta'ak had considered that wording carefully. It should be delivered privately but formally. Although they hadn't planned on Trrk being there, he certainly added credence to the story. Proof positive of the Keloks' existence.

Lee knew this wasn't the end. This was just putting the match to the kindling. No matter how much any of them said this wasn't an official first contact, there was no getting around the fact that they were introducing a new species of persons. Vinz's scheming was just a ripple by comparison. But while she and Seth might still be advisors, they wouldn't be carrying the full weight of the responsibility. Or so she told herself.

She gave up trying to sleep. "Trrk, will you watch and

make sure Adel and Whip stay here?"

"I am able to do that. You are going somewhere?"

"Just to scout around the main house."

"You believe you will find the PAO there?"

"Not now. But I hope we can catch her here tonight and not have to go to town."

"My clan brother can scout when he returns."

"I'll be all right," she said. "But thank you for your concern."

"It should be my responsibility." He tucked the stump of his tail out of sight.

"I know. But we can't risk you being seen."

"Or you."

"If I'm seen, I'm just another visitor in town for Settlement Day." The people who would recognize her would all be in town celebrating. "I won't be long."

It wasn't far to the main stead with the big house facing the road from town and the barn and outbuildings behind it. She stopped at the edge of the trees. The air felt thick, like she had to push through it. Now at least the rain had stopped. The last time she had been there, three years ago, it had been pouring. She'd found Seth in the barn and freed him. He had fled into the storm, lost in the torment caused by the rod Jerdix had used on him.

She waited in the cover of the trees and watched. A skimmer with the ETBC logo on the door sat at one end of the bunkhouse. Caretaker? Someone had to be maintaining the property. The corrals were empty, and the barn looked shut up tight.

The house was closed up too, but that would be

normal on a summer afternoon. Open everything up overnight to cool things off, then shut the coolness inside for the day. She tried to picture the inside. That corner of her brain opened reluctantly. She'd been in and out occasionally when she worked for Jerdix in her undercover role as Anni Dulce, mostly in the office off the main living area. And once in his bedroom.

Breathe. Breathe. He was dead and gone. No big harsh hands grabbing, controlling. No one would ever do that to her again. She proven that to herself with Whip.

She forced herself around to the front door and walked in like she belonged there.

Silence.

The room had been redone, more lobby than living room with a half-door to the office/reception room and small groupings of chairs around the main space. She kept her eyes off the big staircase to the bedrooms and went into the back hallway to the formal dining room and the kitchen. Still no sound of anyone moving around.

Through a mud room and storage area she found the back door. They could come in that way and wait for the PAO. She could do this. A few demons put to rest. But not enough.

She turned around and went back inside. She strode to the lobby, up the stairs to what had been Jerdix's master bedroom, and tested the doorknob. It opened onto an entirely different room than she remembered. Lighter, brighter, everything in different places. A luxury guest suite.

She stood there and for the first time in a very long

time, played out the rape in her mind. His violence and anger, Anni's fear, and, deep under that persona, her true self knowing she could stop it if she just gave up her role and fought back. She had chosen not to. She had walked into that room that night knowing he would take her — Anni — and thinking she was prepared to let it happen. That he would take such pleasure in hurting her was beyond her expectation. She was reminded again and again in counseling that she was conditioned to be Anni. But she hadn't regained her sense of control until Whip Willemsen had grabbed her, and she had left him on the ground out beyond the Whitewater.

She closed the door without entering the room, no doubt the room the PAO would occupy later. She went down the stairs, through the lobby, and out the front door without looking back.

Chapter 49

Lee

Lee was sitting under a tree outside the hideaway when Seth got back from town. She knew it hadn't taken him that long, but it felt like forever. She got up and met him before he reached the building.

"Nice outfit," he said.

"Clean and new. Too much to ask that they'd fit." She ran her hands down the shirt. "Are we set?"

"Pa is going to get Emmerling and Vinz here after dinner. And probably bring Doc and Dougherty along."

"The boss is here?" Good. Dougherty was always steady.

"Coming in this afternoon sometime. Pa let him

know we had showed up."

"I checked out the main house," she said, not sure how he'd react to that.

"You did what?"

"I watched to be sure no one was there. I wanted a look at things. Anyway, there's a big mud room at the back where we can wait out of sight."

He cupped her face in his hand wordlessly.

"I slayed some demons." She quirked a smile. "Everything is different inside. A pleasant guest house now."

"Funny," he said. "I can't even remember the layout of the buildings."

She kissed his palm. He'd worked hard to put his own demons to rest. "Did Joe believe you? About Vinz?"

"You know the marshal. He only wanted to hear what I knew. He wants to talk to Adel and Whip himself."

"No surprise."

"But he sees what things look like. Hard for him. He and Vinz have been friends for a long time."

She sighed. "I wish we could separate that from the presentation to the PAO."

"I asked if we could introduce Trrk first. He agreed."

"Good. You said after dinner?"

"Emmerling is supposed to meet with the district arbiters over dinner."

"So about dark?"

"I think we need to be ready by then. And prepared to wait."

"I hate waiting." She took his hand. "Let's see whether this shack is still stocked with anything worth eating." They went inside and rummaged together food for them all while they waited.

"They come," Trrk said. He stood by the hideout door, listening. "A larger vehicle." He hid his nerves well, but the ruffling of his crest gave him away.

"A jumper," Seth said. "I hear Emmerling has a nice set up for travel, fully self-contained. Let's her get around in a hurry. Here to Portside in a couple hours."

Lee felt a flutter of anticipation, took control of it. All that time with the Keloks, Trrk's injury, the struggle to get to Under Rim, her commitment for evaluation, the events at Lickskillet that morning — everything led up to this.

"Time to go," she said.

"For me. You wait. Give them a few minutes to get settled."

She followed him out onto the porch, put her arms around him, and kissed him. "For luck."

"You look stunning."

She smoothed her wrapped dress of silky bronze shot through with gold, taking courage from the elegant costuming. Just right for a meeting with the PAO. "Bet you didn't see this need when you got this for me."

"It just made me think of your eyes." He ran his thumb along her cheek before walking away through the failing light into the stand of trees between the hideaway and the main stead.

Lee went back in. "Ready?" she asked.

"I don't think I can do this," Whip said. "Who's going to believe me?"

"I do," Adel said. "Tell them what you know and let them put all the pieces together."

"Trust Marshal Reilly," Lee said.

"But Vinz will be with Emmerling," Adel said.

"This is about introducing Trrk. Vinz can't very well say we are imagining him."

"No."

"Joe will decipher who did what with the survey programming. You'll see. First, let's go shake things up."

Adel tossed her braid behind her back and held out her hand for Whip to take. "Let's."

They passed through the woods. The PAO's van was parked between the barn and house. Lee looked at Trrk. "No one is close," he said.

Trusting his senses, they walked past the vehicle and went in the back door. Lee stopped there and took off her borrowed boots. They spoiled the impression she made in the wrap dress. And once Trrk appeared, who was going to notice she was barefoot?

"Come on. You can wait in the hall. I'll come for Trrk when I'm sure I have their attention. And then Adel, you two can follow him in and stop by the foot of the stairs where you won't miss anything."

"This is one time I am glad to let you have front and center." Adel flashed a grin.

Lee grinned back and turned to Trrk. "Please carry

the satchel for me."

Trrk held back, his crest tight on his neck. "I am not fit to represent my people."

"After all you've been through? Of course you are."

He dropped his head and tucked the tip of his tail out of sight.

"Oh," Lee said. "Your tail. Wasn't that injury earned honorably or something?"

"I cannot make Eta'ak proud when I am incomplete."

"When we see her again, Eta'ak is going to be very proud of you. Please, I need your help with this."

Adel mouthed, "Eta'ak?" Not the time to explain.

"Eta'ak is relying on us." Lee walked away, hoping Trrk's commitment to his spouse's plan would overcome whatever restraint his injury placed on him. She was relieved to hear his footfalls behind her.

She stopped in the hall before she could see into the main room. Finger to her lips, she gestured for them to wait. Trrk, Adel, and Whip. She couldn't miss the irony of her being backed up by three people she had considered opponents at various times recently.

She eased forward until she could hear Joe encouraging everyone to get comfortable. Seth came into view, standing near the foot of the stairs. He glanced her way and waved at her, keeping his hand behind his back.

"Okay, son, what is it you found that you want to tell us about?" Joe said.

Their cue. Seth turned and held his hand out to her. Lee smoothed her dress, flipped her fingers through her hair, and walked forward.

Chapter 50

Lee

Lee walked out of the hall to join Seth. Her heart pounded. There was too much going on. She narrowed her focus to priming her audience for the message she had to deliver and tried to smile.

Joe Reilly sat near the front door with Kieron Dougherty. Lee nodded to them. She owed Dougherty a lengthy report about the exploration she and Ike had undertaken for him. Right now, she trusted he would be an ally.

Doc watched from a solitary seat on the edge of the room. She wished she knew what his evaluation of her mental health had told him. The smile he gave her suggested another ally.

Planetary Administrative Officer Charlyn Emmerling stood by the big, cold fireplace next to the stairs with Rodahl Vinz beside her. They were quite a pair, both short and stout, Vinz pale-skinned next to Emmerling's ebony. Her silver hair was braided tight to her head. She wore a long sun-yellow and copper tunic over loose malachite pants that gave the impression she was floating on a breeze for all her bulk.

"So here are the missing riders," Emmerling said. "The marshal tells me you discovered something you want to bring to my attention." She smiled, a formal smile without personal warmth.

"Yes, Administrator." Lee came forward. "Thank you for your time."

Vinz laid a familiar hand on Emmerling's arm. "You don't have to trouble yourself. This person is on a medical suspension from the Rangers. Last night she escaped from involuntary commitment for evaluation."

"Why didn't you mention this sooner?" Emmerling asked.

"I thought it better to wait until we had her where we could get her back in custody."

Lee stood her ground and cultivated calm. She should have expected this from Vinz. "I'll be happy to go with Doc Legat as soon as we're done here."

"There's no need to disturb the PAO with wild stories," Vinz said. "Come, Char, sit down. Doc can take her back into care. I apologize for involving you at all."

"Thank you, Ro, but I am curious. I would like to hear what she has to say."

"Trust me, she's been traumatized in the past, and now she's suffering again. She wants to tell you a story, standing there in her fine dress and her bare feet."

"Someone took my spare shoes along with the rest of our packs," Lee said, looking him straight in the eye. She could almost see the wheels turning in his mind.

Vinz stepped between her and the PAO. "Doctor, please remove your patient. Marshal, I know she's a friend of yours. Can't you see she needs help?"

"Ro, what is this?" Emmerling came up beside him.

"I should have dealt with her problems a long time ago. I was too generous."

"Hey," Lee said. "I can step aside and let Seth speak for us. Or do you suspect him of something too?"

"Well, yes." He turned to the marshal. "Joe, I know he's your son, but I have to say this. He was involved in the same traumatizing incident that she was."

Joe got to his feet. Lee waved him off. Time to stop Vinz and his interference. "Seth, we're going to have to do the other thing first. Have our witnesses come out."

Seth left her side and went into the hallway.

Lee turned to Joe. "Marshal, you wanted to question a couple people about some allegations you had heard. Well, here they are."

Adel entered, her ice-gray eyes stabbing at Vinz. Whip trailed behind her, encouraged by Seth.

"What's this?" Vinz demanded. "Marshal, take these two into custody immediately. You have notices on them both. They are dangerous."

"I'm here to dispute that," Adel said. "In fact, we've been piecing together what we know."

Vinz looked from her to Whip and forced a laugh. "You and him? I gave him a chance with a restitution detail, and he ran. He's an escaped criminal."

"And already in my custody." Joe spoke for the first time.

Vinz barely hesitated. "Verlane should be too. You saw it. The P-and-P rod we found in her skimmer."

"*Your* rod," Adel said. "You had it at Lickskillet this morning. And you provided the programming for me to have Will install." She held out her hand. Whip took it and came up next to her.

"Of course I did." Vinz didn't say anything more about the rod.

"Will found problems in that programming, algorithms designed to skew the survey results to look like Carico is failing to meet milestones."

"Ridiculous. What would he know about algorithms anyway?" Vinz shook his head.

"Let him answer that himself," Lee said.

"Go on, Will," Adel encouraged.

"Obviously he's been coached." Vinz crossed his arms.

Whip stepped forward with something of his old strut. "Nobody's telling me what to say. I may be just a rider, but I've been around these districts, and I grew up in the mines. What's in that programming doesn't match what we're supposed to be measured against. And as for that rod, you'll answer for using it on my partner."

"Are you threatening me?"

To Lee's surprise, Whip kept his mouth shut. But he

didn't back off.

Vinz looked around the room and shrugged. "It's the word of a criminal and a disgruntled employee. Who are you going to believe?"

Reading the first glimmer of uncertainty on Charlyn Emmerling's face, Lee said, "About the rod. Doc, it causes physiologic changes. How much use does it take to show up on a scan?"

Doc got up and came forward. "One use is enough for short-term effects."

"And can you distinguish that from repeated use?"

"Yes, the effects are cumulative."

"Scan me," Adel said. "Here and now."

"We'll have to go to my clinic. I don't have the equipment at hand."

"Can that wait until morning?" Emmerling asked.

"The effects should be evident for forty-eight hours at least," Doc replied.

"Then at the moment I am more interested in the survey programming."

Vinz faced Emmerling. "It's the first I've heard of any problems. I'll have to check it out."

Emmerling looked troubled. "We have talked about the evaluation. You offered to help me through the process."

"Yes. You know I'm happy to help."

"But you have expressed concern about the outcome. And you have said you think the criteria are too lax."

"And if I do? I'm allowed my own opinion, aren't I? In private, between friends? We are friends, aren't we,

Char?"

"And were you and C.T. Jerdix friends?" Lee asked. "Back when you were overseeing my investigation of him?"

He didn't answer, just turned his back to Lee. Standing by Emmerling, he said, "Willemsen is an escapee; Lee is under involuntary confinement; and I am charging Verlane with possession of prohibited technology. If the marshal and the doctor won't fulfill their obligations, I'll have to take responsibility myself for seeing they are all confined until I can put these lies to rest."

"Now, Ro, just slow down," Joe said. "I told you Willemsen is already in my custody, and Doc is here for Lee. As for Verlane, I'm afraid I don't have adequate evidence to put the rod in her possession. But I will take her into protective custody while we sort out this mess."

"And your son?" Vinz asked.

"So far, I haven't heard anything that implicates him in anything. But my wife will be happy to put him under house arrest now that we have him back home." He smiled. "What about you, Ro? What assurance are you going to give us that you'll be around when we look into the programming issue?"

"Me? I have everything to gain by resolving this."

"I will take responsibility for him," Emmerling said.

"Are you sure, Administrator?" Joe asked.

"I've had enough of this foolishness," Vinz said.

Seth stepped in and asked, "Who's Henry?"

"What?"

"Who is Henry?" Adel reiterated. "And why did you

have me provide him with proprietary information on the survey?"

Vinz looked from one of them to the other. "Char, I'll be upstairs when you are done with this nonsense."

"Perhaps that's best. It doesn't seem we'll resolve anything tonight." She studied Vinz with sorrow. "Do I have your word you will not leave the guest house?"

"My word? You ask that of me?"

"Sadly, I do."

"Char, I..." He looked around the room.

"Citizen Vawn-Cory asked you about Jerdix." Emmerling went to him; laid her hand on his arm. "I want to hear your answer. Please, Ro."

The two faced each other. Vinz paused, lifted her hand from his arm, and kissed it. "I wish you had known him. C.T. was a visionary. He saw ... You can see." Vinz put his arm around her and pointed around the room. "Look at them. Carico was awarded to a bunch of short-sighted technophobes unwilling to grasp the opportunity given them."

"What are you saying?"

"Them. People like Joe and the doc, settling for this bare existence. People like Kieron, with all the backing of JT Land and Livestock, and his only ambition is to expand the tarbh operation?" He took her hands. "Carico has so much potential. Commercial production of the medi-botanicals and palm-pine sap. Room to house laborers brought in to harvest and process cheaply. Rare minerals that return ten times as much as copper for the effort they take. And this evaluation is the time to open up all that."

"By making us fail," Lee broke in.

He spun away from Emmerling. "By putting Carico back out for bid and bringing in new management." He ran his eyes over his old friends. "Can't you see the benefits?"

"Benefits? Destroying everything we've built?" Dougherty turned away, shaking his head. Joe put a hand on his shoulder.

Emmerling sagged into a chair. The look on her face was devastating.

Vinz took half a step toward her. She looked away. "Fools," he said. "I've had enough of all of you." He barged across the room toward the hallway.

Joe started after him. Seth held up a hand and said, "He won't get far."

Chapter 51

Lee

Vinz got as far as the entrance to the hallway where he stopped like he'd hit a wall. He froze there, poised to run, a man confronting a dangerous beast.

Trrk stepped into view. "Principal Advisor Vinz, you will not leave yet." With his crimson crest and arm feathers straight up, he filled the doorway. He snapped his beak. Vinz backed up.

"Meet our friend Trrk." Lee took in the reactions around the room. Doc was the only one who stayed seated. Dougherty looked to Joe, next to him, for an explanation. Emmerling rose slowly to her feet. Lee said, "I'm sorry for the surprise. We had planned to warn you all before bringing him out."

"This is why you asked for a private meeting?" Emmerling asked.

"It is," Lee answered.

Trrk folded his feathers down, lowered his eyes respectfully, and bowed. "Administrator, I am honored."

"As am I." Emmerling struggled to recover her composure. "Ro, please join me over here." Vinz complied, moving cautiously and watching Trrk.

Lee bowed slightly. "Administrator, we met Trrk back of beyond. As you can see, he is a non-human person of a previously unknown species. And he is not alone." She kept her eyes on the PAO, resisting the temptation to catch the other reactions around the room.

"Carico has endemic people?" Emmerling asked. Her face spoke of near panic, of one too many new weights on her shoulders. Settlement rights weren't granted to worlds with endemic populations.

"No, no." Lee hurried to reassure her. "They are castaways here."

"You're certain?" Emmerling asked.

Lee nodded. "His people have asked me to give you a message that, under their customs, Trrk cannot deliver himself." She glanced around then, at Joe and Dougherty exchanging surprised looks, at Doc studying his recent patient with new interest. Vinz stood behind Emmerling, looking stunned.

Emmerling squared herself. "Then we will abide by his custom in that." Lee had to admire the woman's resilience. She was an administrator on a frontier planet, not a trained diplomat.

"We need a moment," Lee said. Giving Emmerling a chance to gather her thoughts. Lee went to Trrk. "It's time," she said. Her heart pounded; her mind went blank. She felt Seth's hand on her shoulder. With grave formality, Trrk handed the satchel to Seth to hold and withdrew the stole-of-office from it. He placed it around Lee's neck. Then he handed Seth the two copies of the written invitation and kept the story cloth. She laid one hand on his shoulder and the other on Seth's. "Ready?"

"We'll be right behind you," Seth said. He ran his thumb along her cheekbone. "You are beautiful."

"I wish Eta'ak could be here," she said.

"As do I." Trrk drew himself up tall and carefully straightened the stole around her neck, making sure the long ends hung down evenly. He stepped back. Lee turned and walked to the PAO with her escorts at her shoulders.

"Planetary Administrative Officer Emmerling of Carico." Lee bowed with human courtesy. "I carry an invitation from Prime, leader of the Kelok Gra'a Tral, the exiles of Blue Canyon, to meet to discuss our peaceful coexistence on this world." She took the two invitations from Seth. "Here are the written words of the invitation in our language and in that of the Keloks." She kept her eyes on Emmerling, not sure she could face all the others just then and risk losing her focus.

Emmerling took the rawhide sheets and studied the pattern of colors on the Kelok version. "You have my attention."

"We bring you a gift as a sign of good faith," Lee took the story cloth from Trrk. "The Kelok story is woven into this. Prime hopes that one day you will learn to read it for yourself."

"It is lovely."

Lee was suddenly lost. She'd run out of plan.

"The stole," Seth whispered.

Oh, yeah. Lee took off the stole-of-office and folded it carefully. "And this. It is a symbol of authority for the Kelok. You should wear it when you meet with Prime. It indicates peaceful intentions." She held it out to Emmerling. "If you accept the invitation, that is."

Chapter 52

Lee

Lee held out the folded stole-of-office. Emmerling laid the invitations and story cloth aside, took the stole, studied it for a moment, and put it with the other items. Seth passed over the satchel to hold them. The room was silent. Everyone was still, waiting. Vinz looked about ready to collapse.

"Citizens," Emmerling said, "This is a momentous occasion." She looked around the room, catching each person's eyes before moving on. "I am not going to say yes or no to this invitation tonight. I would like to hear more from Trrk directly."

Trrk edged back half a step. Lee nodded to him and

turned to Emmerling. "In Kelok culture, it would not be appropriate. They have very rigid roles. But he can assist me with answers when I request it."

"Again, I will respect their custom, for now, even though we are in our house."

"Thank you," Lee said.

"You have gone to some trouble to carry a message for people who you can't know very well."

"Sometimes it doesn't take a lot of time. We three trust each other with our lives in spite of many differences."

"So you believe they are sincere in this invitation?"

Lee hesitated. She needed to be as honest as her promise to Eta'ak allowed. "There is not consensus among them, but I believe they will meet and negotiate honorably. And I believe this meeting is in the best interests of our settlers."

"Who are these people? What is their story?"

"Trrk and his people were stranded on Carico when their navigation system failed several years ago."

"Years? And how many of them are there?"

"A full ship's complement." Lee heard a sharp intake of breath behind her. Adel, she thought. And Doc's eyes were wide.

"Why didn't they approach us for help earlier?" Emmerling asked.

Lee shrugged. "Distrust. Fear. They want to keep control of their lives. They don't want to be packed off like refugees."

"So they want to remain on Carico?"

"In the homes they have built. They want

recognition as settlers."

"And to mix with us?"

"That is one of the things that needs to be negotiated," Lee said. "I am just a messenger."

"It does appear that they qualify for aid rendered to castaways at very least. Let me think about what you have told me. It's a lot to take in. We can talk more tomorrow."

"Absolutely."

"May I speak with Trrk informally at some point?" Emmerling stood up and half bowed to Trrk.

Lee looked to Trrk who bobbed his head. "Yes," she answered for him.

"I look forward to it." Emmerling looked around the room. "I gather that no one else was aware of this?"

The invitation or that there were more than one? Not that it mattered. The answer was the same. "Just Seth, Trrk, and me," Lee said.

"Let's keep it that way for the moment," Emmerling said. "Marshal, please have Verlane and Willemsen removed and confined without communication until we can decide how to proceed; for security, you understand."

"We are happy to cooperate," Adel said. Whip didn't look happy. She tucked his hand into her elbow and patted it encouragingly.

Trrk hissed, drawing Lee's attention from Emmerling. "The Ranger." He pointed his beak. Vinz was edging away around the stone fireplace.

Emmerling caught him with her eyes. "Ro, my dear friend, I must ask you to go with the Marshal as well."

"I ... give me a chance to explain."

"It might be best if you didn't until you confer with an advocate."

He stiffened. "I have done nothing you can hold me on."

"No? Then do it because I ask you to. To help me as I address the questions about the survey and this unprecedented invitation."

They exchanged a long look. Vinz dropped his head. "Yes, of course. For now."

"Thank you." Emmerling placed the invitations, stole, and story cloth into the satchel. "I will leave you now. Forgive me, everyone, especially you, Trrk. I look forward to speaking with you at length tomorrow. But I have had a full day and a fuller evening." She climbed the stairs slowly. Lee felt for her, losing trust in someone she had obviously cared about and relied on, just when she needed support the most.

Chapter 53

Lee

Lee watched Emmerling labor up the stairs. She felt Seth's hand on her back. Trrk stood close on her other side. They'd done it. The invitation was delivered. She should feel like celebrating. But they couldn't rest yet. Around them the others shifted uncertainly, trying to make sense of the evening.

"Trrk," Seth said. "Watch Vinz. Make sure he stays here."

"Be assured he will not leave without escort."

"Thanks," Lee said. She took a firm hold on Seth's hand and went to Adel and Whip. "Are you two okay, going with Joe? I can try and get him to leave you in your room here."

"It's all right," Adel said. "Better do what the PAO wants. At least everything is coming out now. And I have Will back."

"Come on, then." Lee crossed to Joe. "They're ready to go," she said.

Joe nodded. "Doc, would you take Adel and Whip back to town with you and keep them under wraps until I get there?"

"I can do that. And I'll run that scan for rod use on Adel while I have her."

"Good," Adel said. "I want that evidence on the books."

"We'll get you and Whip off the hook." Lee could hardly believe she was worried about them. It had been a day of changes.

"Can we drop the nickname?" Adel said. "He's Will. And he's not off my hook."

Lee did something she hadn't thought she'd ever do. She hugged Adel and meant it. Adel hugged her back and whispered, "So much could have been different."

Lee chuckled. "But it wasn't." She stepped back. "Whip — Will — I still think you're a waste of space, but Adel has different ideas so prove me wrong."

"Why don't you and Seth use my room here tonight," Adel offered. "Or do you have other plans?"

"Trrk's with us," Seth said. "Maybe Fallen Pine?"

Joe put his arm over his son's shoulders. "The three of you are coming home. Where I can keep an eye on you."

"But what about Kiri?" Lee asked.

"I don't keep secrets from my wife. She knows about Trrk. And I'll warn her we're coming."

"What do you think?" Lee asked Seth.

"Security, a whirltub, and a real bed," Joe said.

"I'm sold," Seth said.

"Good. Get loaded up and head home. Kiri will be expecting you. You did manage to keep track of the old Steadhand?"

"Safe and sound. Along with a couple horses," Seth answered.

"Leave them here. You can collect them tomorrow."

"Along with two at Tobin, and our gear if we can even find it." Lee tucked herself in against Seth.

"Worry about that later," Joe said. "Get out of here. And Adel and Whip, go with Doc. He'll keep you safe for now. I've got my old friend Ro to deal with."

"You need help?" Seth asked.

"Kieron will go with us."

"Speaking of Dougherty," Lee said. "I'd better have a word before we go."

"Do it then."

Dougherty waited off to the side of the room. Lee and Seth joined him.

"Why is it you two always cause me more grief than any other five riders put together?" he said with a grin.

"You probably won't have to worry about that for a while," Lee said.

"Not coming back to the Wells?"

"I'm afraid I'm going to be tied up with this. I can't speak for Seth." She squeezed his hand, hoping that wasn't entirely true.

"I figured," Dougherty said. "But you do owe me a briefing on what you and Ike found before things got whirly."

"I managed to hang onto the recorder with my notes. I'm not sure about our map. It's in the packs if we can find them." The packs. Scorch it. So many loose ends. "I can fill in most of that from memory though. Ike said it might be good seasonal country for tarbh. It's great for nutgrass." Such a relief to be able to talk about something straightforward, but she couldn't ignore some realities. "Boss, I'm sorry about Ike."

"Me too. Look, we'll have time to talk about your trip later. Quite a bomb you dropped on us tonight."

"We'll tell you the whole story one day."

"I'll hold you to that." He turned to Seth. "Any idea when you'll be going back to Rock House?"

"No, sorry," Seth answered. "I guess I can say goodbye to my garden for this year."

"No worries. I left two riders there, in case you showed up. They're keeping it watered and doing some scouting for a new headquarters while they're in the neighborhood."

"Thanks. I'll get things set up as soon as I can so they can go back to the Wells."

"No hurry. Now, you two get going. Your friend is waiting for you. Never been so surprised in my life."

"He's good people," Seth said with a smile.

"I'm glad you two are okay. And back together."

Lee leaned against Seth. "Right and tight."

"See you tomorrow."

Lee and Seth joined Trrk. Joe had taken custody of

Vinz, leaving the Kelok on his own. Lee could see the toll the day had taken on him. Time to get him and themselves somewhere they could rest.

They headed out the back, stopping in the mud room for Lee to pull on boots. Outside in the rain-clean air she paused at the edge of the woods in the dark to shake off her nerves.

"Eta'ak would be proud," Trrk said with a bob of his head. "You bore her words well."

"I can't imagine Emmerling not agreeing to meet. She certainly is good under pressure. Barely batted an eye when she saw you." Lee straightened an out-of-place feather on Trrk's arm.

"Let us go," Trrk said. "I am exhausted."

Seth laughed. "Anyone who disturbs any of us before noon tomorrow might not survive."

They helped Trrk into the cargo bed of the old skimmer, and Seth climbed into the cab with Lee. "Are you going back to work at the Wells?" he asked.

"I am still on the books," she said. "But I'm afraid we aren't done with diplomatic affairs yet."

"Think we can set them aside for one night?"

"Okay, for one night. Just you and me and a real bed."

Chapter 54

Eta'ak

By the time the sun dropped near the western horizon on the First-Comers' Settlement Day, Eta'ak longed for the days before she had learned of the pending survey. All those from Village of Rushes and Village of Grasses had arrived in Village of Lichens before dawn, forty-four adults and thirty-seven children filling up the plaza. After a night of travel most females and children slept through the day, if restlessly. The males disappeared behind the walls of the men's quarters to sleep or plan or whatever they did out of sight of the females.

On the rare occasions Eta'ak allowed herself to look around from her monitoring station, Prime's eyes immediately froze on her. And the broadcasts still had no word of missing riders or a found alien or unusual activities by the planetary administrative officer. Just celebrations somewhat overshadowed, if Eta'ak remembered previous years correctly, by uncertainty about the upcoming evaluation.

Tired, hungry, and fearful of what was to come, Eta'ak finally left her post to get the food and water she couldn't request. Wordlessly, one of Second's hunters slipped into her place to watch the broadcasts. She balanced between relief and annoyance. She would have taken care of her needs sooner if she'd known someone would take her place.

The male relinquished the monitoring station when she returned, again without a word. But his eyes were properly lowered, telling her she still had some status. Or maybe it was just long ingrained respect to females.

Before dark, males placed shielded lights in the back of the cavern where they would not show from a sky view. They screened Eta'ak's station near the front with mats and blankets to hold in what little light the viewscreen produced. The shielding overlapped leaving a gap for access while revealing little light. Through it she could hear the clans coming to the kitchen area nearby for food, visiting, and trying to keep the children to the back of the village. She felt like a hatchling peeking out the first split in a shell.

But that image was far too hopeful when the very air smelled of fear. Just a hint of where her spouse and the envoys were — that was all she desired. Some small shard to suggest they might still succeed before all devolved into conflict beyond resolution.

Those from Village of Reeds trailed in as the broadcasts of the First-Comers' celebrations closed out and only the few overnight entertainments continued. The port status board showed the ship bearing the satellite array parked in orbit to await the return to business on the morrow.

At last, her clan from Village of Canes arrived. The sound of familiar voices should have cheered her, but they were not directed at her. Except two, those who had been her spouses. Though she couldn't see them, she heard them. They settled in just outside of her enclosure and spoke with grumbles about the difficulties of relocating. Soothed by their presence, she set the monitoring to alert her to the usual key messaging, curled up, and tried to sleep.

Chapter 55

Seth

Seth sat on a stool at the kitchen counter, a tall glass of cool roundfruit juice at hand. He had missed fruit juice. On the other side of the counter, his pa was busy fixing a big breakfast with Kiri's help. Kiri, who Seth had ridden with at Seven Wells before she'd met Joe, with her thatch of dark red hair, deep brown eyes, a splatter of freckles, and now a belly round with his half-brother.

"What?" she asked.

"Just thinking, Mom."

"Don't 'mom' me. I'm not that old." She flashed a smile. It was a standing joke between them.

"Happy?" he asked.

"Now," she said. "With you and Lee here."

She and his pa had their shared-kitchen dance down. They rarely passed each other without Joe's hand laying on Kiri's belly and both smiling. The big house might get a little crowded when the baby arrived. Good thing he would be back in his own place soon. Maybe. Lots of loose ends still to tie off.

Lee stood with Kieron Dougherty behind the big dining table where a map of Carico's settlements west of the Mardukai River covered the wall. Lee traced out the route she and Ike Allred had followed across the plateau to Stampede Spring. She left off there. That was where she had been captured by Trrk and his hunters. She had promised Eta'ak not to share the details of the Kelok settlements. That was for the Keloks to reveal.

Trrk lounged on a couch in the living room where he could see everything. He had insisted he would rest better there than hidden away somewhere. A Kelok was rarely alone. Trrk must be missing his clan brothers' support.

Kiri leaned on the counter across from Seth, her eyes on Lee in animated conversation with Dougherty about something she had observed on her travels. "Are you two going to be okay?"

"Hard to say," Seth said honestly. "So much is up in the air. But I intend to find some way to make it work."

"Does she know what she's going to do?"

He grinned crookedly. "We have a diplomatic meeting to set up. At least I hope so. After that, all I'm sure of is she won't be at Rock House with me full time."

"And you? Is Rock House still your dream?"

"It was never more than something to do while I waited."

She patted his shoulder. "Joe would be thrilled if you two settled at Fallen Pine."

He shook his head. "Too far from the action."

"Well, we can hope, can't we?"

"Hey, Seth," Lee called. "What happened to that data pendent? Is it still in my saddlebags?"

"You're asking me?" But he got to his feet. "I'll look." He trotted up the stairs to his childhood bedroom. He paused to remember the night before, their first together in a real bed since he had left Seven Wells a year earlier. They would find a way to make it work.

The little recorder was in the very bottom of one of Lee's saddlebags, wrapped up with Ike's journal. He left the little book and took the recorder downstairs.

She met him at the bottom of the stairs with a thank you kiss.

"Going to share the images Eta'ak added?" he asked.

"Later. With the administrator. Sales pitch."

Seth took over the kitchen to make sure Trrk had a good selection of food. Joe Reilly made his own sausage. Seth didn't recognize the spice blend in this batch, but it caught Trrk's attention along with the seared strips of tarbh loin. "Hey, Trrk, do you want spinxi eggs with this?" he asked. They hadn't seen any spinxi at Village of Canes.

"Eggs?" Trrk's crest flared. "I believe I will not. It seems too near to ..." A shudder ran through his down. "Our females lay eggs."

Oops. "Sorry. Sausage and loin strips it is."

"Just what I require," Trrk said. The Kelok did look

more alert. "Food and knowing you are representing me in the discussions. When will your female meet with the administrator?"

"Later today. Lee is sure that the PAO will accept the invitation. Then it is up to her and Prime." If Prime showed up. But Seth kept that uncertainty to himself. He'd half-forgotten that they were still envoys only because no official word from Prime ever reached them. Thanks to Second taking care to not see what was nearly in front of him.

Seth joined the group sitting down at the table for breakfast and tried not to stuff himself on the bounty. Lee sat next to him, her leg firmly against his while she talked with Dougherty about plans to expand JT Land and Livestock holdings, the reason for her and Ike's trip in the first place. Across from him, Kiri resisted Joe's encouragement to eat more.

Boots on the porch interrupted. "Now who can that be?" Kiri asked.

The door opened and a little boy toddled in. He looked at the people at the table and then saw Trrk on the couch. He cocked his head in curiosity and headed that way. Trrk stayed very still as the boy reached up and stroked his tail above the injury.

"Davy," Joe said. "Say 'hi' to Trrk,"

"Tuk." Davy moved on to explore Trrk's feet.

"What under the moons!" A young woman came in the open door and rushed to scoop up her son. "Dad, what are you thinking, letting him play with, with whatever this is?" She stopped then, her eyes flitting between Trrk and the table. "Seth! And Lee. Why am I not surprised?"

"Hi, sis." Seth got up. "Hi, Davy."

"Uncs." The boy squirmed to get down.

"Gwyn, meet our friend Trrk. Trrk, this is my sister and her son, Davy."

Trrk rose slowly. "I am pleased to meet my clan brother's sibling. And the boy child."

Seth couldn't figure out what Gwyn was thinking. She probably hadn't figured that out herself. "You can sit," he told Trrk.

Gwyn focused on Seth. "So, you're home."

"Right and tight," he said.

"And with her."

Gwyn had never liked Lee, even less so after he and Lee had split up a year ago.

"Morning, Gwyn," Joe said. "What brings you over early?"

"I, uh, I was going to ask Kiri to watch Davy for a couple hours. The comm site on Snowstorm is down again. I didn't realize you had a houseful."

Kiri got up from the table. "We were going to fill you in this evening at dinner. Or didn't you get our blip?"

"Yeah. And we plan to come. But Nick's helping his mom with something this morning."

"Well, we'd be happy to look after Davy."

"But —"

Seth lifted Davy from her arms and set him on the floor. He immediately trotted back to Trrk. "He'll be fine, sis. Like I said, Trrk is a friend. Now, can I at least get a homecoming hug?"

"Oh, Seth." She hugged him tight although her eyes

never left her son. "Why can't you just settle down where we know you're okay?"

"I'm sorry you worried."

"You are sure Davy's okay with ... what did you say his name is?"

"Trrk. And Davy is safe."

"I would defend the young one with my life," Trrk said. Davy was on the couch with him, checking out his downy feathers.

"He means it," Seth said.

"Go take care of your comm site," Joe said. "But keep quiet about our guest for now. Administrator Emmerling will be here this afternoon for some high-level diplomatic talks."

"Yeah, sure. Why can't I have a nice, normal family?"

"You do," Joe said. "Or at least you were smart enough to marry into one." Her father-in-law was his second in command at the marshal's office, and married to Lee's Aunt Teri.

"Yes, I did." Gwyn tore her eyes from her son. "Kiri, anything you need for Davy?"

"All set," Kiri said. "As always. Now go so you can finish and get off that peak before the afternoon storms."

"Okay, okay. And Seth, you will be here when I get back?"

"I'll be here for dinner. Promise."

"Davy, baby, you stay here. I'll be back in a while. Bye, bye."

Davy was too busy learning about feathers to pay attention.

"Not like you don't leave him here all the time," Joe pointed out. Gwyn left in a rush, like she needed the momentum to get out the door.

"That is the perfect picture to introduce Trrk to Carico," Joe said, nodding to the Kelok and the toddler together on the couch.

Chapter 56

Seth

Not long after breakfast, Charlyn Emmerling arrived at the Reilly house. Seth joined the group at the dining table, but it was Lee's show. He planned to sit back and listen. Joe and Dougherty sat across from Lee and him. Emmerling sat at one end of the table, and Trrk sat at the other, mostly because that gave him room for his healing tail. Kiri sat on the couch, trying to keep Davy busy.

"I couldn't have a better group of advisors if I was in Portside," Emmerling said.

"The mining districts might disagree," Dougherty said.

"All the districts will get their turn," she said. "But last night I was presented with a unique invitation." She nodded to Lee. "I don't see how I can refuse to open communications with Trrk's people. I can hardly brief the General Assembly without firsthand knowledge of the Kelok. Is that the correct name?"

"As good as a human can do," Lee said.

"I trust you are satisfied with the honesty of the request."

Seth felt Lee tense next to him. "It is honest," she said. "Admittedly not all of them agree about making contact with us, but they will follow Prime. She was their ship's captain."

"They follow a military hierarchy?" Emmerling asked.

Lee looked at Trrk for his okay before going ahead. "Not anymore. Each clan selects a representative to their council, and each representative has an equal voice but, in practice, old ways persist. People listen to those who were ship's officers."

"So Prime is the force behind making contact now."

"Actually no," Lee said. "She doesn't like the idea. But she understands the need, and she did agree to the plan."

"You and I must talk at length before the meeting," Emmerling said. "I need your insight and Trrk's, if he'll agree."

"Of course. We're here to help," Lee said. She took Seth's hand under the table, and he gave it a squeeze. She went on. "Their culture reflects their extreme sexual dimorphism, almost like two species. As a male Trrk stands at my back as escort and advisor rather than in front."

"Subordinate?" Emmerling asked. "My apologies if that question is rude."

"More a division of roles. I have observed that the males are fully able to influence outcomes." She held up the data pendant. "We have pictures of some of the daily life."

Emmerling's face lit up. But she shook her head. "Later. We have things to do first. How do I notify them that I will attend? And where am I going?"

"They will be monitoring our news broadcasts," Lee said. She couldn't help but smile at the expressions of shock and surprise around the table. "Any time Damele is in the sky, they can pick up our broadcasts."

"A comm relay on the moon," Emmerling said.

"They set it up before they grounded. It probably needs maintenance."

Seth admired Lee's grasp of things as she set up that possible negotiating point — transport up to maintain it in trade for bandwidth maybe. It would virtually double Carico's satellite communications capability. She would be wasted if she went back to riding at Seven Wells.

"They are expecting to meet no more than eight days from the time the invitation was delivered. You don't have to address them directly," Lee added. "A news release about a meeting with castaways will do it."

"No, no." Emmerling shook her head. "This must be done formally. We have a message to craft. I'll record it so we can add visuals and broadcast it this evening."

"If that's what you want."

"And where is this meeting to take place?"

"Neutral ground, far from any settlements," Lee said. "The big rock where Seth buried Ike Allred."

"The middle of nowhere," Seth said.

"Truly. But fair, I suppose. As long as you don't expect me to get there on the back of a horse." She smiled. "All right. Let's get busy then. I will need to forewarn the district arbiters and a few individuals before my broadcast. Notification to the Sol Terra Alliance can wait, I think, until I have spoken with Prime and better understand the situation."

"The Kelok are not looking for recognition by the Alliance or the Coalition," Lee said. "Not yet anyway."

"Keep it local? I can't promise how long we can do that."

"As I remember the First Contact statutes, the new species must request recognition and can control the extent of contact." Lee had done her homework.

"Make a note to discuss that when we meet. We will want to establish their status and that will depend largely on what they want." Emmerling looked around the table. "But before we talk more about that, I'd like an update on the survey issues. Marshal, I expect you are following up on the alleged sabotage?"

"I'll conduct interviews this morning and see where it takes us."

"Good. We need to resolve that quickly. The satellites will be ready to deploy any time now," she said.

"I know," Joe said. "But after Vinz's admission last night, I'm hoping we can clear Verlane so we can let her get on with the project."

"That would be for the best," Emmerling said. She

lifted her chin and squared her shoulders. "Now I would like some time with our three Kelok experts if Trrk feels up to it? We can gather in the living room."

"Trrk?" Lee asked.

"As Administrator wishes," he said.

"If it is acceptable to you, please call me Charlyn. We are not a formal people."

Trrk bowed his head in a nod. "We are. However, I will try to adapt."

"Boss," Lee said, "do you want to sit in?"

Dougherty shook his head. "I'll leave the high-level talks to you. But I'll be around if you need me."

Seth found the morning difficult. Finally, he excused himself. Trrk had the synthesizer, so he didn't need a translator, and Seth felt that fewer voices were better. They were still treading a narrow path. Emmerling needed a certain amount of knowledge, but they had committed to preserving the Keloks' privacy. It would be Prime's choice, in the course of negotiations, how much to reveal and when.

Kiri and Dougherty had retreated to the front porch where a pleasant breeze kept the morning from being uncomfortably hot. Davy was playing in the yard under Kiri's watchful eyes.

Seth joined them with an offering of iced tea.

"Too much talk?" Kiri asked.

"Too many people. Not much I can add to what Lee and Trrk will say."

"I just keep losing good riders," Dougherty said. "Kiri, it's a sure bet that you're not coming back. And I'll really miss Ike. Now it looks like Lee will be off on another trail.

What about you, Seth?"

"Hard to tell what I'll be doing."

"JT hasn't given up the idea of a new stead," Dougherty said. "And I still think that basin near your place is the perfect headquarters."

"What are you suggesting?"

"I get the feeling that your castaways are actually a pretty well-established settlement, and I'm thinking that, however the negotiations work out, there will be trade opportunities."

Seth let that sink in. "Five Canyons — that's what Lee and Ike called the basin — it's not that close to Trrk's people."

"But Ike's Rock and what you call Stampede Spring must be. Lee called that neutral ground. Perfect for a trade site."

"And you think Johannesson and Tecknir would be interested?" he asked. They owned several enterprises on Carico in addition to Seven Wells.

"They have an eye for opportunities. Especially if one of the two experts on our new neighbors is involved."

"Are you offering me a job?"

"Something to think about. If they go ahead with Five Canyons."

Seth smiled. He liked working for Dougherty. He'd only left because he and Lee had split. "You know," he said, "the Keloks distill a fine drink from buttonweed."

"JT makes some excellent wines. And it looks like the Keloks have weavers."

"And rawhide braiders." He held out his arm to show

off the bracelet Trrk had made.

"And medical knowledge," Kiri added. "Trrk asked me to cook up a batch of that lichen for his tail."

"So, not only do we snuff plans to sabotage the survey, we potentially add new development, technology, and resources to help meet the milestones." Seth leaned back and propped his feet on the porch rail. "No wonder the PAO was so ready to accept the invitation."

Chapter 57

Lee

Lee met Joe and Dougherty on the porch when they came back from town, where Joe had been interviewing Adel, Whip, and Vinz. Dougherty had gone along to try and track down the missing packs and gear.

"What did Vinz say?" she asked.

"What can he say after his admission last night? He stands by thinking what he intended was in Carico's best interests." Joe shook his head. "*Properly exploit potential* was how he put it."

Lee vividly remembered Jerdix saying that exact thing. Still ... "I hate to be the voice from the void, but is he right?" She looked to the two men for a lifetime of insight she didn't have. "Has Carico been too slow to develop?" The lack of reliable communications had bothered her since she had first gotten on world.

Dougherty rubbed at his face. "Maybe. To a point. Maybe we should take this as a wake up. Except for the mining industry, we've avoided importing technology we can't maintain or build here. But we also chose to limit our impact. I think a lot of us like it that way."

"I expect the presence of Trrk and his people will jolt some of us into new ideas. This fall's General Assembly should be interesting." Joe grinned.

"If we can count the Keloks toward some of the milestones, it'll help us out," Dougherty said. "I do hope we can settle things with them here before the Coalition wants to talk recognition."

"Poor Ro," Joe said. "To have his whole plan discovered and to lose out on laying the foundation of relations with a new species, all in one night."

"I never guessed he was so ambitious," Dougherty said. "But I always wondered why he didn't push you to deal with your suspension, Lee. I tried to make up for the support I thought he should have given you."

"She was always a threat," Joe said. "When she came here undercover, he had to make sure she didn't succeed in finding out what Jerdix really had in mind."

"You think Jerdix knew all along what I was there to do?" Lee hadn't considered that possibility.

"I would guess Ro told him. No wonder Jerdix seemed to go to lengths to parade his control of you — of your 'Anni' persona — in front of me."

"Can we not get into all of that?" she asked.

"Sure." Joe laid a hand on her shoulder. "Just tell me you and my son are going to be okay."

"Yes." She nodded. "We're good. I mean except for needing a few days without sleeping on the ground and eating trail rations." She caught the look he gave her. "Oh, you mean 'us'. We're right and tight."

"Good."

"And you don't owe Seven Wells for those missing packs and gear." Dougherty's mahogany face wrinkled in a laugh. "Ro told us where to find it. We brought it with us. Including your boots and one lone sock."

Joe grinned. "We took the liberty of stopping by the store for new boots for both you and Seth. Yours looked too far gone. We figured his looked about the same."

"Thanks." She couldn't argue with that. "And the boots I borrowed?"

"I left those at Lickskillet just as you asked," Joe assured her.

"It was Ike's place, wasn't it?"

"A long time ago."

"He would want to be buried there, next to his wife," Dougherty said.

"You knew his past?" Lee asked.

"Some, but I never knew why he left Under Rim. Or why he never came back."

Joe frowned. "He made some decisions on the heels of the pandemic that I guess he found hard to live with. Best let the past lie."

"Lee, Lickskillet is yours, you know," Dougherty said. "Ike left everything to you."

"He what?"

"I had a letter on file to be opened on the occasion of his death. All his possessions go to Lee Vawn-Cory who reminded him every day he knew her of his late wife, Lori."

Lee let that sink in. "I read a little of his journal," she said. "We were finally beginning to get along when..." she let that hang. "Horses. What about the horses?"

"You did leave a few scattered in your wake," Joe said. "I had a deputy collect the two at the guest house. They're at the livery in town. The two at Tobin should be fine for a few days."

"Boss, we lost Pokey. He broke a leg in the stampede." She hadn't actually seen that. Trrk had told her.

"Sorry to hear that," Dougherty said. "Ike had used him and Tinker for a long time."

"I know." She pulled herself back to the present. "What about Adel?"

"She'll be free to go after Emmerling's announcement tonight," Joe said. "I'll have to hold Willemsen. He did leave his restitution detail without authorization. You seemed on pretty good terms with them both."

"Who'd believe that?"

"She's truly been worried about you."

"I guess she really was. You know, I think she'll do a good job filling in behind Vinz while they sort out how to replace him." Vinz. She still had trouble grasping that. "Seth said something about a visitor Adel had, a man Whip had seen with Jerdix. Henry?" That piece Lee hadn't been able to figure out.

Joe shook his head. "I'll keep working on that one, but Adel said Vinz had her give him proprietary information about the survey. She thought he was from the PAO's office."

"Could even be legitimate. The PAO connection should be easy enough to check," Dougherty said.

"Willemsen said he'd seen him with Jerdix back when." Joe frowned. "But not everyone Jerdix dealt with was a crook."

"What'll happen to Vinz?" Lee asked.

Joe shook his head. "The survey programming is probably an administrative issue since it was discovered before any damage was done. Unless the PAO wants to push it, which I doubt. Even so, his career with the Rangers is certainly over. Central Services will dig into his background for any connection to Emerging Territories, but I think Lee nailed it. Jerdix got to him."

"What about the rod?" Lee shivered at the thought of it.

"Doc's scans showed Adel had experienced minimal use. Surprisingly Vinz showed none."

"He was pretty vocal with his opinion of Jerdix and his addiction when that came out," Dougherty said.

Joe shrugged. "Possession alone will get him some serious rehabilitation time."

"What about Whip — Will?" Lee asked. "Adel thinks he's redeemable."

Joe grinned. "He may get an extension of his restitution detail, because of his escape, but he was sharp enough to pick up on the skewed algorithms. Let him clean that up. And he knows his way around Carico.

He can help with survey validation. A good mentor seems to be what he needs."

"Is that what Adel is?" Lee chuckled.

"Assuming she gets a temporary promotion, that'll leave the survey lead open for you," Joe said.

"I have a job." Lee looked at Dougherty.

"Got to admit that the Rangers always had first claim on you," Dougherty said. "But I think Charlyn is going to need your help for a while."

"She and Trrk's people both. Until this first meeting." Lee's head was spinning with the options. "After that, we'll just have to see." Seth came first. This time.

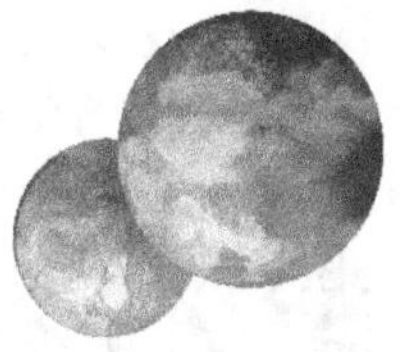

Joe called the whole family together for dinner. Lee and Seth spent lots of time assuring everyone they were okay. At least Trrk's presence was a distraction. Hard as Gwyn tried to keep Davy close at hand where he was used to running free, it was impossible to keep him away from his new friend.

"Let him go," Kiri told her gently. "He'll be fine. Or go with him and have a talk with Trrk. He doesn't bite."

"He looks like he could," Gwyn answered. But, to Lee's surprise, she took Kiri's advice.

Seth managed to get Lee aside while the steaks grilled. She didn't know what to say to him. So much was happening; so many changes coming at them. But he just put his arms around her and watched the activity. "One day at a time," he told her. "And know another will come along."

After they ate, as the sun dropped toward the ridge to the west, Emmerling set up to record a broadcast for Carico. She had already sent blips to all the district representatives in the General Assembly to let them know that she had been contacted by some non-human castaways who wanted to meet, that they should watch the broadcast for more, and that she would be in touch with each of them in the next few days.

"This is too sensitive to do live," she said. "Let's make sure it's perfect before we release it."

She directed Dougherty to a storage bin in her van for the necessary equipment. They had worked with Trrk on the script for the broadcast. Emmerling planned to edit in images that Eta'ak had recorded of daily life in the Village of Canes. And Trrk had even agreed, reluctantly, to appear on camera. Lee thought that was mostly so Eta'ak would see him and know he was okay.

"Ready," Vinz said.

"Trrk, where's Trrk." Lee looked around the yard for him. He'd been resting as much as possible, though he seemed glad to be surrounded by activity. She spotted him stretched out under a nearby tree with Davy curled against him, worn out by the day's excitement.

"Get that," Emmerling said quietly to Dougherty. He turned the camera on the pair before Gwyn ran in to collect her son and free Trrk to join them.

"Okay, let's do this." Emmerling took her place against the backdrop of her van.

Chapter 58

Eta'ak

Eta'ak wondered how they had all lived in this one cavern, back in their first days on this world. The village was awash in clamor and the tang of many bodies. Not enough space for looms or martial arts that gave people focus and calm. Back then, at the beginning, one hundred thirty-nine of them had sought a way to exist. Now there were ninety-nine adults. No, ninety-eight with Trrk absent. And the children, sixty males and twenty-one of the precious females that represented their hope for the future. If they survived the next few days and weeks.

All through the long day after the First-Comers'

celebration day, Eta'ak huddled in her enclosure, more and more grateful for its shelter from the fear and the anxiety beyond. Late in the afternoon, she heard Second's voice speaking with those who had been her spouses, assigning them to protect the monitoring station. That sign of support made her smile for the first time in days.

Still no word of Trrk or the envoys but also none regarding deployment of the satellites that would reveal them to the First-Comers. They could not hide forever in the one cavern. Food had to be gathered and hunted. The fungus gardens at the other villages needed tending. And adults and children alike needed activity. Crowded together, fear fed on fear, anger on anger. She was glad of the presence of two males to discourage those who would pour that out in her direction. She was the one who had sought a solution, to give them some control over their future, but now she was the messenger to be blamed for the message.

A tray of food appeared in the entrance to her enclosure as the sun's light began to fade. Eta'ak turned aside from the viewscreen to eat what was provided, little as it was. Supplies were tightly rationed. They were under siege by ones who didn't even know of their existence. Yet.

The light in her booth changed. She looked to the screen. All the images from all the feeds coalesced into one uniform feed — Planetary Administrative Officer Emmerling with the envoys at her back.

Eta'ak drew a long breath and watched Administrator Emmerling accept the invitation to meet and the images of Kelok village life displayed for all of Carico to see. Emmerling confirmed the time and place for the meeting over a backdrop of Trrk — beloved Trrk — with a human child snuggled in the curl of his tail. A tail that to Eta'ak seemed oddly short.

Eta'ak set the segment up to replay in a loop. "Remove the barrier," she said. "Everyone must see."

"What?" Second appeared in the opening.

"The invitation is accepted." Eta'ak was careful to speak to the rock wall to not offend Second.

"The barrier," he said. In the corner of her eye, she saw him helping pull back the mats, revealing the screen to the cavern.

And Prime was there with all her people gathered around her. Would she refuse to acknowledge the acceptance? Would everything Eta'ak, with Trrk and the two humans, had tried to achieve for her people come to naught?

Eta'ak turned up the volume and started the replay, standing aside to show the First-Comers' leader. Few of the Kelok had ever seen her, a short, stout human with skin as dark as their own females. Eta'ak let the message play through twice, then froze it on that final image of Trrk with the child. She could do no more. It was in Prime's hands now.

The cavern erupted into confusion. When they had been gathered together, it seemed all hope of peaceful resolution had gone. Yet now it reemerged. The cacophony echoed off the rocks and filled the space. In the midst, Prime stood as a statue.

"Here," a voice said in Eta'ak's ear. Second handed

her a folded stole of office and a copy of the printed invitation to the PAO. Puzzled, she took them.

"For Prime, to remind her of her decision." Second lowered his eyes respectfully, as if she were not an outcast.

Eta'ak strode through the villagers. They turned aside from her, clearing her path to Prime. On the screen behind her, the PAO's acceptance replayed. Saying nothing, Eta'ak held the stole and document out to Prime and waited.

Chapter 59

Lee

Lee waited with Seth and Trrk on the undulating plateau on a sunny morning. It had been eight days since Settlement Day, since they had finally reached Emmerling. "You really think Prime will come?" she asked.

"Have faith in my spouse," Trrk said. But his crest ruffled, and his tail twitched restlessly.

Lee walked off. They had gone over it all before, many times, in the days since extending the invitation to Administrator Emmerling. But they had kept that fear between the three of them.

Eta'ak had accomplished much in getting Lee and

Seth to Blue Canyon in the first place, in overcoming cultural prohibitions so they could use the hearing facilitation devices and begin to communicate, and in positioning Prime to agree to meet with the PAO. All that was left was for her to bring Prime to this meeting. After that, it was up to Prime and Emmerling.

Lee placed her hands on the lone boulder at the edge of a depression covered with chartreuse nutgrass and verdigris soil. Ike's body was gone, reclaimed from the earth when searchers had found him. She had been at his old stead three days ago when they had reburied him beside his long-dead wife. "Old man, you were right," she whispered, "about Seth and me. We couldn't have gotten through this without each other." She climbed up to perch atop the rock.

Emmerling's van sat out of sight in a swale to the east. Trrk had assured them that, when the time came, she could arrive at the meeting site by skimmer. Right now, the skimmer mimicked a second boulder on the landscape close by. In the back were the makings of an awning and an assortment of seating. Lee teetered between wanting to start setting things up for the meeting and abiding by Trrk's advice to let a Kelok delegation take the lead on preparations since they had issued the invitation.

If they ever showed up. They hadn't had any direct message from Blue Canyon, just Trrk's assurance that a delegation would arrive before midday to set up for a late afternoon meeting as he and Second had planned back at Village of Canes two cycles of Damele — just sixteen days — earlier. Trrk said this first meeting would mostly be a chance to exchange pleasantries and feel things out before getting down to business the next morning. Kelok invitation. Kelok protocols.

Trrk, still recovering from the stink bear bite, moved restlessly, pacing out possible places for the awning. Lee was certain the amputation of part of his tail disturbed him deeply. Maybe he had confided in Seth but never to her. Among the fiercely ritualistic, hierarchical Kelok males, what would it cost him?

Seth got to his feet and began the batayr martial arts form. He had done that a lot in the last few days and, as had become routine, Trrk joined him. The Kelok was making progress on a style poorly suited to him physically. When they reached the end of what he knew, they switched to the Kelok style where Seth was seriously limited by his total lack of a tail.

It kept them busy and calm. Lee was tempted to join them, but it made Trrk uncomfortable. Kelok females did not practice the forms.

Lee had tried to explain the gender differences to Emmerling. In many ways, the Keloks were two species, one predatory hunters who expressed their competitive natures in ritualized combat and the other growers and weavers and planners. But the PAO would have to see for herself before it began to sink in.

Lee stood up on the boulder. A band of Kelok males crested the rim of the wide depression. "There," she called out and pointed. "They're coming."

Seth came and gave her a hand down. She carried a synthesizer so they would be able to understand what was said. Emmerling had a second one, built from Seth's hearing facilitation device.

Trrk stared at the approaching hunters, keeping his tail tucked out of sight beneath him. "I should not have come. They will not acknowledge me."

"Your injury?" Lee asked.

He bobbed his head. "And I betrayed Prime when I warned you that she would rescind her support for making contact. I must be outcast now."

"Why didn't you say something sooner," Seth asked.

"My intent was to face them and accept whatever punishment they decreed, but now I know that must not interfere with the meeting."

"Seth." Lee laid her hand on his arm. "It's up to you to talk to them. It's one of those male things. I can't help, but maybe Trrk can stand back with me as my escort. Okay?"

Trrk bobbed his head slowly. "That should suffice for now."

"You owe me for this," Seth told Trrk. "I never figured on being the lead here."

"Speak now as Administrator's representative," Trrk said. He moved behind Lee. His crest told Lee how uneasy he was.

Seth went forward to meet the Keloks. In the lead trotted Second, Prime's spouse and the highest ranking Kelok male. Lee was relieved to see he wore a hearing facilitator.

"We have come," he said. The synthesizer translated his rasping phrase, and he started.

"Welcome." Seth bowed his head. Then he held up the synthesizer. "We added a speaker to one of the facilitation devices so we can understand any of you who speak within its range."

"Convenient," Second said. "Where is Trrk? Where is the one who abandoned his people?"

"Trrk assisted me — his clan brother — and my spouse — his clan sister — to deliver Prime's message," Seth said. "Today he escorts my spouse."

Second's crest flared. "His answering will wait. Now we prepare for leaders to meet."

"We brought some things you can use to set up."

"We have come prepared. What things would you contribute?" Second followed Seth to the skimmer.

"Items for the comfort of the leaders." Seth showed him the awning and seats.

The rest of the Keloks laid down the rolled mats they carried. Lee recognized one from Village of Canes. He wasn't one of Trrk's co-spouses. The other three were strangers. She guessed that, including Second, there was one from each of the five villages.

Trrk edged around the boulder from Seth and Second and pointed with his beak. A lone female crossed the depression. "Eta'ak?" she asked. The Kelok female walked across the dusty ground with her body forward to balance her stout tail, her face a mask of black, her tail fan tightly closed.

Trrk bobbed his head.

"Can we go to her?" Lee asked.

He bobbed his head again and crowded after her eagerly but stayed behind her until they had passed the males. Then he ran ahead, his tail raised behind him.

Lee hung back and gave the couple time. When Trrk

tried to hide his tail away, Eta'ak reached out for it and handled the stump gently. Then she carefully groomed his arm feathers into place and waved to Lee with the fanned tip of her tail.

Trrk raised the end of his tail to her as she approached.

Eta'ak cradled the stub and pointed to it. Lee looked closely. He hadn't let anyone but Doc near it. "It's regenerating!" She reached out a finger and didn't quite touch the ring of new flesh under the peeling temp skin.

Trrk bobbed his head rapidly.

"I'm so glad," Lee told Eta'ak. "I've been worried."

Eta'ak touched the hearing facilitator around her neck and pointed to Lee.

Lee held up the synthesizer. "We adapted the facilitator so it broadcasts the translation."

"Your technicians discovered how," Eta'ak said. Her face flashed purple. "We have such for monitoring broadcasts."

"Trrk told us. He has been a huge help in spite of being badly injured."

"The lack of familiar tools was a challenge." Trrk stood just behind Eta'ak's shoulder with his eyes respectfully lowered like any good Kelok male, but Lee didn't miss that their tails entwined.

"He saved Seth from a stink bear," Lee said. "But he needed medical treatment, so we had to take him with us."

"There will be time for your story later," Eta'ak said. "Now the meeting between leaders is the important thing."

"After what Trrk told us, we weren't sure Prime would come."

"She did not believe your leader would listen to you after the Ranger assaulted your credibility. She was surprised when you succeeded."

"Administrator Emmerling is eager to meet Prime."

"Then you have portrayed Prime sympathetically?"

"Of course. You said yourself that the events have not been easy for her. I can't blame her for wanting to hold on to whatever normality she can for all of you."

"She has seen the ship in the night sky and listened to the broadcasts about the satellite array to be released. She understands."

"And you?" Lee asked. "Will she listen to you now?"

"No more than is needed. She could not banish me and lose a reproductive female. I believe she intends to remove me as an influence by assigning me as liaison to your people."

"What about your family?" Lee knew she had two spouses in addition to Trrk as well as a small daughter and probably sons. The males raised the male children, so she wasn't sure how many.

Eta'ak's face feathers went to black. "The children are with the clan, as is our way. Trrk will stay with me. His brother spouses have distanced themselves from me at my request. A smaller price for them to pay than if they stood by me."

"I am sorry for you and Trrk both," Lee said. "But we would love to have you as an intermediary. You've earned that."

"My thanks."

The males, Seth and Trrk included, erected the awning like a great sky-blue wing and spread woven mats colored tan and bronze and copper on the ground beneath it. Lee and Eta'ak helped set out a table with two benches suitable for humans or Keloks. And that was it, the simple setting for the first meeting between leaders of two groups of settlers on Carico, between two alien species.

When everything was ready, Second and his hunters gathered. "Eta'ak will return to our camp with us," he said. "Trrk will accompany her."

"I will go," Lee said. "I recommend you send Eta'ak with Seth to explain Kelok expectations and protocols to Administrator Emmerling. And I will answer any questions that Prime may have."

Second considered that. "Yes, I believe that is acceptable. A thoughtful gesture."

"Are you sure?" Seth whispered in Lee's ear.

"Look after Eta'ak," Lee replied. "I'll take care of Trrk."

"See you this evening then."

They separated, and Lee strode away with the Keloks, leaving Seth and Eta'ak to take the skimmer. Everything was in place.

Chapter 60

Lee

Lee stood with Seth on one side, Eta'ak on the other, and Trrk beyond her, their backs to Ike's rock. Bystanders, observers at a meeting they had struggled so hard to bring about.

Before them a single table sat under the sky-blue awning, bare except for one of the speech synthesizers Trrk had helped construct and one of the units the Keloks used to monitor the human broadcasts. Two identical benches sat across the table from each other, neither facing into the sun. Fair and equal.

Nearby, Planetary Administrative Officer Emmerling waited in the skimmer with Joe Reilly and Adel Verlane as her escorts. Kieron Dougherty was acting as videographer to live broadcast the momentous event. Seth and Trrk had discussed that with Second. Second had agreed with one stipulation, that the Keloks could watch too. The little moon, with its hidden communications site, was in the sky, and he had provided their version of broadcasting equipment. He explained that the events would be translated for the Keloks at Village of Lichens.

"Flaming frog-eels." Seth pointed his chin to the far side of the depression. "What is that?"

Trrk's crest flared in laughter. "You still have much to learn about us."

"It looks like your people appreciate the importance of first impressions," Lee said.

A vehicle glided down the slight slope, a floating chariot without horses. Second squatted at controls in front, and Prime stood tall behind him. Four Kelok males trotted in escort. The group came to a stop opposite the skimmer and precisely the same distance from the awning. The craft settled to the ground.

Prime stepped off and waited for Emmerling to get out of the skimmer. Then she strode forward, standing upright with her tail swaying low behind her. A heavy torq of intricately braided copper wire lay over the stole-of-office around her neck. Second followed at her shoulder.

From the other side, Emmerling, accompanied by Adel, matched her timing. She wore a long, ivory-colored dress that set off the multi-colored stole-of-office and her jet skin. Shorter than Lee and twice as broad, she moved gracefully with what Lee could only describe as presence.

Prime bowed her head slightly. "Thank you for accepting my invitation."

Emmerling touched the stole-of-office Prime had sent for her to wear. "I am pleased to be here." She swept a hand toward the table. "Here is the written record of your invitation in both our languages and the story cloth. I look forward to a day when I can read that for myself."

"For now, we will have to tell you our story."

Emmerling took a piece of fabric from Adel. "This was made by another member species of the Interstellar Coalition. Its threads don't tell a story except for our love of beauty." She shook out a long scarf of iridescent gold Jelwyn spider silk. "Please accept it as a symbol of sharing between peoples."

Prime took the scarf and draped it over her shoulders. It lay on her raisin-purple skin like jewels. "This I will treasure." She took a basket from Second and placed it on the table. "I am told you have a custom called 'breaking bread'. We also share food to show good will." She opened it and took out a loaf of bread and a small container.

"Beulah bread," Lee whispered. Made from Ike's yeasty starter that she had left with Eta'ak. "Your contribution?" she asked Eta'ak.

"Prime has developed a taste for it. The spread is made from fungi that we raise. Quite savory."

Adel handed a bottle to Emmerling who put it next to the bread. "And I have brought a bottle of wine, a drink made from fruit. I am told your people share our taste for fermented beverages."

And so it began with a pleasant chat between two leaders over yeasty bread and chilled verdejo wine. The real work would begin in the morning, days or weeks of negotiations to settle how the two species could co-exist. But Lee was confident that Charlyn Emmerling saw the value to the human settlers of treating the Keloks as additional settlers and ignoring their uniqueness for now. Until someday in the future when they could no longer avoid introducing the Keloks to the Sol-Terra Alliance and the Interstellar Coalition.

Epilogue

Seth

Seth parked the skimmer by the Visitors' Quarters in the Central Services compound in Portside. Before he could open the door, Lee came out. She threw her bag in the back seat and climbed in next to him, hurriedly shutting out the chill winter wind.

"Ready?" he asked.

"More than ready." She pulled off her jacket and settled into her seat. "Are you sure this beast will make it home?"

Seth patted the control panel of the aging Steadhand. "She'll do fine."

"Nice of your father to give it to you."

"Nice of Kiri to insist he get them a new one before their baby came." He put the vehicle in motion. "We'll be down in the hot desert soon. Dougherty is expecting us at Seven Wells tonight. That'll give us plenty of time to get home tomorrow."

"To your Rock House?" she asked.

"No. Trrk and Eta'ak are settled in there — the sole contact point for the Kelok enclave at Blue Canyon for now. Although it's a little crowded since Trrk's brother-spouses showed up a few days ago."

"Oh, did they? What about the children?"

"Trrk says they are best raised by the clan, as is the custom."

She nodded. "Then where are we staying?"

"We've got a nice new prefab that Dougherty moved into Five Canyons until the new stead has real buildings."

"We do, huh?"

"It's all ours for the next month, one full cycle of Lander. Until Adel expects you back here."

"I'm going to have to insist on fast transport so I can commute more often. I always swore I wasn't going to end up like my parents, apart more than they're together."

He fingered the rawhide bracelet he wore, the twin to hers. "If that's the only way I can have you, I'll take it. Besides, anticipation spices things up." He had sworn he would take as much of her time as he could get for now and not complain.

"She keeps promising to find a replacement for me. Scorch it! I thought she was just going to hand it over to

Whip. Give him something to do that he's good at and he's almost a tolerable human being. Then they credited him with the time he was on the run, and Dougherty took him on when his restitution was done."

"So he and Adel split?"

"No. Adel suddenly developed a deep interest in spending her free time at Seven Wells."

Seth reached over to lay his hand on Lee's leg. "You know the only way Adel will let you out of the survey project is to promote you to Kelok liaison. Someone is going to have to shepherd Prime and friends through the official First Contact."

"They still say they don't want that."

"It's inevitable. A lot of them didn't want contact with us either."

"You're right. But I think you're better at the interspecies relations than I will ever be."

"I'm better with Second. But not Prime."

"Okay, it's going to take co-liaisons. One of these days. Right now, I'd like to concentrate on that spice you were talking about."

"It's taken three and a half years," he said, "but we finally have a little time all to ourselves. No one else to answer to; nothing that can't wait until later."

"Except training horses."

"They're on vacation."

"And visits with Eta'ak and Trrk and spouses."

"Once in a while, just for a change of pace."

"And going to meet your new baby brother."

He looked into her brown-gold eyes. "Whatever you want."

She smiled. "Just you. And me. The rest can wait."

THE END

About the Author

Nan C. Ballard's *Under Carico's Moons* series of science fiction cowboy stories reflects her love of places where vehicles yield to cows, towns are hours apart, and hills climb clear to the sky. She's written and edited environmental assessment reports, written an  arts column for a small town paper, and collaborated on adaptations of plays for community theater. Her poetry has been published in the online *Willawaw Journal* and the anthology *Mount Shasta Reflections.* She supports her fellow writers as a chapter co-chair and online coffee co-host for Willamette Writers. She does quick pen-and-colored-pencil doodles to practice mindfulness. Her current just-for-fun project with her husband is to visit interesting places in every county in Oregon.

You can find her at nancballardwriter.blogspot.com or @NanCBallard on Instagram.